THE VIRGIN'S DAUGHTER

AN HISTORICAL NOVEL
By

Jennifer Levens

The Virgin's Daughter

An historical novel

By Jennifer Levens

ISBN:9781686805585

This publication is designed to entertain. It is a novel and not necessarily historically accurate concerning people, places or things.

Dedicated to

Ken Levens who keeps everything on track.

Coast of Northwest Wales—Present Day

Llewelyn, Lloyd and Lelah Lewis played on forbidden land-an escarpment overlooking the Irish Sea. Time and erosion had dispatched parts of the old dirt road, a road that had seen the hooves of many military mounts and the feet of the smugglers they sought for the noose. A misstep would result in death by rocks at the bottom of the steep cliff.

Lloyd went to the edge and looked over for the hundredth time. There was a small ledge and the children were brave this damp cloudy day. The boy lay on his stomach and yelled to his twin brother. "Welly, there is a hole back of the ledge. Hold my legs. I want to see more."

Llewelyn came over and slammed to his stomach next to his brother. "You hold my legs. I am older." The two boys wrestled at that edge. Lelah, their younger sister crept over. She was small and redheaded like her brothers, but more cautious in nature.

"Welly, Lloyd, stop that. I'm gonna tell ma. We needs go back to the house. It gets to be time for breakfast."

The boys stopped wrestling and propped their heads on their elbows and looked at their sister. "We are going to throw you over, if you don't shut up, Lee." Welly started to push himself to his feet and his hand slipped. He wound up on his back and Lloyd pounced. That was all it took. A chunk of earth let loose and Welly was hanging his upper back over the new edge. Lloyd crabbed backwards off his brother. Lelah screamed. A few more chunks of dirt dropped to the rocks below. Welly turned over onto his stomach and stretched over the edge. He wiggled so his head and upper torso were hidden from sight. "Hey, Lloyd, there is a hole here. It might be a cave. Lelah will fit down there if we hold her. Lelah, come here."

"I don't want to go in some old hole." She stomped her foot. Lloyd came up behind her and picked her up.

"You be going in that cave. Who knows, there may be riches in there."

"There may be spiders and biter things, too. Why not send Lloyd. He's not as big as you. Maybe he will fit." Lelah tried to pull away from her brother.

"Nope, you're going down, little sister. Why do you think we kept you all this time?" Welly laughed. "Ya know we love, but you're going down. You keep sayin' you're a big strong girl. Prove it. Come on

Lloyd, bring her here. I've got a bit of rope to tie around her so's we don't lose her."

The twins looped the rope under their sister's arms and lowered her to the ledge. "Stand there and don't look down. How big is the hole? Don't worry. We won't leave you there. Hurry up. The house is awake, and we must get back soon."

Lelah had more room on the ledge than she thought. She turned and peered into the cave. "It's bigger than from the top, Welly. It's a great hidey-hole. I'm going in." She crawled into the cave opening. She couldn't stand up, but there was plenty of room for her to sit. There was room so that even her brothers could sit inside. She wiggled back a bit further. Then she stretched her arms a bit further still. Her hand hit a soft lump. She screamed and withdrew her arm. Nothing came at her, so she stretched some more searching for the soft thing. It was there and it didn't move. She clutched it in her hand and pulled it to her. She returned to the ledge and called to her brother, "Pull me up, Welly. I found something." She put the pouch into her sweatshirt pocket as the boys hoisted her over the edge to safe ground.

"What did you find? Buried treasure?" The boys laughed.

Now safe Lelah teased her siblings. "It's all mine, you goons. I was the one who went in. It's all mine."

"I saw the thing first," said Welly. "and it was my life that Lloyd tried to take pushing me over the edge like that."

"You lie, Welly. The ground broke or we wouldn't know of it at all. Open the thing, Lelah. We want to see. You can keep it if it ain't dead. It was the custom long ago for pirates to bury treasure in the caves further down the coast. They said it in class last year. Let's have a look, Sis."

Lelah pulled the package from her pocket. They all looked at it. It was a leather pouch tied with a decaying piece of string. Lelah pulled on the top of the pouch and the string fell to dust. "Move you goons. Either of you got a hankie?"

"I do," said Lloyd. He pulled a cotton scarf from his pocket and spread the square on the ground. Lelah dumped the contents of the pouch on it. All three drew back in amazement. Several gold pieces lay on the hankie surrounding a blue stone the size of a robin's egg but much, much bluer and a faceted red stone of almost the same size. A large cameo pin was in the middle of this hodgepodge pinned to a hand drawn picture of a girl with curly hair.

"I'm going to get Da," said Llewelyn. "We all need to get Da and show him this. This is more than I ever thought...."

They heard their mother's voice ring out. "Breakfast, kids, breakfast. Come and get it."

Lelah gathered up her treasure and the three of them ran pell-mell for the house.

London 1559 Late Spring

"Oaf! Move! Git yer arse outta the street, now or I'll let Nancy here drag us over yer worthless husk!" the wagoneer shouted as he drew up his nag as not to hit her, a shadow in the late dusk. "Filthy wretch. Move it I say."

She looked at him. No use revealing her identity with a stupid comment. She headed toward the walls of the shops, her face down and her head covered in a hooded cloak. The slums of London swirled around her like a dark, dank cloak stinking of sewage, garbage and unwashed bodies, all of which fermented in the heat of the day, to a miasma of stench and disease filling the warm nights of summer and early September.

I can take no chances, she thought. She approached the door of The Witch's Brew, the door that would lead to a life of challenge and fulfillment, a life lived in the sun and not in shadows.

Witch's Brew? The name should be outlawed. She'd think about it, but not right now. Right now, she had to find the one person she'd heard of who could help her. She pulled her rags closer to her body and reached up to feel her head to make sure that none of her identifiable hair was showing.

She looked around her. No one was watching. *Keep your head low*, she thought as she opened the door and went in. There was no outside light and her eyes had to adjust to the almost black interior lit only by a small fire in the large fireplace. The smell of urine and old sweat coupled with burned meat made her retch. Nothing came out, thank God. A hulk of a man appeared in front of her. "Git yer arse outta here. We don't truck to no beggars here." The deep masculine voice was loud in her ears as she felt rough hands grab her shoulders to turn her around ready to boot her out the door.

"I am here to see... Morvyn? My...me mistress sent me," she said in a small voice she hoped indicated her service.

"Morvyn ain't seein' nobody today. Git yer scrawny arse away from me establishment, ya whore's leavin's. We's got royalty today. Come round tomorra." Jack Hoggins started to shove her out the door. She slapped him away, but as she started to leave, he gave her a kick in her behind and sent her sprawling face down in the filthy alley. Her hood fell away for an instant revealing a glimpse of red hair. She reached for her hood, glancing around for witnesses. There were none. *Thank God,* she thought. The door slammed behind her as she rose, muttering a low-class curse in his direction and feeling her knees bruise on the spot. "The nerve of that..., remember what you are. You cannot let anyone know what is happening. Pull that cloak around. Keep your head covered. Think, girl. You have that... Just get home. Nurse will help you today and we will get through this," she muttered to herself. She bent her back to look older and hobbled back down the alleyway toward home.

***

Morvyn Hoggins was seconds behind her husband to answer the door. She'd heard every word he spoke and was poised with the great log poker to bash his head in. But she had to give him a piece of her mind before she eliminated him. He had no right. Maybe that lass wanted a love potion or to get rid of an unwanted, ill-conceived brat. It would keep them in food for a month.

"Yer an ass, Jack Hoggins! Someone for me talents and ye send em away? Ya ain't got no royalty here today or any other day, fer that matter. Ye take me business away and what d'ya got? A dead-end pub! Ye give away the ale and ye want me to do the cookin' to feed the scrabble what gather outside yer back door every night. I should bust in yer head, ya old bogger, and take back me place to meself. It were me Da what left it ta me. It be mine an' don't ya fergit it."

1534 Northwest Wales

Matilda and Morvyn Evans were born three months apart. They were opposites in looks, Matilda red-haired and blue eyed and Morvyn dark and mysterious. The girls were first cousins on their fathers' side, sharing the fine Welsh name of Evans, and raised far enough from the mainland to be unnoticed by any but the locals. Both girls were best friends as youngsters and maidens. Both loved to dance and sing. Both attended the healer's lessons. Both were introduced to academics in the schoolroom of Lord Maurice, a member of the nobility, whose crofts housed a population of about one hundred people, mostly farmers' families.

A progressive thinker, Maurice thought men and women of all classes should have reading and writing skills as well as mathematics. So, to that end he invited the children of the crofts to come to the estate house three times a week from the time they were about four until they were needed on the land or in the house. A tutor taught reading, writing, French, mathematics and music to the manor children and crofts children in the same classroom.

A healer and midwife in one of the crofts taught females about healing herbs and potions. To some of the 'talented' she taught spells from the old religion. Lord Maurice knew nothing of these lessons. Witchcraft was punishable by burning, if the practitioner were caught and found guilty. Morvyn sought the healer's lessons far more than the academic lessons. Her natural touch made her adept at the 'practice' in a very short time. She helped the healer with births on the estate and even went to the big house as an aide for the lady of the manor. Because of her talents, she saved the lives of both mother and child in a difficult birth. The less talented midwives started calling her witch.

Morvyn had the sight and touch. Matilda had the green thumb and delicate hand with the herbs. Matilda was not as astute as Morvyn in the "arts", but she was an excellent student and gardener. Her herbs and vegetables were larger than most in the area, and sweeter, too. Her baked goods had natural flavors that could go from savory to sweet without the use of sugar from the Indies. Her pies and stews were the talk of the crofts, and she often went to the big house to help the French chef with parties and gatherings. Matilda was on her way to becoming a baker in her own right, but for the unfortunate situation that a single woman could not own property or have a business of her own.

Morvyn helped the crofters. She assisted the midwife and as she grew older, her skill with herbs and potions redoubled, until she was able to make a living from all of the lovesick maids and lads in the crofts. Her healing skills helped sick children and animals. She used the herbs and balms she made herself when she found that many remedies the official healer made were less effective. She could set broken bones and wrap them, so they healed faster, and the patients had full range of motion and no outward indication of the break. She was a wonder with birthing mothers.

Matilda sealed her fate the night she met Evan Lewis in the kitchen where Lord Maurice bade servants of guests sup, while their employers enjoyed the fete in the halls above. Matilda eyed the muscular, red-haired blue-eyed lad just as her slim body and red hair attracted Evan and several other youths. A short bout of fisticuffs with an older man bent on having Matilda for himself settled the matter, and Evan and Tildy (for that was Matilda's day name) were inseparable the rest of the night and into the early morning when the party was over, and Evan need to serve once again. He vowed to see her again after he bought an inn from his uncle, and she vowed to wait for him. Of course, they would meet when Lord Maurice entertained and invited Evan's employer to attend.

Both Matilda and Morvyn reached young maidenhood with skills far beyond any of their peers.

Both seemed destined for fine independent lives until the day a farmer got angry with Morvyn and accused her of not healing but of killing his cow with a spell.

Morvyn denied it. "I am not God and cannot heal everything. You called me and then refused my treatment. You are not blameless by any means. You let the poor thing graze on wet grass. She got the bloat and you let her explode."

Morvyn was right, but the farmer refused to admit his responsibility. Just as she was to plunge the knife into the cow's side and release the air, the farmer forcibly stopped her and told her to leave. He swore before the magistrate that Morvyn, a witch, laid a curse upon the cow and caused her death. Morvyn, frightened for her life, ran to Matilda. Matilda begged her folks to take Morvyn in. When they heard the story, they refused. " Matilda, you will make us part of a coven. If you do this, you can both get out," screeched Matilda's mother in fear.

No one on the estate would give Morvyn sanctuary, including the church. The accusation 'witch' was a death sentence to any who harbored one so accused. The priest did offer to exorcise her of her evil spirits. Morvyn said she was not possessed, and the priest threw her out of the church. Morvyn, instead of accepting her fate, got angry. "Burn in Hell, you heathen, for condemning an innocent girl." She said it in front of witnesses.

Morvyn hurried home and gathered what few things she had. She left the estate and Matilda's family for good. London would be her new home. She would join her father, if he were still alive, and work for him.

***

Her trip was long. She was farm-bred and knew the edibles along the byways and paths. She walked many miles for several days. She saved her coin for lodging when it was available. Tildy had given her bread and some dried meat to take with her. The first few nights she slept in caves or wooded copses to avoid prying eyes from the estate.

The town of Bryn a Cywd lay to the west on the road to the Queen's castle on the wild northwest coast of Wales. Edward II had built it in 1100. It still stood today as a part of the holdings of the Queen of England. Henry VIII used it for a hunting lodge and a stop off before going to Ireland. A mile or two east of the town lay a little inn. The Cock and the Sow was the only establishment on this road.

The pox was rampant in England's larger cities, and occasionally it traveled to the more countrified areas of the British kingdom. Morvyn found not food and bed at this inn but the owners sick and dying. She nursed them, gave them comfort until the owner died. His wife, Margaret, survived but was horribly scarred and very weak.

Margaret's three children were gone from the inn, married with children of their own. Morvyn urged Margaret to contact her children to help with the inn until she had the strength to work it herself. The good wife thought she could run the inn for a while and use the time to make up her mind. She offered some coin to Morvyn for nursing and getting someone to bury her husband despite the pox. Morvyn explained she needed a place to stay for a few days and some good home-cooked food. The wife invited her to stay as long as she wanted. Perhaps Morvyn could serve the clients and save Margaret from appearing in public, her scars so severe as to frighten young children and small animals. Morvyn shuddered at the thought of people paying for food she cooked. "Margaret, you cook, and I will serve. It would help to keep business.

Morvyn took care of the woman and burned all the cloth that came in contact with the infected couple. This meant that Morvyn's dress as well as all of the old woman's clothing would be ashes. New would have to be made. The old woman said she was handy with a thread and needle and, if Morvyn would rip, she would sew. There were plenty of clean sheets available for fabric. "I have my best dress, what I would be buried in. That be in a safe place in the eaves over the rooms. I can wear that. I will make a few chemises and aprons. You'll lose your dress as well."

"I have a spare or two. My sisters gave me one each that fit me well enough. I'll take a chemise and an apron, though, to get me through for the service. And thank you very much." Morvyn gathered all she could and went outside to do the burning. "Your husband did all the stable work?" Morvyn called over her shoulder on her way out.

"Yes, " responded the old woman. "Please, you have to go to the local kirk and let them know what has happened. I will also need a lad to do the stable work. Let them know when you go to the priest for the other. Right now I need a rest. I am weary after just this short time. Please take over should someone

come for a night's rest. Thank you for all you have
done." And the woman fell back and slept.

"I will cart the body in a shroud and have them
bury him," Morvyn said to the silent room. She hung a
"Closed" sign from the door and prayed that
customers would heed the sign. She went to the local
church for the mistress and told them what happened.
One of the families sent a lad over immediately to
help. The priest asked if she wanted a blessing on the
grave of the husband. "I think yes, but I will ask.
Thank you for the lad. The old woman can use him. I
must get back in any case. Let all know the inn be
open again." Morvyn left with a lighter heart knowing
help was on the way.

Morvyn stayed for a month while the woman
recovered her strength. Morvyn wished Tildy were
there to help with the cooking. The mistress was not a
good cook. The food she made tasted like swill and
was worse than Morvyn's. Morvyn said to the woman,
"Let me do the cooking for a while. It seems to tire you
too much. I will stay as long as you need me." Morvyn
proceeded to cook simple fare. At least it was edible.

In that month Morvyn looked around at the
building and the grounds. The stables were sturdy and
in good repair but needed cleaning. She set the boy to
that. The great room of the inn was a large area, dark
with one or two windows and filled with tables and
benches. The tap area had a small storage for the
drinking vessels and an alcove underneath that could
hold two casks at a time. There was more storage
behind that. The guest rooms were generous for the
day and fairly kept, even though a light film of dust

covered everything. That was easily remedied. Each room with a large window in each of the four and a fireplace with the wood set for lighting. Each room had a bed, a small table, a chair, and a clothes hook.

The building consisted of add-ons with the great room beneath the guest rooms. Beside the kitchen area were two rooms that caught the heat from the hearth and had a window that was covered in the cold weather. This was where Morvyn found the old couple and nursed them. The kitchen was large and well equipped, but the woman used only a small space. She used coarse wheat flour for her breads and pies. Morvyn saw no herb garden. The vegetable garden was limited, so stews were limited. Many sheep occupied the area and mutton was the meat at hand.

"Where do you get your milk for cooking?" Morvyn asked.

"I milk the ewes when they are in season. Sometimes a farmer brings cow milk to me. Another will bring goat milk, but that is very rare, and you can't make butter from goat milk. And before you ask, I get my flour from the mill about a mile hence. I can't afford his white, but this is good. He sells me barley for my stews, too. The apple tree in the back gives me apples once a year and I make sweet pies in season and what I can't use I dry. I don't like the inn, nor do I like cooking. It were my husband's dream and I loved him, so it were mine as well. I am good with a needle and with the loom. I spin my own thread. I can't read or write and or do sums. I am in a right poor place trying to run this inn, so your help is very welcome."

Morvyn heard that and stored it away in her mind. She could not stay here forever. Her reputation would catch up to her and she would have to run again. She knew that London was much safer for her. She told as much to the old woman but gave no reason.

"I have needs to get to London soon now. I have my Da there and will have permanent work. I also need a husband. This inn keeping isn't too bad, but the business is very short. Maybe you need to think about selling it after all. I will stay with you for a few more weeks until you are all on your feet, but then I am gone." Morvyn fulfilled her promise.

Back at the Crofts

Tildy stayed on the estate and did the baking and cooking for parties. She helped her parents with the farm and baked for them as well. They sold some of her bread at market for an excellent price. The house on the hill paid her well for her services and her father allowed her to keep all that she earned to build her trousseau. She and Evan saw each other regularly at croft gatherings. She never understood why the priest avoided her. She had no idea that he equated her with Morvyn as the same kind of woman.

Tildy's plan was to marry Evan and have a large family. Evan only wanted to have Tildy and give her whatever she desired. There was no question that they were kindred spirits and soulmates. It was the very heart of their relationship.

Neither one wanted to stay on the estate of their employers. The goal was to find a business that would make both happy and lend to having a happy family.

1552

Tildy and Evan were married in January of 1548. Tildy bid her parents farewell and moved with Evan to the estate where he worked. Tildy's reputation as a baker and a cook preceded her. She started baking a month after the marriage. Several months later they were overjoyed when Tildy found she was with child. Three months after that they mourned the miscarriage of their first child. It might be the first but would not be the last.

No child, no family to mourn with her over the loss made Tildy droop. The heart went out of her, and she went through the motions of everyday life. No longer were there songs of joy on her lips or a smile on her face. Every day dragged by while she carried the failure of her womanly duties on her shoulders. Months went by and it was close to All Hallows Eve that Tildy got word from her cousin. Morvyn wrote and said she was as safe in London as she would ever be since she was married to a man named Jack Hoggins, who owned the Witch's Brew, the pub she would have when her husband died. She had a running business with her herbs and potions and did a bit of the illegal on the side, though she said she would never kill a born babe.

Morvyn wanted a break from the city. Her husband was not the man she thought she should marry, but then she was no prize either. She never turned to the streets for a living, but the pub was in the dregs of London, and she served many of the women who took to the streets to survive.

Morvyn asked Tildy if she could come back for a visit, now that all were settled with spouses and such. London was about a week's ride, but if taken faster without stopping could be done in about four days. Tildy wrote back, delighted that her cousin could come. Evan approved. He hoped that Tildy would cheer up with this visit and lessen the loss of the child.

Morvyn's Arrival

Morvyn's arrival started a great visit for the two cousins, so long separated. Tildy had a neat herb garden behind the croft. Evan kept a cow and a horse in the small stable. Tildy had all the milk and cream she could use. Evan's brother and his family came for supper once a month since all lived on the same estate. This visit was the first from Tildy's family. There would be no children to grace this table.

Morvyn listened to Tildy's recount of the child and recommended she chew on some St. John' Wort from her garden to help relieve her spirit. They went out and Morvyn showed Tildy which leaf to chew. "The wort helps the spirits to lift and put a smile back on your beautiful lips, cousin. Do this every day and you will feel more of your old self once more," Morvyn told Tildy as she glanced at the rest of the garden. "You have bonny plants here, Tildy. Do you have the dried in the kitchen?" Tildy nodded while chewing on a leaf of the plant Morvyn recommended. "Let's go look and smell," Morvyn said, another thought coming to her.

Tildy opened the box of sage she'd hand-dried from the spring. "This is from the last spring, Morvyn. I use it to rub on the sides of meat for the big house and in the bread filling for the fowl, when asked for. It keeps its flavor for about six months or so. This is just about done. Take a sniff. What do you think?"

Morvyn took a long sniff and smiled. "Tildy, this is grand. If this is six months old, then what I get from the merchants in the city is very old indeed. None has this fragrance or strength. Can I take some with me when I go home? You have some other plants I can sorely use for my balms and such. I will pay you well for them."

***

The parties were frequent in the estate house. Tildy baked breads and cakes. She helped in the big estate kitchen preparing the meats and fowl. She always used her own herbs for all of the recipes. She saved the pennies she earned for her service and from the sales of her baked goods. The Lord and Lady were generous, and her savings pouch filled quickly and often. There was a party two nights after Morvyn's arrival. Tildy was in the middle of preparing the sweets for the party. She was done with the scones and biscuits for the teas served before and after the party. Morvyn helped her in the preparation as best she could. She helped Tildy and Evan deliver the baked goods the day before. She went with Tildy the day of the party. Morvyn carried the herbs, and on the walk to the house, sniffed them, bringing the aroma of them deep into her body. "Tildy, you need to be selling me some of these. Remind me, I have something to

propose to you and Evan when you are through here."
The Cock and the Sow was one of the reasons she'd
come.

"Morvyn, I can sell you the herbs dried or not. I
am saving my pennies so that Evan and I can get an
establishment of our own. You know he makes the
best ale and with his own hops at that. We can grow
precious little of it here. Now don't go telling Evan
that I am doing this. I want it to be a surprise, when
he decides the time is right."

"Of course, you silly! I love secrets as well as
the next person. This time I will take the fresh herbs
and dry them myself. You can dry the next batch. I
will try to come two times a year, so you always have a
fresh crop.

"Now, about what I have to tell you. It is your
dream, yours and Evan's. We can talk later. It will be a
wonderful surprise." Morvyn knew The Cock and the
Sow was still standing and that the woman wanted to
sell now more than ever. It was hard work running an
inn even with the help of the youth that did all the
stable work and a girl that did the heavy work in the
inn. Cooking, cleaning, replacing straw and washing
linens took a toll on one's body. Morvyn figured the
young couple had a sure thing in this inn.

That night the three of them sat around the
kitchen table and supped on one of Tildy's meat pies.
The pie was left over from the big house party and
Tildy warmed it for them, so the taste was delicious.
"Tildy, this is wonderful," Evan pronounced after
wolfing down a couple of bites. "Just think, if we
owned our own place, this could be a good seller, and

it doesn't even take much to keep with a proper ice house and such. I understand there are some inns that fetch in ice in the winter and it stays all year until the next winter. And this ale we got at the big house is nothing to what I can make with my own ingredients. We can grow the hops and have a sweet filling ale. It is all in the growing beasties and hops to make a good ale. Oh, what I wouldn't give for a place of my own." He then proceeded to tuck away the rest of his plateful and then another.

As soon as supper was done Morvyn told them of her idea. "Listen you two, I don't know what your savings are, but I know of an inn that is for sale on the way to East o' the Sun, the Queen's castle. I know not what the old lady wants for the place, but it is worth looking into. You would have to leave this place, but the inn would be your own. You would own the land and the buildings and some farmland behind. It is not part of any estate I know about. What do you say?"

Evan looked at Tildy and said, "I've been saving to buy my way into my uncle's pub, but my cousins are interested too, and they are his blood kin. I don't stand too much of a chance of getting it. Morvyn, where is this place exactly?"

Morvyn said, "It is a two-day travel time from here. We could make the trip when I leave, and I can introduce you. This is the old lady I nursed before I went to London after the cow incident. You remember, when I was named a witch." Morvyn laughed.

Evan replied, "It is always nice to have an income and not having to work. She might be happy to have an income from this place for as long as she live." Evan made it sound like a done deal already. Tildy looked at his face and saw the hope and desire there.

"My darling Evan, can we dream upon it for tonight? It is a big task, keeping house for lodgers and such. It is a lot of cooking and cleaning and you would be around people all your livelong day. Do you want that kind of life?"

"We will sleep on it, Tildy. That is why you are the wise one in the marriage. Morvyn, thank you. What is the name of this inn?"

"It is called The Cock and the Sow. I would think you could change the name if you willed," Morvyn answered. "I stayed there a night on this trip just to see how she was doing. She bellyached about the work and how she didn't like it or the inn even though she had help. Her business is poor, her cooking is worse.

"Sleep well on it. It is a big undertaking," said Morvyn. Tildy worked at the sink and Evan went out to make sure the animals were in the enclosure. He returned and had a pipe and another pint of ale before they retired for the night.

Before sleep in the loft Tildy whispered to Evan, "My darling man I needs show you what I have here." She went to a small shelf and uncovered a smallish box hidden in her aprons and chemises. She brought the box back to the bed and opened it. "I have been saving for low these many years from the bread and parties. It is all yours, if you really want the inn of which Morvyn speaks."

"Nay, love, it be ours. If we both use our savings, ye could have the finest linens and cloths for yerself. Ain't too many women would do what you have done. We will go to this inn and take a look around. That old woman may have what we want. It is good for us to investigate." Tildy went to speak, but Evan covered her mouth in a kiss and for the first time in six months enjoyed his marriage bed.

November 17, 1558

Queen Elizabeth I is twenty-five years old and Henry VIII's legitimate daughter. She is crowned Queen of England and Ireland.

1558 The Cock and the Sow—On the Road, Again

Morvyn Hoggins dug her heels into the side of her hired mount. "Come ye beastie. It's only a few more miles and then you can rest on my cousin's clean hay and eat the finest oats ever to reach your poor gut. Give me a bit more and we will be there." Old Jesse shook his head and plodded on at the same speed, his only speed. "You old nag, Jack will needs get me a better ride for my next trip. The faster the better. Oh, to have a carriage, even better a coach and four. Aye, Morvyn now you want to be Queen of England. That new one, might be the queen of the whole world someday. I heard of that New World, ya know, Jesse," Morvyn gave her little history lesson to the plodding horse. His head went up and down as though he were agreeing with her. At least she had something to listen to her here. Better than talking to herself like she did most of the time.

"Ah, Jesse, these visits to Tildy are a godsend. If only I weren't so stubborn, I would still be here in the green country and the fresh air. But no, I trusted that me Da would get me safe in this world. That no good swine! I am there a few months and a better offer comes to him-Jack Hoggins. Thank goodness, I have my trade and my good reputation. Those what can't afford a doctor come to me and I apply the poultice or give the potion. Those lovesick girls drink my recipe and think that they are going to live happily forever. Jesse, ye should see some of the wounds that come my way and the pregnant maids, I could list them forever. That old harridan next to the Witch's Brew had a poison that poured down the baby chute. Took care of a lot of unwanted even if it were against the law. Money and goodness have never been good neighbors. Thank God she taught me well. All but two of the whores survived. One died probably because of the sores on her body. I told her to get well first, but she insisted. Said she needed the money and to get on with it. 'Tis an art, Jesse, to get rid of unwanted brats."

Morvyn mused on. She was the healer of the area now that the witch, her neighbor and her mentor was found dead of a well-placed blade to the throat. The authorities came round, but they questioned Jack and left her alone.

Jack Hoggins was an abomination in a city full of abominations, pure evil clear through he was. After the first few years of taking Morvyn, her newness wore off. He was now onto other younger girls who would have him for a few pints of ale. He never knew of the three babes she rid herself of during their few years of mating. She didn't want any brats, especially not his. She would not bring more evil into her life. Jack took her healing money. She hid her other earnings so she could restock with herbs and have a little put aside just in case. Her trips to Tildy's were her salvation and her sanity.

Morvyn inherited the pub when her da got himself killed in a street fight over one of his whores. Jack was not happy about this, but Da had been very clear. If Morvyn did not get the title to the pub, it would mysteriously burn down and Jack with it. If he did not burn, he would work to support both of them or leave Morvyn alone. The streets were out for Morvyn as well. That was the deal they struck when Da sold her to Jack. That was her da for ya, sell the child and then tie her owner's hands. Jack! Just looking at him left a bad taste in her mouth. Someday! SOME DAY!

Morvyn urged Jesse on. There was the sun rock; not too far now. She was tired and thirsty. This trip was hard, yet it brought her profit like staying at home never could. She thought about Evan Lewis, a strong silent man with average looks who loved her cousin Tildy with all his heart. The only thing the two of them wanted was a child of their own. It was the one thing Morvyn could not give them.

Her pony trotted on. Morvyn daydreamed of a life in this country or maybe the New World she'd heard about from one of the Southern merchants from whom she bought spices. The New World—what would it be like there?

1559 London: Early Summer

"If he don't let me see her today, I'll get Nurse to take over. How can these people be so adverse to gold?" The young woman muttered to herself as she knocked on the alley door. "This is the last time. I will find another way," she said, her lips barely moving. She looked as though she were in prayer.

The top half of the Dutch door flew open and a woman peered out. She was tall and very skinny, drawn and unkempt. Her eyes darted back and forth then focused on the person in black. "Whadya want?" she growled.

"I need to see the witch, Morvyn. Allison sent me." The girl stopped. To herself she thought, *I will give myself away before time with this speech. I didn't realize.* Aloud she voiced, "Be ye the witch, Morvyn?"

Morvyn looked at her and then glanced around. "Git yer ass in here afore anyone sees ya, lass," Morvyn growled again as she opened the bottom part of the door for Elizabeth to pass. "Ye need to hurry afore we get caught here. My husband will be out for a little while." Morvyn shut and barred the door. "Allison, the whore?"

"Uh, aye the whore." Elizabeth's word stumbled. She knew only the court women who were called whores by the more religious pious men in the Chamber. This woman did not remember her nurse, a sweet older woman who cared for her and shared her joys and woes, woman to child, then woman to girl then woman to Queen. Elizabeth learned very quickly that her power was worldwide, and she could not afford one single mistake, a severe penalty for one as naïve as she. She was royalty, born and bred. She knew that her legacy was the salvation of the country, and she knew she was of strong stock, but a child would ruin her as a woman and as Queen.

"Come in. What is your will—a potion for love, a poison for a wastrel mate, what will ye?" Morvyn walked past the kitchen boards to a small niche hidden by the shadow of the larger room. She reached into her apron pocket and pulled out a small key.

"Allison says ye keep yer mouth shut. True? If not, I needs to go now."

"Aye, my lips are always sealed. I don't want to know you, just what you want and the color of your gold."

"Gold is always gold, no more no less. Is there a privy room? I can pay." Elizabeth stated. Morvyn unlocked the door and pushed Elizabeth in.

"Get in here and be quick about it."

"Here is a sovereign fer yer trouble." Elizabeth offered. Morvyn snatched the coin as Elizabeth passed.

She held it to the dim light. "Ah, the Queen's currency! Move it, girl. We can't be caught here." She snatched an ember from the fire, closed the door and went for a candle in the dark room, sure in her movement. This was not the first time for this act.

Elizabeth did not move until there was light enough to see. Morvyn moved from sconce to sconce until the room was bright with candlelight. It was a large room by most standards. A table covered in glass vials and beakers and small flame coal cookers took up the middle of the chamber. A bed with a mattress filled with straw and covered with a very clean white sheet stood in one corner. A cupboard with locks on all the doors took up one wall.

"What is this place?" Elizabeth asked, wonder shading her voice. "This is not of our time. Ye truly are a witch and a sorceress. Ye must be of Merlin's line."

"Keep your voice quiet. Now what is your will?" Morvyn asked in a quiet tone. She could see the girl was about her own age and scared.

"I...my friend is with child. We must be rid of it. Can you help? There is much payment to be had." Elizabeth whispered.

"You are with child? Let me feel. Remove your cloak." Morvyn reached up and pulled back the hood. Elizabeth pulled the hood back up but not before the witch saw the copper halo around her head.

Elizabeth knew that this moment revealed her secret. This could be the end of her reign. The Catholic bitch would rule, and the civil wars would rend her beloved nation into pieces and open it to the infection and domination from foreign sovereignties. Was this the answer? "The brat is not mine, but that of a lady. I told you that. This needs be kept in the utmost secrecy. Do I have your word?"

"Milady, I cannot talk about my clients." Morvyn gave her a most courteous bow. "It means my head if I am known. We both have secrets, it seems."

"Your tongue—it has changed—you are not a low born as you seem."

"Yourself as well, milady, but that is not the problem at hand. You have an unwanted brat to dispose of. How far along is this lady? I can't promise anything past four months. By that time the child has a hold that is hard to loosen."

"I...I don't know. I would assume 'tis not past two months by her own reckoning. Tell me what needs done and I shall prepare for it."

"You need to bring her here before the next fortnight lest I be gone on my journey and put the cure beyond the time. Send a messenger and make her ready. I will await your signal."

"Thank you, good woman. You shall hear from me soon. I bid you *adieu.*"

Morvyn closed and locked the door. *This will be a pretty package tied with gold. Mayhap I shall have that coach and four sooner than I thought.* Morvyn went back and locked her privy room. She took the kettle of hot water and brewed up a pot of tea. As she did all this, she dreamed about her bright new future.

London: Court

Sitting quietly in her boudoir, the young queen and her nurse whispered to each other. Allison encircled the Queen's shoulders and pulled her close. "Do not worry, my love. Perhaps you will lose it on your own. Most stop bleeding after conceiving. But, my sweet, we must remember you are the Queen of England, and you must do things as you see fit, even to having a wee child of your own."

"Nurse, the witch said I must bring my lady in need to her within a three-month time. Oh, Allison, what am I to do—I have not seen Robbie low these last four months. I am past the time."

"Hush, my child, there are other ways— remember you set the fashion, you don't follow it. We will not lace you quite so tight, and we will pray for a small child to grow inside you. Why did you not tell me when you stopped bleeding? With all else, I did not notice, you not bleeding every month as it is."

"I have not stopped bleeding every month. Each month I show a bit and you have washed my bandages and I have stayed in chambers. There has not been as much as usual."

"I must caution you. The child cannot stay in court. Raise her as you were raised, apart from all this. A country life is healthy and simple. This child cannot know who she is, and neither can the parents you choose. We raised you knowing that you could possibly be Queen one day. You stayed with the King's younger cousin and her husband. You were not a bastard, though made one for a while by those royal imposters. This child will be one. There can be no connection between you. Please trust me to take care of this in my own way and all will be well." Allison stood and in a loud voice stated her usual morning lines, "Milady, 'tis time to rise and shine your radiance upon your world; give your subjects hope." She pulled on the service cord and together they waited, queen and nurse, for the daily ritual to begin.

***

"This is not the way of the French court, but *cie la vie,* this is England." Lady Marie Saltworthy, married early by her merchant father to unite the two countries for greater profits and to save his ships from English marauders, had few kind words for her adopted country. That she was one of the queen's ladies was a feather in her cap even if she was the lowest ranked female in the room. Her appointment was only by suffrage of the demands of Albert Saltworthy, Duke of Avon and Minister of Trade in the Chamber. His marriage was disappointment to both parties and to Henry VIII, but Henry died, not from disappointment but dissipation. After some religious and political unrest Elizabeth inherited her ladies from Mary I, who ruled before her. Saltworthy had a good head for trade agreements and saved the country from small but expensive skirmishes. France was quiet now due to this marriage and the possibility that Elizabeth might marry Phillip I. Spain was a great obstacle as well since both governments looked to their monarchs to unite them in the marriage bed. Elizabeth wanted nothing of it.

"Marry that worm, I think not. I will not have England speaking Spanish and idolizing the Pope," she told William "Willie" Cecil. She was adamant, and both governments wrung their collective hands over her decision, working constantly to change her mind. The 'Scottish Bitch' as Elizabeth called her half-sister, Mary, was a constant threat even ensconced in prisons inland. Should she decide to start an up-rising, she had many who would do her beck and call. Mary would marry that Spanish bastard at the drop of a whim. Elizabeth said it was the quickest way to war with Spain. Who wanted a wife who was perpetually on her knees but not for his pleasure? Elizabeth knew she was playing a dangerous game. This child was a piece from another puzzle. It did not fit Elizabeth's picture of her reign. The sooner it was done and over the better.

The latest courier from Spain indicated that Phillip II would be making a visit to ask in person for Elizabeth's hand in marriage after his attack of gout abated. The sea air would be welcome on the voyage and perhaps a personal proposal would soften her stance on the union. What greater honor could he bestow upon her than himself? Elizabeth worked on an answer that would not antagonize his minister and at the same time prayed for a very long and very painful bout of gout for Phillip.

"Kat," Elizabeth hailed her first lady-in-waiting, "What is my first stop, the Chamber or the audience room?"

"Madame, I will inquire. Generally, it is your choice, but you have not been available low these thirty days." Kat gave her a prying look.

"I prefer the audience. This illness has taken me from my people. The Chamber always has my ear, no matter how ill I am. My people seem to go wanting."

"I will tell them, Madame." Kat exited and Elizabeth dismissed all but Allison.

When she was sure there were no lurking eyes or ears, Elizabeth whispered, "Allison, did you get that wig? I am excited and worried at the same time. We must hurry. The Lord Chamberlain will be here shortly with my list of petitioners. I will sit in front of the glass and you fasten it on."

"Close your eyes, Madame. I want to see the surprise in your eyes when it is on." Elizabeth closed her eyes and Allison drew out the long, dark-haired wig. She bade Elizabeth sit still and when she was settled, slipped the hand-sewn wig over Elizabeth's carrot-colored curls. She tucked and primped and set the large bent wires used to secure the piece.

"Ouch, Allison, take care. That hurt! Me thinks my skull bleeds. They will think you have slaughtered the Queen. Better yet, now we can dirty the monthly bandages and you can wash and hang them...." Elizabeth giggled.

"My Love, I stuck you but a little, " said Allison. "Give me a second and you can look." Allison poked a few more times and set a cap on her creation. "Open thine eyes and behold. You look like an Irish gypsy with your blue eyes and dark hair. Oh, and notice the cap! It is a Scottish tam. You could infiltrate that land and pass. What is thy will, Madame? Open thy eyes."

Elizabeth's mouth formed an 'O' as she stared at her reflection. Where was Elizabeth? It was not possible that this raven-haired beauty was she. "You have changed me completely. I am no longer Elizabeth. Who shall I be called, Rowena, Wild Jessica of the Heath? I am so free," she exclaimed.

A knock sounded at the door. Allison snatched the head gear and stuffed it up her sleeve. "A moment, sir, and she will see you." Elizabeth mouthed that she see who it was. "Who comes anon?" asked Allison

"'Tis only me, Willie, with the lists."

Allison rearranged Elizabeth's hair and placed a simple gold circlet upon it. "Enter My Lord," said Elizabeth. "I have only my overdress to place, and we may proceed. You can explain the lists as we walk."

"You are feeling much better. I have not seen you up for several days and your ladies said you languished ill and would not see them either. You are a welcome sight and your beauty will grace the court once again." Willie smiled.

Willie was a leftover from her father and Mary, but he was the best friend she had in the Chamber. She trusted his advice above all others. She loved the way he flattered her. She knew she had the vain streak inherited from the Tudor line, but it was nice to hear the compliments, true or not. She smiled at him and honored him with her arm as they entered the Great Room that held the throne of England.

Elizabeth was dressed simply in a sapphire blue gown edged in gold. She looked upon the Lords and Ladies in attendance at Court and marveled at their exhibition of snobberies. "All Rise!" rang out over the room, and the noise level rose to deafening level.

"Silence!" Elizabeth roared over the crowd. "Silence, I must hear the petitions from my people. If I cannot, you will all be banished from this room." The court bowed and was quiet.

Willie approached the throne. To Elizabeth he said, "Robert Dudley has come to pay homage, Milady. What willst thou?"

She whispered back, "I did not know he was back in London. Let him come. I always have a few moments for an old friend."

Willie announced, "Sir Robert Dudley, Earl of Leicester."

Elizabeth's friend and lover bowed to the Queen. He walked the full length of the hall and bowed again. Elizabeth stood up and offered her hands to her friend. "Robert, it has been months since you were to court. We have missed you."

"As I have missed you, my Queen," Robert said, and they looked at each other a fraction too long. "There have been certain swellings from unwelcome realms. I have been taking care of them. Please accept my great apologies for my long absence. I will be here more often now. Please beware and take care. Listen to Willie. He will council you well." Dudley dropped her hands, bowed and retired to the side where the rest of peerage stood. The family lost all titles and holdings for supporting Mary, Queen of Scots against Lady Jane Grey, who held the throne for seven days and was a long time dead.

"Thank you for your service to the Crown, Robert. Willie, who is our first petitioner?"

"A Welsh sheep farmer looking for a piece of land to graze his sheep," Cecil said in a loud voice. "He was not terribly clear," he whispered to Elizabeth.

"Proceed."

A man in his finest wool coat and long work pants with cobble boots clattered up the aisle and bowed to the Queen. His face was red from embarrassment. He rolled his cap around and around in his hands in a nervous gesture. "Ye Majesty, yer Honor, Ma'am, I, er, we needs to have a place to put the sheep to graze. Me neighbor thinks his cow should have all the land, mine included. Our Lord, he decided that whichever one o' us to go before the Queen, why he would abide by her rulin'. I been waitin' low these two months jest ta git in here and me poor woman, she be takin care a the youngins' and the fields and the sheep. They be needin' shearin' and I needs ta get home afore she decides to do the shearin' herself and then kill the cow fer food. Ya' see yer Majesty's Honor Ma'am, my woman makes the softest threads and weaves the warmest cloth. I don't know how or why. Some say she be a magic woman wi' the wool. I think she treats it wi' som'pin differn't. Here be a wrap she done wi' our wool.

Well, I lay it afore ye yer Majesty, Ma'am. We jus' need a small piece o' the land for the sheep. There be only one cow ya see an' four sheep." The poor man bowed and curtsied looking backwards to make his embarrassed escape.

It was all Elizabeth could do not to laugh out loud. Some of the Court was sniggering behind fans. "Quiet," she said to the Court. To the man she said, "Please don't run away. Thank your woman for the wrap. I will wear it proudly. Tell your Lord to make sure you get your piece of land for your sheep. If she has time, have your dame weave me a neck warmer from her fine thread. Thank you for coming. Ask the doorman to show you to the kitchen for a bite before your journey home." To Willie she said quietly, "That Lord needs to make those decisions himself." Aloud to those congregated in the hall she said, "Lord Chamberlain, record this decision and call the Lord before me on another day. I must see this man, who lets his Queen do his job for him."

The day dragged on. The list of petitions was interminable. For seven hours Elizabeth sat and listened and squirmed but did not excuse herself for food or drink. At the end of the seven hours she was faint with hunger. She had a headache that would kill a man. She put an end to the public day and bade everyone waiting to be heard to come back on the morrow. "Lord Chamberlain," she whispered, "I do believe my legs and feet have fallen asleep. Please empty the hall of all and when done come and grab my arm that I may walk to my chambers in a modest manner without stumbling."

"Yes, Your Majesty," and to the assembled said, "Please go to your homes now. There will be another public day tomorrow. Please return all ye who have business before the Crown."

The hall emptied rapidly. Elizabeth tried stomping, first one side then the other. Pins and needles attacked her feet and legs. She waited for Willie to come and get her. "Willie, everything I heard today should be the work of the estate. Why are not the peers taking responsibility for their lands? Did my father give too much to too few? Did Mary ruin it for the poor folk who live on the lands? Ask the Privy Council to sit this week—not tomorrow, perhaps the day after. I have much to discuss. All must be present unless they are at war or on the high seas." Elizabeth stood and hobbled a few steps, grasping Willie's arm for support. "Damn these chairs, Willie. Have a small soft pillow on the throne for tomorrow and have a few knightings ready. I must stand up occasionally during the day. There, the other foot is now fully awake. I can walk without the support of your arm.

"Oh, Willie, I do get so lonely. Robbie is back. At least now I can talk to him. Why will you not give permission for us to marry? Oh, I do rattle on. I know, unite kingdoms. One would think that was all a woman monarch was good for." Elizabeth and William Cecil made their way to Elizabeth's chambers. "Thank you so much Lord Chamberlain. It has been a most interesting day."

"My Queen," said Cecil with a bow. He turned heel and left.

She entered her room. It was full of ladies-in-waiting and servants. Elizabeth glowered with displeasure. "What is going on here? Who dares be in my chambers without my permission? Where is Allison?"

"Madame," Kat Ashley curtsied. The rest followed suit. "We were summoned to meet here and await your return."

"And who summoned you, Milady?" the Queen queried.

"Why Cecil of course, Madame." Lettie Knolleys broke in.

"And when did this request occur, Milady?" Elizabeth worked hard to hide her smile.

"Why an hour or so ago, Madame." Kat Ashley took over again.

"And how did he summon you, Milady?"

"Why he just came to the outer chamber and requested that we be here, of course." Kat Ashley's cheeks were red with the lie.

"That old rascal!" the Queen grinned. "He is simply magical. He can produce himself in two places at once."

There was more than one red face in the room now. Lady Marie Saltworthy started to speak, but Elizabeth stopped her. "Do you know the penalty for treason, any of you?" Elizabeth's cheeks were pinkish in the light. "Do you? If you don't remember let me refresh your minds. The penalty for treason is death prefaced with a rather long and tedious stay in the tower. Lying to your Queen is treason, especially if she knows the real truth of the matter. Now, who summoned you to my chambers and when. Pray, tell me the truth as to why you are here and do it now."

Allison appeared at that moment from the inner chamber of the Queen's boudoir. "Milady, these women wanted into your boudoir, but I locked it and myself in. I know what you told me a fortnight hence and have strived to obey thee. Naught have been in there this day, but thee and me." Allison was ashen with embarrassment and shame at having to address Elizabeth in front of her appointed and trusted ladies.

"You have done well, Nurse. I am glad you were here." To the rest of the room she announced, "The least of you is trustworthy. If there is a reason you want access to my private quarters, avail yourselves now. Be aware that you will be followed from this day on until one of you reveals the spy who called you to my household without my permission. Go now and search to your hearts' content. Allison, I am in need of drink and sustenance. Summon it now and make haste. My innards grumble and gnaw at themselves with disuse and they beg me to help them fulfill their duty." Elizabeth reclined on the chaise lounge by the fire. Sighing, she closed her eyes for a short rest.

The ladies availed themselves to a short and unfruitful search of her private chambers. She overheard whispering, "I did see the monthly rags hanging by the fire fresh washed. There can be nothing to that rumor at least," said one and another said, "Yes, but Mary said there was some more to look for." A third commanded that they hush or bring the axmen to their door.

Elizabeth allowed a small smile to reach her lips. The door closed on the whispering women and Elizabeth touched her stomach in the age-old protective caress of a mother-to-be.

1559: Late Summer: On the Road West

"This should help with the disguise," said Allison as she draped the Welsh Flag over the Queen's shoulder. Once we get to East o' the Sun, we wait. It should not take too long. You have done well, Milady. You carry high. These cloths have hidden your small belly, the extra fabric in the petticoats as well. How are you feeling?" Allison and Elizabeth dispensed with the daily ritual for over a month now inviting the ladies of the court in after Elizabeth discarded her nightgown and put on her bloomers and camisole. Nurse was in charge of lacing and not one of the ladies-in-waiting questioned the Queen's vagaries.

This trip to the Welsh castle of her father's was a necessity to the security of the country. Smugglers were assaulting the northwestern Welsh coast. The practice was age-old, but now taxes were important to the maintenance of the military establishment. Elizabeth's reign was not without its financial difficulties.

Elizabeth and Allison made the trip over four days. The coach was comfortable, and Elizabeth wanted to make the castle in as short a time as possible. There was one short stop made for lunch. The foot man went to inquire about the menu and brought the news that not only was lunch available, but bread and cheese for the trip and sweets to satisfy all. Elizabeth requested that the food be brought, and they ate in the coach to complete the trip that day.

"What was the name of that inn, Allison?" Elizabeth asked with her mouth full.

"Why the Cock and the Sow, Madame. Were you pleased with the food?" Allison stopped eating long enough to answer.

"Whoever cooks there is worth his weight in gold. I should bring him back to London. The French have nothing over him. I will talk to the footman, when we are through with our business at the castle." Both women continued with their meal.

1559 London—the Court—Fall

The long days passed. Elizabeth, home from the Welsh land hold and with some ingenuity and planning, set about a long-term idea to help fight the smuggling and piracy plaguing the western fronts of the kingdom. It would take time, but eventually with the right people in place, the station would run smoothly and enhance the military strategy of England.

Her days were getting short. Elizabeth felt more and more clumsy. At seven months she became 'ill' again. Once more the ladies of the court were bade by a spy, still unknown to Elizabeth or Allison and denied by William Cecil, to search her apartments after this latest 'illness'. The monthly rags were found with fresh blood, yet unwashed, and the Queen complained of an ache in her lower belly. Once more all were satisfied. Rumors wafted around the Court that she was ill. No one dared confront the Queen.

In private she asked Allison, "Why is it so different for a woman to birth an infant without marriage than it is for a man to start a child outside of it? The child is still a bastard, and we know that even legitimate birth is changeable by the whim of the church or a misbegotten law. God save me from misbegotten laws." Elizabeth talked in a quiet voice after this latest visit. "By the by I have made a show of eating more and your expert lacing distributes much of the child away from my front. That new layer of petticoats helps as well, and I have noticed more fullness in the skirts of many of my ladies. Oh, Allison I do wish this child were out and gone."

"Milady, I do wish you would let me see my cousin to dispose of this baby."

"Allison, you cannot go. She knows you. We made arrangements. It will cost a purse of gold, but that woman in the Witch's Brew can take care of everything. She has all to lose and will not talk.

I need to be out of this castle and away from prying eyes for a short while. Why not dress me in that wig you brought low these many months ago? I can then check on. We can go to East o' the Sun. We will go incognito. We will be as two travelers and see the countryside, too. It will be a lark and have a purpose. We must needs make that coach as common a carrier as possible and see who rides with the Queen. This journey will take ten days at least. We may hear more of the real news than we do now. Cecil is only as good as his spies and they are in foreign lands. I want to know what my people think. That is just as important as foreign doings." Elizabeth hugged

Allison, part from love and part from the insecurity the monthly searches made. Her government did not trust its Queen in all ways and that was not permissible. If only she could find the person who questioned her behavior. She knew that Mary was informed at all times, but by whom, and how was that bitch giving orders in her house? The questions haunted her.

"Yes, Milady," Allison returned her hug. "One can learn a lot in ten days. I am not sure a trip so soon before the child is wise, Madam. Can we not make it a few weeks after and make other plans for the birthing? Milady, ye have a devious mind. Ye are so like your father ye are." Allison rinsed and hung the monthly rags dipped in the chicken blood fresh bought from the market. "Are you receiving today or are you going out?"

"Allie, today I should go and see the witch and see if she recognizes me from the time before. If she does not, I will be the proper one to make the arrangements for the disposal of the child. Oh, please dear God, let her be born bald and with brown eyes and darkish skin. The further from me she can be seen the safer we all are. I don't want a child placed like the Fitzroy bastard; God rest his soul. I can never recognize and honor her with a title and say 'all's well that ends well' as could my father. It will ruin my reputation. I can have a lover, but no blow by. Allison, I am married—married to England."

Elizabeth cried and Allison held her making the cooing sounds of comfort. Elizabeth could never have anything of her own. Even by marriage to a foreigner,

her children although legitimate would belong to the
country; be England's children. They would be torn
between France or Spain, whatever country their
father ruled, and she would never truly be Queen of
England again. The demand by the Papist hoard
would demolish her church and England would once
again march into the background of world power.

1559-The Cock and the Sow

Georgie, the stable boy all of six years old, was
apprenticed to Evan by his father, Evan's twin
brother. The child was magical with livestock, horses
especially. Tildy loved what he did with her sow, the
cow and the three sheep, all of which kept them in
food stuffs and wool. Georgie was there only a month
or so when a rich nobleman came through for a bite
and draught and a good night's sleep. Georgie took his
team and when the nobleman started to speak,
Georgie interrupted and asked him what he wanted to
feed the steeds. The nobleman was aghast that one so
young knew enough to ask. When he left in the
morning, the team was shining as was the carriage,
the interior dusted and the leather polished to a soft
gleam. Each of the team got an apple and gave a
nuzzle to the little stable boy. The nobleman flipped
him a coin and told Evan that boys twice his size did
half as much for a larger price and that Evan should
keep this one around. He had a talent with the great
beasts.

Since that time more gentry and peerage had
stopped at the inn, sometimes for luncheon or tea and
sometimes for the night, but all were pleased with the
treatment of their livestock and recommended the

place to others who might pass by. It did help that Tildy's cooking was superb, with delicately herbed meats and stew, beautifully baked breads and sweets to make one drool. Her cream cakes were known far and wide as the most delicious confection in the country.

Late Summer: The Cock and the Sow

At long last the sign for The Cock and the Sow came into view. Morvyn breathed a sigh of thankfulness that the long ride was over. As she came to the yard, the young boy, Georgie, took her bag and helped her from the pony. Evan scooped up the bag and handed the leathers to Georgie, who marched the tired beast to the stable. "Come ye wee beastie. Ye look tired and wore out from your long walk. Let's get you some warm straw, dry hay and a nose full of oats." Georgie gave the pony a pat on the nose and one of his never-ending apples. The pony trotted alongside the little boy, contented.

"Come now Morvyn. Tildy is waiting for you long these few weeks. She said it was your time to come again. Have some tea and set a spell before dinner." Evan tolerated this skinny, ill-kempt cousin of his wife. He did not like her or trust her, but he could put up with a few days twice a year, and Tildy never asked to go to London for a visit. That suited him just fine. "Tildy probably has some warm water for you to wash up with and get the road grime from your face and hands. She knew you were on the way. It's like she has a sense for you. I'll take your things up to your room."

Morvyn looked at the pleasant face and alarming blue eyes of her cousin's husband. "Ach, Evan, you're treating me royal you are. Thank you. Do you have a full house? If so, I can stay in the stable. It doesn't hurt me none. I appreciate it when you let me sleep in a bed. That damn Jack sometimes makes me sleep in the stable, and it isn't near as nice as yours, so I am mighty thankful to you for anything." Morvyn meant every word. Tildy was waiting by the door as Morvyn entered. She opened her arms to her cousin and enveloped her in a grand bear hug.

Tildy had long, lustrous, red hair, which she wore in plaits under a coif. She told people she wore the coif to keep hair out of her cooking. As good a cook as she was, she was slender and showed her bodices and petticoats to an advantage. Evan adored her and bussed her often of the cheek or lips in front of customers almost like a warning for interested males to stay away. Most, observing this, smiled and nodded and resumed eating. Who would have thought that The Cock and the Sow would garner such attention because of the cook and the stable boy? Evan didn't mind. They came and spent their money.

"We are so pleased to have you again, Morvyn. You are a little late this time?" Tildy smiled and hugged her cousin again.

"Nay, I had some things to collect, but we can talk tomorrow when we go to the garden. Oh, Tildy, it is good to see you again. A little drink and some bread would be good, as well. I ain't had nothing since this morning. That pony doesn't have any speed but slow and I didn't pack enough to chew on. Ah, but it good to finally be here. Cute little stable boy. My pony took a shine to him, he did." Morvyn giggled at her thought.

Tildy said, "Come along Morvyn. The food is ready, and it is more than a crust of bread. There is no one here now. Let's all sit down and have a bite. I'll call the lad."

They all sat down at the kitchen plank. Evan gave a short thanks, and they dug into lamb stew with bread, butter and ale. As a finish Tildy brought out her apple fig pie and a pot of tea. They chatted awhile over the tea, then Georgie yawned. Evan took him out to the stable and Tildy took Morvyn upstairs and kissed her good night. "Sleep well, cousin. We'll talk in the morning.

After the morning nip was off the air and a cup of tea and some raspberry scones were safely ensconced in their bellies, Tildy and Morvyn went to the garden. Morvyn looked in awe at the full beautiful herbs Tildy grew. "You are Tildy, the Goddess of Herbs, cousin. I will take all you can give me. Save your seed plants and that which you need for your own use." Morvyn touched the growing plants with reverence. "Tildy, look, I have me some seed I got from a merchant from the East. I got some root stock, too. Do you think you can make it grow? These are some spices what come from warm, wet climes. I don't ken how much ye can do but try it. These are some strange and wonderful spices. We can do so much with them. Jack don't know I have this, so should it ever come up...."

"I can keep a quiet tongue in my head, Morvyn. You should know that by now."

"Aye, these come from the East and India. Merchants say they are warm countries where you don't want to wear even a bodice, but only loose and flowing cloths of the finest silk to keep the body covered. I took a chance that just maybe...oh just try. If naught shows, then my loss. If there is bloom, I get first fruit free."

"Morvyn, you know I like to try new things. What kind of spice be these, none poison for I canna grow poison around the wee boy and the animals who might graze?" Tildy looked at Morvyn for a face or expression. Tildy, smart woman that she was, did not always trust Morvyn's judgment.

"I don't think any be poison. Humans eat them. They are normal but tasty, cinnon and nutmeg and a couple that yield a hot flavor and the gingerroot and the clove root, but I think that it is the buds you want from the clove."

Tildy agreed that she would give the new wood and seeds a chance. She did not hold much hope if they needed a wet warm climc, but she would do her best. Morvyn left within the week, loaded down with herbs to dry. She carried two large cloths one on either side of the animal she rode, and her ride home was redolent with the scent of sage, lavender and much more.

1559 The Witch's Brew Mid-Winter

A knock on her door drew Morvyn to open the top half. A woman with long black hair, bent slightly looked up at her. "Expect a child within the month, my girl. Expect a child." The old woman coughed. "Yer ta git rid 'o it. There be gold in it fer ya. Just git rid 'o it. The old woman pulled her skeletal hand from her cloak a velvet pouch in it. She offered it to Morvyn, who took it. Morvyn opened the pouch and looked in. Gold! Her mouth agape she looked up. The old woman was gone.

1559 The Cock and the Sow—Winter

The weather had grown cold. Even now there was a chance of snow. The traveler, a young lad, stopped at The Cock and the Sow. Georgie ran up and asked for the ribbons of his horse. "I be looking for Matilda Lewis and a bite, and yes, ye may take me horse."

Georgie took the reins and led the horse to the barn for a rubdown, but not until he yelled into the inn, "Aunt Tildy, Aunt Tildy, man ta see ya." Then Georgie hurried away, the day being chilled with a coming snow.

This was unusual. Travelers didn't ask for her specifically. Tildy hurried out to the courtyard. "Whence come ye?" she asked, "And what do ye want of me. I be Tildy Lewis, Matilda that is."

"I have a message from a Morvyn Hoggins of London. Ye know of her?" the lad said.

"What business be that o' yours?" asked Tildy. "Yes, I know her. Is there a note or did she tell you to say her message?"

"There be a note." The lad dug into his sleeve and dug out a greasy piece of paper. "I be on my way to the Queen's castle. She knew of my trip from the

Witch's Brew. I agreed to deliver this to ya. I just
wanted to make sure this were the right person."

"Oh, you poor lad, where are my manners? I
have some soup or a bit of stew before you go. 'Tis
cold out today and will get colder. I hope you have
more to wear, a warm cloak or so." Tildy bustled the
lad into the inn and into a seat. She went to the
kitchen and cut some bread and dished up some
savory lamb stew. "Here, fill yer belly and rest a while.
You will need all you can get. Here is a travel snack,
some bread and cheese with some dried meat. I'll
leave you to it. I have bread rising in the kitchen."

"Morvyn said there might be a meal in it fer me
here. Thank ye," the lad replied with a grin.

Tildy smiled and then ran into the kitchen. She
pulled the note from her bodice and looked at it. She
had a hard time reading Morvyn's scrawl.

Will see you in two fortnights. Morvyn

Two fortnights? Tildy thought. *It is near the
dead of winter and that will put her here around
Christmastide. Something must have happened to
Jack or even to her. I have no herbs for her. Besides
she never sent a note before.* Tildy's mind raced.

Something was afoot. Morvyn was always a
little wild. When she up and married Jack Hoggins, it
was to get away from the mess she created in the
croft—the two boys and a dead cow. She wanted to go
to the big city. Tildy knew she practiced witchcraft,
but it was not the evil kind, just the old religion.
Morvyn was a sort of grey witch, neither good nor
bad, and now she sends a note for the first time in all
the times she visited. Yes, something was definitely

afoot. Tildy warmed some apple tart and brought it to the young man. Evan brought Georgie in for a break and a taste. Tildy went and got each a bowl of stew and some bread and then said to Evan, "I must talk with you and soon. Something be going on."

Georgie looked up from his bowl and asked, "Auntie Tildy, who be that man?"

"Georgie, 'tis not your business. Did he come with a horse?"

"Yes, Auntie, and he asked fer ya on his dismount. I sent him right in after yellin' after ya. I took his horse straight to the stable and rubbed him down and give him some grain and hay. That were alright weren't it?"

"He is a traveler from London, who brought a message from your Auntie Morvyn. Just eat you tea and get back to your chores. We don't feed you for nothing, you know." Tildy ruffled his hair. Poor babe, his da could no longer keep him and sent him to his Uncle Evan as an apprentice. He was a wonder with the horses and as sweet and kind as a small angel. He helped Tildy with the pig and had it trailing behind him everywhere he went. Ah, to have a child of her own. All those times she and Evan tried and all those near gets and then the one who died in childbirth. She wanted to try again, but Evan said they had each other and what more did they really need. Tildy tried to convince him that a babe would be even more, that she wanted a family, but Evan was adamant. No more babies for a while. She would make do with Georgie, even if he weren't really hers. Best get back to the traveler. "Have ye had enough?" she asked. I have a warm tart for ye to take as well as what I gave you. Let me get it and you can be on your way."

"Thank ye, kind lady. The stew were better than I could get in heaven, I warrant. The bread and cheese and now this tart will last another day, and I should be at my journey's end afore that. Your husband give me some ale and it is the best yet. Thank ye again and goodbye."

"Ye should be on your way. The weather is turning. There be no highway men that we have heard of along this way. Take your leave with the good weather. Your mount should be a happy one after Georgie is through with him. God go with you," Tildy said. The boy walked out the door,

Tildy picked up the dirty dishes and took them to the kitchen. "Evan must know of this," she said to no one as she cleaned the tea dishes." Ay," she affirmed, "It is his business too." She prepared the plate for another pie. "Might just as well get the evening meal started." She went to the larder for the last of their beef. "Time Evan slaughtered another calf. We'll be having chicken for the next few days." Tildy went about her chores wondering what possessed Morvyn to travel in this weather. It must be important.

1559 London—New Year's Eve

"Allison, I must get to that safe house you found. There is no one there now?" Elizabeth felt very strange. She could bear no laces today. She felt as though her whole inside sank to her thighs.

"Milady, here is your wrap. I have a small cart we can use at the end of the tunnel. No one need know ye are gone"

"Bring the hair, Allison, bring the hair. I must be well enough to bring the babe to the Witch."

"Aye, Milady, I will bring it all. Make haste, my love. Ye have little time and we must get out. No matter how you feel or what happens, try not to make a sound."

"Allison, can we take the back door? Ye know the one—my escape door? Ye are sure the cart is at the end outside the castle?"

"It has been there a week now. Who knew ye would last so long?"

"You have the hay and the cover?"

"Yes, Milady, all is in order. Hurry now. Ye must make it on your own for most of the way. I am not strong enough to carry you that far and hold the candle high. I have your bag and the other wrap so I must follow."

Elizabeth, clad only in a chemise and the long black cloak, led the way down the dark tunnel that led to an outer gate of the castle. It was that tunnel that saved many a life in strife-torn England in earlier years. Elizabeth learned of it as a child, her mother napping, she exploring as children do. Then her mother was gone, and she was sent to her aunt's house for raising.

The candle Elizabeth held gave little light, but she and Allison had rehearsed this escape several times before. This trip was the real thing and Elizabeth felt both joy and dread. She could not keep this child and keep the throne. The throne was more important. *This would all be over tomorrow or the next day and that would be the end of it,* she thought.

Elizabeth felt a cramping in her belly. "Allison, something is happening. My belly is cramping."

"Can ye still walk or is the pain too much to bear? We can rest a short time."

"I need to stop a bit to catch my breath. It was took nigh away from me." Elizabeth leaned against the tunnel wall. It was dry to the touch. In fact, the whole tunnel was at a pleasant heat for the winter months. "A person could live in here trust no one know of it and food could be gotten," Elizabeth said, "but we can nay stay here. We must be on the mo...." She stopped in mid-word. "My God, Allison, I have a flood between my legs! What is happening?"

"Come mistress we must be gone. It will not be too long for you now. You have lost your waters and the pains will start very soon."

"How many children have you helped into the world, Allison? Be true."

"Only two and a doctor were at one of them. Sad to say both the babe and the mother died. The other was got by the village woman. She done it right and all lived. We must keep moving. It ain't too far now. I needs you lying down soon."

"Allison, O-o-o-of...." Elizabeth dropped her candle and doubled over. The candle rolled a few feet and sputtered out. Elizabeth panted like a tired dog.

Allison put her hand over Elizabeth's mouth. "Ma'am, you must be quiet. Someone could hear. This tunnel has its own voice. Now, you need be the

Queen of All England. You have started to have your babe. When the pain subsides, arise. I will get your light and re-fire it. We have not much time to make it to the cart. It is but a little way now."

Allison passed the Queen and dropping to her knees, felt around on the floor. The candle was under her fingers. She reached around in her pouch for another light. A couple of strikes of the flint and the candle shone again. "Come, Mistress, I'll lead, and you lean on my shoulders. We will get this done."

Elizabeth obeyed. The two women made their way to the end of the tunnel. The cart was as Allison left it over a week ago, hidden behind the closed exit from the tunnel and the castle. "Get into this cart, Ma'am. There is straw aplenty for you to rest. I brought the monthly rags. They are clean, but ye might want to wad one in your mouth should another pain strike on the way." Allison was in charge, but she was worried. She had a ten-minute journey pulling the cart and with Elizabeth hidden in it, it could take longer. This was one thing that slipped by in her planning. Allison prayed! "Here we be, Ma'am. How are ye?"

Allison reached for the Queen's forehead. Elizabeth was damp with sweat but cool to the touch. That was good. There was no fever and she prayed there would be none. Allison shuddered to think what would happen if the Queen should get the childbirth fever and die, away from the castle with no one knowing but her. She envisioned her own beheading and moved more quickly.

Allison saw the cart outlined in the candlelight. "Just a few steps more, Milady, just a few steps more. Then you can rest a spell. It may be a bumpy ride, but you need to rest as much as possible. The cart be old but sturdy and light enough for me to pull."

Reaching the cart, Allison drew back the coverings revealing fresh straw. A small woman sized space outlined with crates and a barrel or two, all empty, took up the very middle of the cart. "Here, Madam, let me spread this cloak for you. It be old but soft and warm. Lay upon it. Ne'er mind what happens to it. Aye and here is a rag to stop your noise should there be any from now on. I expect you will have more pains soon enough."

"Aye, and here is one...," Elizabeth drew her knees up and held her belly. She tried to turn on her side, but the boxes prevented her.

"'Tis better you stay on your back, Ma'am, 'tis easier. 'Tis easier still to sit or kneel, but that can't be until we get to the house. Don't forget the rag. It could save your life." Allison covered Elizabeth with a dark cloak and then with a covering of straw. She stowed the purse with the rest of the equipment into a corner. She dug around in her pouch for the door key. Freeing the door, she slipped out, looking for any sign of human life in the darkness—guards or passersby. It was night. The pubs might still be full, but the streets were empty.

The curfews put an end to those midnight gatherings led by rabble rousers and religious persons who knew the new church would send them all to perdition by-passing purgatory, a favorite resting place for all before the final determination. The idea of a consignment immediately after death to either heaven or hell was too much to comprehend for some folks.

Allison saw no one—no guards, no people, no one. *Didn't anyone guard the castle? It was almost too quiet, as though the night waited for some big event. Where were the soldiers? I need to get the Queen out now,* she thought. She pulled the old shawl up over her head and went back to get the cart. "God, give me strength," she prayed under her breath. She lifted the rails of the cart and stepped out of the castle into the shrouded alleyway. She locked the door and went back to her task of pulling the Queen of England, pregnant with a possible heir and ready to give birth, to the safe place for which she'd planned. Elizabeth was ensconced upon the straw much like the Mother Mary awaiting the Baby Jesus. A second silent prayer went up to the heavens, *and please dear God, let it be a girl.*

The cart was lighter than Allison thought it would be. She pulled it through the back ways of London, a bent and cloaked old lady lost on her way to market from the country, should she be stopped. She heard a muffled groan from the cart and stopped for a minute to whisper gentling words to her passenger. Groaning straw was a give-away. Elizabeth quieted, and she was on her way again. Ah, Tripock Street and the watchmaker's store, Allison's safe house was right next door.

Allison drew the precious key on a ribbon around her neck and unlocked the door. She turned the cart so the unloading would be quicker. Elizabeth groaned again. The pains were much closer together now. *Please let me do this one right*, Allison prayed silently again as she helped Elizabeth out of the cart and into the warmed kitchen, kept that way this week by Allison in preparation for this event. "Come Milady, lean on me. A bed be on the other side away from peering windows."

"I am having another. Quick, Allison, I cannot step too much further."

"Just a few more steps. The cot is just a few more steps." Allison almost dragged the Queen the rest of the way to the cot and helped her lie down. "Keep the cries muffled, Milady. We need no one interfering before I close the door."

"It hurts, Allie. Please make it stop hurting. Why do women do this?"

"It is the curse of God for Eve's sin, Milady. Ye are doing well. Let me close up so you can do this right." Allison let go of the Queen's hand and went back to the cart and got the purse. She turned the cart against the building and covered it with the coarse woven cloth. Tomorrow morning would yield a child and a tired but freed queen. She hung the heavy covering over the one window and closed and barred the door. She stripped herself of her cloak and lit another candle. "Let's get down to work and get this child born." She bade the Queen to let her look to see what progress. There was some blood and a small shiny dome appearing from between the nether lips of the Queen. "Milady, the child should be only a few minutes more. Please push. I know it must hurt, but it will be only a short time before you can see it yourself. Push, Milady, breathe and push."

Elizabeth pushed and then in the great pain of splitting apart, she pushed again. Sydney launched out from between the Queen's legs and Allison caught her in clean rags reserved for this moment. She laid the child on the Queen's belly and tied off the cord that attached the two. She checked it to make sure she had it right and then centered the knife and cut the cord. "Hold the child to your breast, Milady, so's I can clean you up. 'Twas not a long confinement for you. You do get down to business in all things, do you not?" She thought a moment and as if remembering another step said, "The child has not cried. Let me give it a little tap on its royal behind." Allison took the child and gave its back a cupped tap. The child let out a wail to wake the dead. "Ye have a wee girl, Madam, and she is bald as an egg, just as ye ordered." The Queen reached for her child and with one last shudder passed the afterbirth which Allison dumped into a bucket held just for the purpose. She looked at the mother and child, a picture she never imagined and one she would never see again.

Within minutes the child suckled at the queen's breast, then nodded off with a content smile on her face. Allison cleaned up the rest of the mess, burning the bloodied rags but keeping a few of the monthlies. They would come in handy later on. Three hours later Allison looked upon her handiwork, a swaddled child in a lowly rough cloth, a gypsy woman bound top and bottom and wrapped in a cloak and ready to give up the child which could bring down a kingdom if it were known. The fire dying, Allison told the Queen, "We best be gone, Ma'am. Can ye walk?"

"Of course I can, and I will get stronger with a little more rest. Do not forget I must walk to the witch to give my child away. Allison, there is so much less of me. Ye must know I have named the child Sydney. I have wrapped her in cloths I prepared myself. Her name is on one. I will tell the witch that the maid that bore the child wanted that name to go with it." She giggled at her little joke. "Let us go now Allie. You have the gold? Are you sure you can pull the cart with us both in it again?"

"Of course, Madam. I have had the gold for a month. But you know it came from thy purse as 'twas given. If I pulled you here, I can pull you back to the street for the witch. We must get started. We are very close to the sunrise and people will start to populate the streets."

Allison was relieved. The birth was simple. The Queen would bleed for a few more days, but as blood went, she did not produce that much of it at the birth. "Thank God you are healthy, Ma'am. It made your birthing much simpler." Allison helped the Queen back into the cart, the dark wig in place and the babe covered with the soft cloak. Things were more dangerous now that dawn was upon them. Allison reversed her path, holding the cart rails and the much-relieved Queen, who rode within.

They could not go back to the castle the same way they had come. There would not be much sleep for either of them this day. It was two hours before the household awakened and the child had to be gone before then. The Queen must be seen in her bed and in a clean chemise.

The alley was still dark. Dawn did not reach this far into these dank streets. Allison woke the napping mother. "Ye must go to the witch now and get back to here. This is as close as I can get you without revealing all. It is but a five-minute walk if you go slow. Are ye able yet?"

"Of course! I have napped and ye have bound me well. I can make the walk to and from and deliver this babe, whom I love already. The good Lord protect her innocent soul!"

Elizabeth disembarked with the child. Allison handed her the pouch of gold. "Go, Rowena the Dark, and make your life whole again." She pointed Elizabeth in the right direction and whispered, "Go in this direction until ye see the sign. Ye'll know the way then."

The Witch's Brew looked worse in the half light of dawn. The sign was faded, and the iron hinges rusted to immobility. Elizabeth carried her sleeping baby close to her chest. Her breasts ached with milk, but she could not suckle the child anymore. Best to be rid of her quick. She walked down the dank alleyway and stepped to the door. She knocked softly at first, then louder. She heard a hoarse whisper, "Who be there?"

"'Tis Rowena the Dark." Elizabeth said in a half whisper. The top part of the door opened.

"What do ye want at this ungodly hour?" The rasping voice asked. The hag looked down on the young woman at her door.

"This is the babe I told you of. Me mistress' babe were born this morning in the early hours." Elizabeth extended the child toward Morvyn. "Take her afore she cries and wakes the street. She be healthy, she be. What a wail she made with a light tap at her birth. Quick, take her. I must be gone back to the house afore I am missed this morn. Oh, and the child's name be Sydney accordin' to 'er ma. 'Get rid of it' she told me."

"Gimme the geld, lass." Morvyn took the child and cradled it in her arms. She peeked under the swaddling to make sure it was real and alive. "The geld, lass, and be quick." Elizabeth handed over the coin wrapped in a rag that Allison provided.

"It all be there, I think," said Elizabeth playing the ignorant servant girl. "Milady said it were all there."

Morvyn opened the rag and her eyes grew big at the large number of gold pieces that lay in her hand. It was more than she ever saw in one place before. "This must be very important to yer lady. Much geld has passed because of this child. Who be she?" She looked up from her hand. Rowena the Dark vanished like a ghost, gone, not to be seen anywhere in the alley. *'Tis just as well,* thought Morvyn. She went to her niche and unlocked it. She lay the babe in the middle of the straw bed. 'Get rid of yer' she say. I'll be 'gettin' rid of yer', but not agin the law." Morvyn whispered to the sleeping child.

Drawing out a small chest from behind the many jars in the large cabinet against the wall, she placed eight of the ten coins in it with great reverence.

"This'll pay fer a fine coach with coin left over," she said aloud rubbing the two coins between her fingers before she concealed them in her bosom.

1560 The Cock and the Sow

Christmas was past. Tildy was worried. Morvyn was late. She should have been there within the fortnight before Christmas. She had written that two fortnights ago. The new moon was in the sky and still no Morvyn. Tildy mentioned it to Evan at breakfast. "Evan, my cousin is late for her visit. She is never late. Remember the note she sent by a special messenger? She never did that before either."

"Aye and you fed that messenger and paid him as well. Did you think I didn't watch you with the change? It is fine, though. That is the first note any messenger ever dropped here. Mayhap Hoggins blackened her eye," Evan continued, "And she didn't want you to see what the brute ha' done, so she waited until the swellin' went down." Evan gave a humorless laugh.

"Evan you jest. That 'brute' be a coward. If any eye be blacked, it be his by her. She packs a powerful punch and she don't let him get away with much. Ye know we both learned our letters together. She were powerful smart. She done her reading and learned how to mix and apply like a doctor. I read the Bible and what books I can get, and I can read and write scrawl. My letters are formed, and you can read them. Morvyn's are true scrawl and illegible. I did learn my sums though, and I am quite good at remembering. More tea?" Tildy defended her cousin more than once.

"Aye, and another cup will top me off. Do you have any more of your pie? T'wer perfect in sweet and tart. Ye have many more talents than yer letters. Ye are the lovingest lass and ye cook like an angel. When ye leave this mortal coil low these many years from now, just bring one of your pies and God'll let you pass through in an instant of tasting it."

"Ach, Evan ye be as sweet as..." Tildy was interrupted.

"Uncle Evan, Uncle Evan come quick. There be a man out here what says I kilt his calf and that be not true."

"Calm yourself, Georgie, think. Ye have not been away from this pub in two years, and ye are magic with the cows. Kill, I ask ye?" Tildy was red in the face and ready to do harm to anyone hurting her little boy, even if he didn't live in her chambers at the inn. She nursed him through fever and colds and made sure he dressed warm in the winter. She showed him how to knit socks with the yarn she spun. He made mufflers, too, but more than not they wound up around the necks of horses or covering flanks that were chilled. Tildy didn't mind though. His work was good, and she even sold some of his newer pieces at the inn for travelers not ready for the cold. She put the coin aside for the little boy's future. She taught him to read and do his letters. Most of all she taught him how to care for the garden soil, so she could grow the herbs and greens. This lad would never kill an animal unless it was in deathly pain and not able to come out of it again, or if he were pushed to starvation. Tildy went out of the inn armed with her temper and her love.

"Killed a calf say ye? And where be this dead calf? There be no blood around this yard or in yon stable. Where be this dead calf?" Tildy started at the man, her fists raised.

"My God, woman, I didn't say *killed*, I said 'yer skilled, lad'. Yer boy saved me cow and her babe. The cow dropped this morn in front of yer pub, and the babe didn't neither draw breath nor the ma try to clean it up. Yer boy come out and saw, and the wee lad cleaned the sac from the babe and pressed its body and the calf drew breath. He brought the cow around so the calf could suckle. Yer lad misheard me is all. He is very good with the livestock, yer boy is. I would like to take him as me own to help with all me animals." The farmer wrung his cap in his hands, his face red with embarrassment and slightly frightened of Tildy's ferocious approach.

Evan appeared with Georgie in hand and heard the last of the man's speech. He looked at Tildy, now ashen with tears on her face. Evan put his free arm around Tildy's shoulders and said, "I be sorry, good sir, but this lad is naught for sale. He is my nephew and a big part of this household." Evan continued, "I am glad for your change of heart. Come in. My wife will fetch thee a cup and a bite. Leave the boy with yer animals. It looks as though ye prosper today.

1560 The Witch's Brew—New Year's Day

From the other cabinet Morvyn pulled a traveling bag into the middle of the room. In it were her herb bag and a clean chemise. She put another warm blanket over all this. Then she made a pap with a small flask and a leather glove finger and tied the glove to the neck of the flask with several wraps of thread. "I hope the baby can suck. If not all these preparation was for naught. The child could not live five days without nourishment. If it cannot suckle, then perhaps it can take the drippings from a clean rag," Morvyn muttered. She put some sparkling white rags into the traveling bag.

     "Now please don't make a sound little one. No one can know you live. We must away from London today. I am already two weeks later than I thought when I notified Tildy. She will worry. I can hire a fast coach and have cover and comfort for us both." Morvyn picked up the child and cradled it in her arms. The baby slept on. "Ye be a peaceful one, it seems. I almost hate to give ye away, but I can't have ye here. Ye need space and fresh air far away from the sin and pestilence of this house. You, child, are sinless. May ye have every bit of love and peace ye can find in yer life. If ever there was a time to be silent and sleep long, this is it. Do it and ye can grow up strong and healthy. Ye ken, I don't even know what ye are, lad or lass. I'll check after we leave London this day. Sleep on little one." Morvyn put the sleeping child in the soft wrappings in the bag. She got a few more rags for swaddling and tucked them around the child. She took another warm shawl and covered the child all but its face. She hefted the bag and decided she must leave in the next hour before Jack woke and looked for her. If she was discovered and she would never get away.

Morvyn packed a couple of things for herself and put the feeding flask into the bag. She could get goat's milk or cow's milk along the way. Escape was the first priority. Morvyn found a scrap of paper in her little-used Bible and wrote '*I'll be back*,' weighed it down with a fork on the kitchen work board. Locking her niche and pocketing the key, she picked up her bag and left by the Dutch doors, shutting them tightly behind her. In the early morning, she went to the stable and rented a carriage spacious enough for one and some inside baggage.

"I need ya to get me close to Bryn an Cydr in Wales. It should take about four days. What do ye ask fer such a journey? Your food and drink will be included as will care for yer animals." Morvyn asked politely.

"It'll take more 'n ye have old woman," the coachman sneered.

"Tell me how much," Morvyn snarled, all politeness gone.

"Half a sovereign. Can't do it for less, time away, missed fares and all, ye ken?" The driver looked at her, a smug smile washing across his face.

"I'll be back in five minutes. Ye'll have yer half sovereign. Just be ready to leave when I get back." She had made the best of the bargain but would not let him know he could have had the whole thing. Thank goodness she knew her sums and a place to change gold on a fair trade. Ten minutes later she was back. "Here is yer money and there'll be no more for ye."

The driver looked at her astonished. "Git ye in the carriage. We be gone," he said as he placed her bag on the floor and helped her in, all polite and such. He closed the door. *Half a sovereign,* he thought, *I would have done it for half that amount!*

Morvyn felt the lurch of the carriage. She hoisted the bag on the seat beside her and opened it. "Here we be, ye sweet babe. Yer on yer way to a whole new life." The trip was so uneventful that driver and passengers dozed with the jostling of the carriage. Morvyn was careful to stop three times a day for the first two days, always getting fresh milk and fresh bread when available. The child was very good with the flask-glove combination and, when not eating, it slept.

The third night out they stayed at an inn. Morvyn got to unwrap the child and found it to be a female, a very wet dirty female. As she cleaned the child up, she said to her "Even better for Tildy, for when you are grown some, she will have another set of hands to help her. Just now she will have the babe she always wanted." The child was now in clean swaddling, the dirty washed and drying over the fire. One strange piece was the red silk band with 'Sydney' embroidered, fine stitching in gold thread. "What a strange name for a girl," Morvyn whispered to the child. "I wouldna told Tildy, but for this. So ye be Sydney. Nice to make yer acquaintance, me little love." Morvyn wrapped another shawl around the child and, cradling it in her arms, lay down on the bed to sleep the sleep of the righteous. Both woman and child woke before dawn. Morvyn used the rest of the milk from dinner and fed the child. She cleaned the child again, only having to remove the large cloth, and redressed the child for the trip. She washed out the large cloth and stowed it for travel in a small pouch she always kept with her. Morvyn got dressed, packed the child and got ready for the final leg of the journey. She went downstairs to the dining area and knocked on the kitchen door. The owner's wife answered and Morvyn stated, "It is on the road I wish to be. The days be colder than I thought. Do ye have a brick or stone to warm the coach?"

"Aye, I'll get my man to make ready fer ye. Do ye want any breakfast?"

"Aye the driver and I will take one. It makes the travel smoother to have a stomach full. Oh, and would ye render me a bill?"

"Nay, I dinna do the sums, but me man will have a price for all when he comes back. Here be yer bowl." The good wife handed her the bowl with the slightly lumpy porridge, but the milk was fresh and sweet. It was a good break and quick.

The coachman was true to his word and the trip was only four days long. She paid well for his service. She'd fed him and provided room for him and his horse and rested enough that no one was exhausted from the trip.

It was early and time to go. She liked to leave by dawn each day. The horse was hitched to the carriage and the warm stone placed for heat within the coach. He got a small stone for his feet as well. Saucy Sue was old, but perfect for this job. He loved his horse, he did. He loaded the oat bucket for her and got himself ready to travel. The inn owner brought him a bowl of porridge with some milk. He'd had better, but some was better than none. He ate and had the coach waiting for the woman. She came out directly with her bag and got in the coach. "As fast as ye can but spare the horse. 'Twould be nice to be there afore dusk. Get on wi' ye." Late that afternoon the coach pulled up to The Cock and the Sow. Georgie met the coach. The coachman helped Morvyn light from the interior. He reached in and pulled out her bag. She grabbed it before he could carry it into the pub. "This be my cousin's inn. Ye are free to do as ye like, but my cousin be a wonderful cook, so ye might like a bite and a tankard. Ye have driven long and I thank ye fer that." She took herself and her bag to the front door of the inn.

     The door opened as if by magic. "My God, Morvyn, ye be here!" Tildy wrapped her arms around her cousin who was alive and well. "We been worried when ye didn't come. It be another two mayhap three weeks since yer message. Come into the kitchen. Leave your things here. We'll have a bite and a short chat, and then ye can unpack. I don't have many this night, later maybe, but not now. Come along, come along," Tildy chattered. Morvyn picked up her bag and followed.

     Once in the kitchen Morvyn asked, "Are we alone here?"

     "Of course, silly. Do you see aught else?" Tildy gave her a little giggle. Then more serious, "Ye know 'tis too early for the mature herbs, Morvyn. They must have six or seven more weeks. What brings ye this soon, love?"

"Aye, Tildy, I ken 'tis too early for the greenery. Tildy, ye look a little plump. Do ye think ye kin be bearing a child?

"I am no plumper than the last time and the time before. What are ye trying to say, Morvyn. Bear a child? Ye ken I am barren." Tildy looked sad.

"So was the wife Elizabeth afore her son John the Baptist were conceived, but she had a child anyway, and ye be not as old as Elizabeth were when she had John." Morvyn gave a little humph at the end of her statement to acknowledge winning the argument.

"Ye are full of blather, ye are. What speak ye of?" A small mewling sound came from the bag at Morvyn's feet. "What be that, Morvyn, a new puppy? That is not what we need around here, another useless hungry mouth to feed that'll chase the chickens right into their nests and no eggs for the baking. Be ye going daft coming all this way for that?"

"Nay, Tildy, 'tis a new mouth to feed, but better than a wee pup. Although this may chase chickens, too. Here let me show you." Morvyn opened the bag and they both looked down and into the bluest eyes either ever saw. Hiding the child as she did and looking in the evenings, Morvyn never really saw its face and when cleaning it, she paid no mind to the child's eyes with wondering about the embroidery and all. Between all that and sleep she never really saw the child at all, and never in good light.

"How wee is she?" Tildy murmured. "When did ye birth her?"

"Don't be daft, girl, I didn't birth her and even if I did, I would never burden you with the spawn of Jack Hoggins. No, I was paid by a gypsy woman to take the offshoot of a lady, who had to be rid of her. The mistress paid me some small amount, but I couldn't take its wee life. My feelings were bad about it from the beginning. I could hang should anyone find out and walls have ears and eyes in Londontown. I thought of thee and how ye yearn for a child of yer own. So, what do you say? Do you want her?"

"I...I don't know. I must find Evan. It must be his decision too." Tildy reached for the child. "Oh, yes, sweet thing. How can I not say 'yes' to thee?" To Morvyn she said, "Evan be in the stable. Hold her. I will get him." Tildy gave the child to Morvyn, tears of joy in her eyes. She rushed out the door to fetch her husband. Morvyn knew that the child had a good home.

Evan came into the kitchen at a run, Tildy gasping for breath and talking a mile a minute as she tried to keep up with Evan. "Evan, ye must say aye. A child, a babe, a newborn birthed low these four days past. It would know no other but we for parents and we be enough out that no local would know if I be with child or not. Look at her." Tildy swept the child from Morvyn's arms. The baby started to cry and Tildy comforted it. She showed the child to Evan. "How can ye say nay to these eyes? They be brighter and bluer than mine."

Evan looked at the child Tildy thrust at him. "Hold her. Feel her heft. She will be a good worker." Tildy looked at Morvyn for reinforcement. Morvyn was looking at Evan's face.

Evan was besotted. He reached for the child and folded the top of the shawl away to take a good look at her face. "She be bald!" he teased. Morvyn knew in that moment that her trip from London was worth it and that she stayed on the right side of the law was of even more value than the coin she'd spent.

" Oh, Evan, a little maid," said Tildy. "We shall call her…"

"Sydney," Morvyn interrupted. "That is the name the mother wanted for her. At least that is what she embroidered on this piece of swaddling. It must'a been done during the waiting. The needlework is exquisite. Her name is Sydney." Morvyn handed over the piece of cloth with the name on it.

Tildy hung on Evan's arm and both looked down at their new daughter, tender smiles curving their lips. Together they said, "Wee Sydney." They looked at each other and smiled even wider. This was Tildy's dream come true, and if truth be known, was also Evan's.

Ignored this whole while, Morvyn looked at the new parents. She was hungry and there was a lovely meat pie waiting. She 'heard' it crying out to her, so she sat and ate and smiled a smile of satisfaction.

***

Morvyn stayed with Tildy and Evan until the herbs ripened to full richness. Morvyn was always overcome with the beauty and fragrance of these herbs. It was only five months since her last visit, but she asked Tildy about the roots she brought in the late summer. "What happened with those pods and the roots from the last time?" Morvyn asked.

"Oh, Evan made me some frames and I buried them under the earth and then covered them with the frames with glass in them. They aren't very big, but we can go look and see if anything is happening." The baby was sleeping, and a short walk to the herb garden would do both women some good. Tildy lifted the first frame where she'd buried the root. Small green leaves seemed to be sprouting up from a tree like plant.

"Morvyn, look, something is happening. Mayhaps we need to wait until the weather gets warmer to uncover this. Let's look at the seed frame. Evan thought this might keep in heat from the sun and give the plants some growing time. It hasn't been overly cold so far. I will cover them with a shawl or two if it gets really cold." She lifted the frame from the second and there were small growths in orderly rows. "We may have some interesting plants come spring. Be patient and we will see. All could go bad you know, so keep praying all goes as well as it has so far." Tildy dropped the frame back down, and the two women went back inside.

"A small house made of glass might hold in more sunlight," said Morvyn.

"That is an interesting idea. We can ask Evan how much that would take in time and materials," said Tildy.

"I have a new seed for you, Tildy. Actually, it is for the babe, when she grows up. I got it from a Dutchman on my trip. I give him some herbs to make his breath sweet, and he give me this. I am glad I kept the herbs with me on this trip. I had them for the child to help keep her sweet and dry. He told me this be called a 'bulb,' and it makes a beautiful flower in the early spring. When you plant it, put the pointy end up and ne'er mind the cold. It likes the cold, so plant it when you harvest, and you should have a flower in the spring. You do nothing after that. They grow fast and it will rise every year after first planting, and he said it might make more," Morvyn finished her story.

"What is it called, Morvyn?" Tildy asked.

"It is called 'two lips'. Maybe that is what it looks like. I don't know. Let its beauty make you happy." explained Morvyn.

Tildy held up the bulb and said, "If this 'bulb' grows I shall name it Sydney's Two Lips in honor of her birth. She will have a flower named for her as the Queen has the rose out back named for her. Sydney is our little princess." Tildy had no idea how very close she was to the truth.

1561 Spring in Wales: The Cock and the Sow

Sydney grew. She went past her first birthday walking and talking and pestering Georgie in the stables. She 'helped' Tildy in the gardens and generally got under foot. She also got lots of hugs and kisses from all the family. She was a bright lively red haired imp loved by all and the core of Tildy's heart.

Tildy rued the fact that she did not really birth the child, and she knew God would condemn her to Purgatory for a very long time, if there were still such a thing in this new English Church, but she didn't care.

Evan and Tildy went to church now and then. They were not regulars. Neither one was much concerned with the afterlife. The afterlife was enough time to get concerned about it. They took Georgie and Sydney to church, usually Christmastide, Easter, and marriages and funerals if they knew the people involved. Other than that, they worked with little or no time off.

The 'two lips' came up a beautiful crimson. Sydney acknowledged her 'two lips' as Sydney's Twolip. *S* was hard for the little girl to pronounce. She dropped her *r*'s as well, and Gauwdy was the best she could do with Georgie. As her brother, he played with her when he was not helping Evan or Tildy. Sydney adored Georgie, her older brother and followed him without stop.

1562 The Cock and the Sow

"Sydney, Sydne-e-e-ey, come to the kitchen, me love. We must prepare." To Evan, Tildy said, "The Queen's Men you say, and she wants tea here?"

To herself she muttered, "Scones—I need the whitest flour, and sweet, I need to check the honey sap. Sydney can churn the cream for a while, I have need of lavender and stevia, ah, that will sweeten, too. So much to do. Fresh strawberry preserves: thank God I gathered and made as I did, but it makes me short of the sugar. Oh, too bad, I will make do as I thought.

Georgie must get the stables ready with fresh straw and Evan needs go to the gorse for the new blue berries and I must bake a loaf, a grand loaf, of bread. I have only a small bit of time, but enough if I hurry."

Tildy yelled for Sydney, "Sydney, Sydne-e-y, come along quickly. Yer Mum needs ya now."

To herself again, Tildy spoke, "She knows I am but a simple woman. I can only do my best by her and pray it is good enough." Tildy gave the stew already on an absent stir and tasted the savory gravy. She dropped in a pinch of the precious salt and stirred again. The Queen would be here tomorrow for tea. Tildy muttered again, "If only I can keep Sydney clean and quiet for the hour.

"Oh, please, Heavenly Father, keep Sydney clean and the Queen happy. Oh, and thank you," she prayed.

The Next Day

"Sydney, what am I to do with you?" Tildy hugged the small girl to her bosom. "Ye can run and play, but not in the fields or the garden or the barn. You may not go to the stables or play with the pigs. Today we must stay clean and neat. I really want you to be my second self, to walk with me and sit with me and never leave my side. I know, you are my right arm today, not Da's nor Georgie's but mine. You did so well yesterday with the butter and the picking just the right sprigs of lavender for the scones and the cakes. So today I need you to do exactly as I ask. We will have a grand day, a day we will remember, my little love. We will have a grand time. Practice your curtsey."

"Ma, Gauwdy is twaining the wee goat to pull a cart for me so I can go to market wif him. Please let me watch him."

"Nay, Georgie is doing no such thing. He is helping yer Da with the stables and the polishing. We are all drawn to this one thing, making our inn the finest in the land for a very special visitor. Sydney, my pet, the Queen of England is stopping by today on her way to the grand castle in the West. Yer ma must have a tea ready and fit for a Queen. Oh my, that is funny if it wasn't so serious." Tildy giggled and tickled Sydney until she laughed. "Let's see your curtsey again."

"What be going on here with my two daft women laughing in the kitchen when the Queen be on her way to our own doorstep? I expect half the village to be by when they hear about this and they will, mind you, they will hear. But to be on the safe side...." Evan joined Tildy and Sydney for a few seconds and all three were laughing. Evan thought for the millionth time how wonderful having a child of their own was. Georgie was part of the family, too, since they had him at such a young age, but his lineage was after all known and they were definitely related. "Tis a beautiful picture I would put on wood wert I an artist," said Evan.

***

"Aye, my love, she will be here in minutes. Everything is in readiness. There are only six guards and two in the carriage. There is stew enough, isn't there?" Evan was nervous. His wife's nervous energy from the last two days had infected him, and he was displaying signs of his own insecurity with every breath.

"My love, all is in readiness. The child knows her curtsey without falling over, the tea stuffs are ready. Oh, the roses, I forgot the roses, but that is quickly remedied. Where is that scamp? Sydney, get in here and let me look." Tildy was the calm one now.

Sydney appeared, not one mote of dirt on her. "Gauwdy, here?" she asked.

"No darling, he is awaiting Her Majesty's coach and guards. Show yer Da your curtsey."

Sydney did her bow. Once again, she did not fall down. For one so young she achieved a very difficult move. Tildy couldn't be prouder. Just then the noise of horses and coaches rolled in through the open door.

"She's here, Tildy, she's here," Evan said, shaken to his core.

"Calm down, sir. What could happen? All is well." Tildy stood and smoothed her best apron over her stomach and thighs. She peered out the window, sparkling clean for this visit. "Evan, the guard is opening the carriage door. Let us go out and give our due." Tildy pulled Sydney by her and Evan followed. They stood beside the open door.

"Her Royal Majesty, Ruler of England and Ireland and Protector of the Faith, Queen Elizabeth!" A short slender woman with bright red hair peeking out of her traveling bonnet stepped down the steps of the coach. Sydney ran to her, stopped right in front of her and dropped her curtsey. The little girl ran back to her mother who was deep in her own curtsey, which she held until the Queen entered the door. Another woman, well dressed, taller and much older, followed the Queen.

"Dothz I bow to her, too, Ma?" Her high child's voice rang out in the silence of the moment. Tildy heard the Queen giggle.

"You might just as well, my love. Can't hurt now, can it?" Tildy laughed nervously. Sydney curtsied again and ran over to Georgie.

"I did good, Gauwdy, didn't I?"

"Aye, lass, that you did, as good as any at court," said Georgie, and he led the horses from the carriage to the stables area and bade the guards to dismount and water their steeds, showing them the accommodations. The head coachman went with Georgie and watched, amazed that such a young boy could do so much and with so much aplomb.

In the inn, the Queen and Lady Kat Ashley, Chief Gentlewoman of the Household, sat at the saw table, whispering. "I had food from here not long after my coronation. I came this way with Nurse to inspect father's castle here in the northwest. The food was brought to us to eat on the way. Before then I had no idea there was an accomplished chef here and a woman at that." Both removed their gloves, glancing around at the accommodations. They smiled at each other as Tildy approached.

"What will ye have, yer Majesty?" Tildy asked with a curtsey.

"Have you that good local ale we heard about, and some sup? We have not eaten since breakfast. I am most hungry for some good food, and it smells very good in here indeed." The Queen smiled at Tildy. Tildy went to the cupboard and brought out the finest tableware she had. She was aware of the whispered conversation between the two women when they first sat down. She asked Evan to draw two draughts for the ladies and bring a pail to the drivers and the guards. Tildy went about the business of dishing up a generous bowl of the lamb stew and brought it to the Queen and her lady. "I have some fresh baked bread and fresh churned butter if ye wish, Your Majesty."

The Queen tasted the stew. It was delicious. She nodded to Tildy about the bread as she ate like a starving prisoner. Tildy went to the kitchen. She cut the bread and brought it with a bowl of butter, both of which she set in front of the ladies. She retreated to the fire and waited as the ladies ate.

"Your name is Tildy, correct?" asked the Queen when she finished her bowl and was eating a piece of the bread.

"Yes, Ma'am." Tildy bowed and curtsied as she answered.

"Do you have any more stew, Tildy?"

"Aye, Ma'am, I'll get it right away and more bread, too."

Tildy returned with the bowls full of the steaming stew. "Do you have enough for my men, Tildy?"

"Yes, Ma'am, I do, and I'll bring bread and butter to them as well, if that be all right with you, Ma'am." Tildy curtsied again.

"Of course, it is or I would not have asked. See if your husband can fetch it for them. They need not have your finest china and tableware, however." The Queen smiled.

Tildy called to Evan to come to the kitchen. "Herself wants her people to sup on the same stew and bread as she eats. All is ready. Just carry out to them. Thank ye, Love." Tildy gave him a hurried peck as she shoved the caldron of stew at him. Georgie appeared and she all but threw the basket at him and told him to go with his uncle.

Tildy asked the Queen, "Is all to your satisfaction? I have sent sup enough for all your men and I can get more ale, if ye wish for you and for them. I do have a cake for your pleasure, if ye want it."

"I would like some cake, if it is as good as the rest of the food even though I am quite full now. What about you, Kat?" To Tildy she said, "Yes, and a cup of tea each if you have it. I do have a question for you, but after the cake is served."

"Yes, Ma'am," replied Tildy.

With a generous slice of cake in front of her, the Queen asked, "Who is that adorable child that met the carriage"

"Ye mean Georgie? He be my husband's nephew. He has a great affinity with the livestock here and he makes all the horses quiet and happy." Tildy blushed. She knew that Georgie was not the child in question.

"No, my dear, I meant the little girl. How old is she?"

"She is about two years old. She is my daughter. She has hair the color of mine even if it is not quite the shade and her eyes are blue like her Da's.

Would you like to meet her? Her name is Sydney."
Tildy was feeling uneasy lying to the Queen about
Sydney's lineage. It couldn't be a good idea lying to
one so powerful.

"Be easy, good woman. I thought she was a
charming child and would like to meet her and gift her
with some small token." The Queen smiled. It was as
though she looked at a mirror and saw her two-year-
old self.

"I'll be getting her for you. I do hope you are
enjoying the cake and the tea." Tildy went back to the
kitchen. She opened the door and called for Sydney,
who was with Evan and Georgie. Sydney came
running to her, a little mussed up with a touch of
straw in her hair, but still fairly clean. "The Queen
wants to meet you, love. Come and I'll comb you up a
bit."

"Ma, Keen Liza has hair the same color as me.
Ith she my auntie too?"

"Nay, darling. Look ye at your ma and da. We
both have the ginger hair and your da has the blue
eyes. I don't think that we are related to the Queen.
Now be a good girl and you can have that piece of the
cake after the Queen leaves." Tildy pointed at the cake
and then brushed the straw from Sydney's hair and
smoothed the apron a little. She cut a slice of cake and
left it on the table to fulfill her promise to the child.

"What a fine-looking child, Elizabeth, "Lady
Kat said slyly, not missing the red curly hair on the
child's head. "Whence came the child?"

"I come from the thtables with Gauwdy, Ma'am
Queen. I gots a bit dirty, but my Ma made me clean

with thpit. Thank you for coming. I made the butter for the bread. It were hard work."

"You are a lovely child. What is your name?" The Queen asked with full knowledge.

"Thydney," whispered the girl, then she curtsied. "And thee, I didn't fall over," she yelled as she ran to her mother.

"Child come here. I am so pleased to meet you. I have a gold sovereign for you. Put it away, and you shall have a fine start to your life."

Elizabeth stretched out her arms and Sydney went toward her. "Do I bow again, Ma?"

Elizabeth laughed and said, "No, my darling, your Queen just wants to give you a hug. I have no fine young ladies to call my own." She reached out and hugged Sydney close, gave her a quick kiss on the cheek and sent her to Tildy with a gentle pat on the bum. To Tildy she said, "Call your husband and have him ready the coach. It is getting late, and I wish to make the castle by nightfall. I will be passing through again in about a month, but others from the court will be coming for visits. I will recommend this place. I should take you back to cook for me, Tildy. The cake was light and delicious. Kat pay for all the meals and the care. Thank you again, Tildy. Hold your daughter close to you. She is a precious gift."

Tildy called to Evan and within minutes, coach and team were at the door. Queen Elizabeth swept from the inn with Lady Kat close behind her. Once settled in the coach, Elizabeth drew back the curtain and waved to the small red-headed girl standing between the two people she called Ma and Da. They were all waving back.

The Queen did not get to stop on her way back to London. Tildy and Evan saw her once more, many years in the future. Elizabeth was good as her word. She recommended that all her court and messengers stop at The Cock and the Sow on their way to and from the castle. Tildy and Evan did very well indeed with their inn.

Tildy watched the coach fade into a dust cloud. She said to Evan, "Evan, put her down. The tyke needs to be running. Sydney, go change your dress. I will be in to help you."

Evan released the child and Tildy took her hand and they went to the family chambers. Evan went back to the stables. Tranquility reigned over The Cock and the Sow once more.

1562 to 1564-The Cock and the Sow

Sydney grew and developed into an inquisitive child, interested in nature and the world around her, small as that was. She now did more to help Tildy around the inn. Tildy taught Sydney from the Bible she used in her youth to read and copy the letters. Sydney mastered the simpler words with ease, but they were all in Latin.

A townsman watching the little girl copying from the Bible suggested to Tildy that the landowner two miles away had a daughter Sydney's age and perhaps in exchange for some of the baked goods or a few pence, Sydney could get lessons in reading, sums and French.

Tildy saw the landowner a week later and he thought the idea was a good one and an occasional cake would be payment enough. He thought it good that his own daughter would have a school friend. The lessons would start the next year when both children were four years old. Tildy couldn't wait to tell Evan what she had done.

Evan had other news for her. "A traveler told Georgie about highwaymen to the west of the inn. Several travelers, peerage, were robbed of all their jewels and money at sword point on the road to the Queen's castle," Evan said.

Tildy was horrified. "What will this do to our business?"

"I don't know. If they move east of us, it could hurt us some, but in general there aren't too many rich folk for the taking in these parts. Warn each of the patrons, if he looks to be of means. The rest will be fine."

Tildy brought the children to her. "Stay close to the inn. Don't either of you talk to strangers afore your Da greets them. That means both of you. Understand?" Both children nodded. "And, since you are here, come in for noonich right now." Tildy hugged both children around the shoulders as she took them to the kitchen plank for their dinner.

"Yeth, Ma," Sydney replied. She was always hungry for the sweets Tildy gave them after their meal.

Georgie asked, "Why do I not greet the customers?"

Tildy answered, "There are some bad men riding around to the west of us robbing people. I don't want either of you to get into trouble. You let your Da take care of things for a while. That don't mean that you can't work in the gardens or the stables. Just stay close to home and don't go wandering around. Things will get better. We just love you both so much."

"We can do that, Ma," both children answered. They proceeded to eat their meal and the sweet then ran out the back-door whooping and hollering, forgetting all that Tildy had told them.

***

As close to the sea as they were, the small family at the Cock and the Sow did not realize that there were nefarious activities and piracy occurring right on the Irish Sea. There was money to be made, a lot of money, but it was not entirely legal.

Francis, Lord Walsingham was stationed at East o' the Sun. The Queen requested that he run a network of spies to track down those who were not on letters of marque (privateers). Those not on the 'letters' were criminals who were stealing from the crown.

Lord Walsingham had a plague in the guise of his brother-in-law, a fawning gorp of a man, whom Walsingham suspected of killing his sister with over-adulation. Harold Lord Bardsley, Second Marquis of Craegelon, moaned and groaned about the loss of his great love. Walsingham was on the verge of slicing the man's throat, when a brilliant idea came to him. Perhaps, just perhaps, the pirates or smugglers would do it for him.

Walsingham sent Harold to catch the smugglers at any cost. Harold Bardsley, happy for a chance to get out, gladly accepted. He left the castle and started on his way to the sea. *How can I get close enough to find these people?* Harold thought. *I will have an assumed name. Hmmm! Gilpin, that's it. Mr. Gilpin.*

Mr. Gilpin wandered away from the castle and out of Sir Francis' hair, or so he thought.

1567 London the Witch's Brew

An epidemic of smallpox scourged London, killing a third of all who contracted it, scarring those who lived through it. Morvyn hoped all was well with Tildy's family.

A drunk sailor who had just landed from the East told her of a way to prevent the disgusting scarring disease. He came into the Witch's Brew for a drink but didn't stop at one. He yelled for more wine and she served it. As she poured, she asked, "Is that a bullet hole in yer arm?"

"Nay, good woman," as he took another swig of wine, "It be a hole from the pox."

"How can that be? "Morvyn asked. She sat down next to him and looked closely at the scar on his forearm. It did not look like a pox scar up close.

"I done it meself," the sailor slurred.

"Tell me! Why?" Morvyn asked with a quizzical smile on her face.

"I kin tell ye how, but the why is another question. The why is because I were five sheets to the wind. The how, well ye might like this one. 'Twer a comely China lady wi' eyes as dark as her hair. She were a beauty, she were. She were a whore, much like yerself, only prettier and younger. Ya know them Chinee think women is a burden, so there be lots of them what ain't kilt at birth, what practice the womanly arts, if ya ken what I mean." Morvyn, bristled at the implications, but forgave him because of his condition. Besides she wanted to hear why he caused that deep scar on his forearm.

"It were a plague there. Many died and were dyin' even as we lay together. I seen the scar on 'er arm. She said it were the pox, so I asked her why she didn't have more. She said a wise woman took pus from a pox from a dead woman, scraped her arm and smeared the pus in. She got a little sick, but nothing compared to others what died. I asked her if she could do me.

"I weren't too much meself just then what with the wine and the loving and such, but," and he took another sip and held his flacon up for a refill. Morvyn complied, fascinated by his story. He continued, eyes drooping with drink, "So I sez... wot were I sayin', woman?"

"Nay, ye don't fall asleep on me now, good man. Continue with the story. There be another flacon on the house, if ye finish," Morvyn bribed him to go on. "Ye were talking of the lovely Chinese whore and the pox hole she had an—" He grabbed her breast. Morvyn slapped his hand, "Keep yer hands off me. I be married to Jack." She pointed at him glaring her way. "He don't take kindly to me being manhandled by any others but himself. Now go on."

Morvyn sat down again and listened. The sailor started again, "Chinee pox hole?" He listed to the left then to the right. Morvyn uprighted him and told him to go on. "Aye, now I gots it. Me Chinee lady. Ye ken I had more 'n one, whore I means. I ha' one in every port, I do. When I ship out agin, I be goin' ta—"

Morvyn interrupted, "The pox hole and be quick afore ye pass out for the night."

"Aye, well for the longest time I held 'er an' looked at that hole. It weren't deep, but it weren't pretty. I sez to 'er, why don't she try it on me. I must say I shoulda been a little scairt of gitten' the pox from 'er or 'er mates. I dinna want me face all messed up, so the ladies wouldn't take me, ya ken? So's anyway, she gits a knife, oh, it were a loverly knife long 'n sharp wi' a fine point on the end. She 'ad it under 'er piller fer protection from men wot weren't as nice as me, ya see? So's she git out a' the bed and goes away fer about a half an hour or so. I dinna ken I were so love-sotted and sleepy. She tells me ta' 'old me arm out. I done as she axed. She shows me the knife be all bloodied, an' then she grabs me arm an' holds it close to 'er body and wi' the knife she starts scrapin' me skin. It hurts an' I try to pull away, but the li'l vixen be strong and holds me closer. She keeps scrapin' til the skin breaks an' I be bleedin'. Then she take the knife wot she bin scrapin' with and rubs the other blood in real good, scrapin' an rubbin'. By that time, I be too pissed ta' care. She wraps it ta cover the wound an' I goes ta' sleep. In the mornin' we finishes our business an' I kiss 'er an' leave ta go back aboard ship.

"The nex' day me arm starts ta' hurtin' and two days later it feels like it should fall off. It be red and twiced as big as usual, really mean lookin' and I know I be wearin' an 'ook afore the week be out, if it git much worse. I covers it up agin and does me work best I kin, an two days later the hurtin' goes away an' the hole starts scabbin' and two weeks later the scab falls off an' I ain't none the worse. I ain't ne'er caught the pox and I been ta places wot people are dyin' all over. Come now, jest one little feel?"

Morvyn automatically slapped his hand away. *I have just learned how to prevent the pox*, she thought. *I'll tell Jack immediately after the close tonight*. He always listened to her advice. He was deathly afraid of the pox, or any disease for that matter. He didn't even sleep with whores anymore for the fear of the great pox or the itching disease and he wouldn't let anyone stay at the inn with a scab for fear of the pox. God help him if the black plague came to the Witch's Brew.

Jack listened to Morvyn that night. He said he thought it was a good idea. They should do it, if she could find a way. And of course, Morvyn Hoggins always found a way.

Morvyn worried about Tildy and her family. They entertained travelers on their way to and from the coast. The pox came from all sources, sea, land and especially from the larger cities. Birmingham was a port town in the southwest of England. Travelers would go to London or cross Wales to get to Ireland. Many passed through and stopped at The Cock and the Sow.

Morvyn remembered the couple who originally owned the pub. She remembered the effects on the poor woman, who was left with the marks which rendered her so marred that customers would not stop if she greeted them. Morvyn always thought it strange that she never got sick herself. Well, the hole in her arm meant she would never get sick no matter what. Morvyn determined she would make Tildy and all her family free of the pox too. Morvyn's mind made up, she made plans to do the trip. It was almost time for the herbs and a couple of days one way or another wouldn't matter to Jack. The pub was quiet because of the disease. The regulars either caught the thing and died or stayed away afraid they would catch it after the deaths of their friends. They would be back when the thirst became powerful enough to overcome their fear.

The bigger question was how to carry the pus, so it didn't dry out on the trip. It still took four to five days to get to the inn even with the roads being better kept by the crown for the passage of troops to the coast. Morvyn headed to her favorite supplier of tools.

***

With France quiet for the time and Spain making small mewling noises, the Queen could busy herself with the pirates that plagued the Welsh shores. She was sending troops and ships every month. So far nothing was working, but the thought was that at least she was doing something. Should there be an attack from another nation, the troops would be closer to the Great Ocean for the fight.

The Cock and the Sow

Morvyn sat with the rest of the family in the kitchen eating a breakfast of porridge and dried fruit. "Morvyn, ye come all this way to purpose the pox? It don't make no sense...I thought ye loved us." Evan did not like the idea of opening the skin let alone putting pus on the wound.

"Evan, ye be daft. Look at my arm. Do you see this hole? It be my pox hole. I did it to myself and to Jack. We ain't got it! You know we be in a bad part of the city. The streets be dank and dark. The people are poor. It seems to get more of the poor. They closed the new theater on account of the threat of the plague. We have all manner of people passing through. Right now, you can hear the groans of the sick and dying. The poor are always the first to suffer. Business is bad on account of the pox right now. This will protect you not sicken you or at least not for long. I didn't tell you this, but the lady you got this place from lost her husband and her looks from the pox a traveler brought to her.

"Let me explain, ya' thickheaded Welshman, the pox can come from anywhere and right now you have many people who come through from London. Your whole family could be gone in a week, should it be brought here again. Now what say you?" Morvyn made her speech and then added, "And Jack be the biggest coward of all, and he were so scared of the pox that he readily thrust his arm out to me for the scratching. His hole is less than mine and mine is less than the sailor what told me the story."

"What story, Auntie Morvyn?" Sydney asked. "Oh, Da, I don't want to die, and I don't want you or Ma to die or Georgie or Ginger, my pig. Please Da," the little girl begged.

"Morvyn, I don't want ye scaring my little girl that way. Now as she asked, what story?" Evan interrupted.

Morvyn recounted the story the sailor told her, leaving out the more lurid parts. She explained how public places were closed and how that really hurt businesses. "Ye probably get people what are trying to escape it," she said. "The royals ran north, but no more. Now the Queen runs to the west and that be ye. She be human 'n God don't protect her any more than us folks. It do work. Please, trust me. Ye remember the woman what sold you this place. Did ya notice nothing?"

"Aye, she were scarred something fierce. That be the pox? But she lived through it. Why wouldn't we?" Evan asked, fear still in his voice.

"Yer a jackass, Evan Lewis. She and her husband had it. He died. It took her two months to get better after the scabs fell off. I know. I was here. I told you as much. You ken I were sore afraid I would git it, too. I were feeding them and soothing them with some of the herbs I had, and he died anyway."

Evan interrupted. "Morvyn, ye got not the pox when ye nursed those two. Why would we?"

Morvyn ignored him. "I would not like to see the wee Sydney's lovely face scarred like that, would you? And what about Tildy and little Georgie. Aye, men kin live with the uglies, but you ken that most die flat out and others are forever hurt, marked life. They can't do their old jobs and so have to beg in the streets. The Queen don't like the beggars neither. Where are your streets here, Evan? An' you ken I were here for two months whilst she got her strength back. That is how I knew about the place in the first place. She only stayed here a few more years. You were married and well that's how things happened and that's honest truth of the matter. And I know in my heart that at least one of you will die and I can't say who."

Morvyn's dramatic presentation got to Tildy. "Evan, it be worth it. I seen some what got it, and I don't want to be looking like that, Sydney neither, nor Georgie. Ye, ye be too beautiful by far to be covered with them things and to lose everything we wear and have to sleep in or so I heard tell. Morvyn, here." Tildy rolled up her chemise sleeve exposing her upper arm. "Ye can do me. This will be one we don't have to bury, like the rest of these stubborn fools; and you can do Sydney, too."

"Auntie, I don't want those ugly marks. I don't want to be sick, neither. Auntie, can I?" Georgie spoke up. "I don't want to scare the horses and the kine. The pigs don't care nor do the goats, but the horses...."

"That is your uncle's decision. I say let's do me and Sydney but I think young Georgie should, too." Tildy was adamant.

Sydney's sleeve was rolled up and ready for the mark. "We are too much in the public to be questionin' this. A Chinamen ye say, cuz?" Evan weakened.

"Aye, yes, Chinamen. Are ye all ready?" Morvyn prepared to give them all the smear of pus. "Ye might as well roll it up too, Evan. Ye know that when she talks, she means business, so you are going to get this."

Georgie added, "Yes, Uncle, I am with the hoi polloi more than the inn gentry. I heard about this pox from a side rider for some nobleman. He showed me where he was branded. His face was full of scars. I be ready for it." With that speech the twelve-year-old shed his vest and rolled his sleeve, exposing a thin but muscular forearm.

Evan looked at his family, all of whom went in the face of his authority. With a disgusted sigh, he exposed his forearm as well. Morvyn scraped each arm and dug a bit of the pus she carried with her. The glass vial was half full, more than enough for the assembled relatives. She silently thanked the chemist who sold her the vial with the cork. The pus was as juicy as when she procured it from the dying body. After the application, she wrapped each wound with clean rags. "This will keep out the dirt. Don't remove it. You will hurt for a few days and then the wound's scab will fall off and you will be as right as the rain. 'Twas a fine choice ye made, Evan."

"If'n we don't die first," Evan grumbled. Tildy got a tea ready, so they could forget the implications of what they just did.

1568 Georgie Gets in the Business

Just before his fourteenth birthday, a couple of men from the coast talked to Georgie about their adventures at sea and how he was young enough to grow into a captain of his own ship.

Smuggling and piracy were common occurrences along the coast and this Northwest portion of Wales had its share of such activities. Coastal villagers were most active in this "sport". Some professional seamen turned to a life of piracy for the money, always for the money. Evan heard tales from travelers who stopped at the inn.

Georgie had heard tales before from the men who worked for the men who slept at the inn. These were the exciting stories, the stories of men who smuggled or pirated. Georgie yearned for the excitement, the adventure, the romance of these activities. He never thought of the danger. What thirteen-year-old would?

Georgie thought that was a great idea and left the stables one night upon a signal from one of the men leaving the pub. He tramped the four and a half miles to the coastal area closest to Bryn a Cywd. There, he was ordered to uncover a lantern if he saw anyone coming from the road. He stayed until the sun came up and saw no one. One of the men relieved him and told him he did a good job. The man gave him a small gold piece. Georgie got home before Evan discovered that he was gone. George continued once a month to participate on some level with these goings on. The men told him it was nothing to worry about. He was doing nothing illegal, but he shouldn't talk to anyone about it, especially not Evan.

He told them when soldiers came to the inn. Once he even heard that those soldiers were looking for smugglers along the coast. The villagers were thankful for the warning and curtailed their activities. Georgie started to get a clue about these night activities and the booty he was given for his help.

Soldiers talked to Evan and he told them that he was not aware of such goings on. "I only go to the village in the summer to sell bread and vegetables monthly at the market. I take my wife and my daughter to help. We make a day of it. My boy Georgie takes care of the inn on those days. We always get back before dark so as to get the night business."

The soldiers seemed to believe Evan. Georgie, eavesdropping on this conversation sighed a breath of relief to hear Evan's words. Georgie never talked to Evan about this either, but he did tell young Sydney in the form of the games they played in the loft of the stales, hiding in piles of hay and yelling 'ahoy ye vasties, ahoy'. They slashed with make believe cutlasses, slitting the throats of those they robbed and pretending to sail away in a pirate ship with the booty, rich as Croesus and happy as clams. They pretended to swing down the rigging by hanging onto the makeshift ladder that got them to the loft and once in a while they would swing on a piece of rope or leather, they tied to a beam.

Georgie kept up this work, once a month for two years. At the end of the two years he was stowing merchandise away in the limestone caves, racing against the tide, so he would not be trapped.

1568 The Cock and the Sow

"Auntie Morvyn, how fares this one?" Eight-year-old Sydney was in the herb garden once again with Morvyn the Witch, who was at the inn for one of her semi-annual visits.

"Ach, girl, ye don't touch that one without ye have something to protect your hands. It is deadly in large doses, and if you get the leaf juice on your skin, it goes right through and kills ya, dead as a door. That one is called oleander. Mind the leaves. Watch for them in other places. I don't want your death on my hands. I must ask Evan to take this one out. It grows all over and could kill your horse or a cow, if they get by the gate. Your animals are sneaky pests sometimes, and they don't watch what they are eating.

"Now, my love, here be a balm to the deep pain when eaten or smoked. Sometimes I put it in pressed oils for a rubbing balm. It is called cannabis. If you dry it, then keep it well away from the heat. The fire robs it of its powers. Cooked in a cake or a scone does help to get to the pain deep inside."

"Then don't the heat kill it if you smoke it, Auntie?" Sydney asked.

"It ain't a long time in the heat and the smoke is not hot when you suck it in, so it does help. Fresh ground and in pressed oil, the plant helps with the outside pain in fingers and joints. This here is arnica, another plant what helps with pain too. It is good for bruising and sore teeth. Now your ma always grows at least two of the cannabis for me every year, and I get it at the fall harvest. Has yer Ma showed you how to keep the seed?"

"Aye, Ma showed me the fruit trees. We have but one of each, but Ma starts for others. It takes a long time, five years at least for the apple and that's after it's set in the ground. The peach is the easiest and the pear next. I ain't seen the plum nor the cherry grow yet, but Ma says I am too young for that. Ma gave me a peach last year for my very own. She said she started it when I was four, but I don't remember. It gave one fruit this last year and Ma let me eat it. It were the sweetest fruit in the grove and soft too."

"Ah, Beware the seed of the apple. It have cyneed, a poison, and if ye feed too much to the kine or the swine, you could kill them, so I heard. I ain't never seen that happen, but I heard. Oh, and don't feed the grape to the dog. I seen a dog drop from eating the grape."

"Oh, Auntie, we have no dogs. Ye be jesting," laughed Sydney. She looked at the pile that her aunt had harvested. "What be this one, Auntie? It smells so different, sweeter." she asked.

"It be basil, but a foreign one from way across the ocean from a land called Italy. I understand Italy is hot and sun-washed, not a bit like our land. This basil is from there and it has a sweetness that regular basil does not. Yer Ma adds it to her stews and savory bread for the wonderful different flavor from other stews. Yer Ma is a great cook but does even better with these herbs. Don't forget the thyme and rosemary to add to all the poultry. I ain't such a good cook, but I sell to some of the big houses in the city and they always come back for more," Morvyn told the girl.

"Sydney, you combine this woodbine and the prickleberry together. Grind them well, rock on rock, then let them dry and blend. When completely dry, use a small firm brush and get all into a packet. Be sure to label it love powder or with a secret code, however ye know what it be."

Morvyn taught the young Sydney each time she came to the inn. Sydney was bright and thought her Auntie Morvyn a wise woman sent so she could learn more than the art of baking with lavender and sweet basil and such. She learned about 'cough stop' and 'feverfue' and how to dry the medicinal herbs to maintain their freshness.

Tildy watched her daughter and her cousin in the garden, their heads together talking and laughing. She was happy they got on so well. Sydney could have no better teacher in the healing arts and potions as Morvyn.

Sydney loved the big people's knowledge. She loved her days with the tutor at the manor. He insisted she pronounce each word with clarity and write each letter and number legibly. He lent her books from the manor library. Every time she brought one back, he gave her another.

She learned of physics and how the earth was round and covered with water. She twirled around Georgie in a great circle to show him how the earth spun around the sun. She told him about the wild people who lived in the new World and Georgie told her of pirates on the high seas.

She did not want to be a wife or an inn keeper like her parents or a 'witch' like her auntie. She wanted to roam about the world and do grand deeds and make great fortunes and fight fierce battles or become a scientist like her friends in the books she read.

Meantime she learned potions from her aunt. She learned how to get the most from each plant from her mother; how to grow and get the most from the garden. She was in charge of the rare herbs and spices in the little glass house that Evan built when she was just a small girl. His design improved on the frames and made tending the fragile plants even easier, for now there were no heavy frames to lift, and in the winter one did not have to freeze while tending.

"Sydney! Syd-ne-e-e-ey," Tildy called for her daughter. "Leave yer aunt do her business and you get in here and clean up. I have need of you. Morvyn, you needs to gather up. There's a storm coming in and you don't want to get drenched.

"Go change your apron, Love. Your Da just got in a grand coach. Do you know where Georgie is? He is not at the stables nor with his Ma, and she don't know where he's got to either." Tildy smoothed the girl's curls while asking.

"Ma, I don't know where Georgie is. I ain't seen him since I worked with Auntie in the gardens." Sydney used a towel to wipe some of the dirt from her face.

"Yer Da can handle this night. That boy needs a stern talking to. Now get on with ye. Put on a clean apron, mind ye, and keep it that way." Tildy was busy preparing stew and a basket of bread for the coachmen.

The peer was already in his rooms. Upon entering the door, he asked for a tankard of ale, a bottle of wine and a palatable dinner, not like he'd got for the last two day, mind you, and how far to the Queen's castle?

"If he didn't like the food, why did he order it. He had the money for a larder in the coach." Tildy muttered to herself during the preparation. "And he can't even eat in the great room. More steps for me at this time of the day with no help." Tildy, angry at his tone kept up her murmurs as she shoved the meat in the oven to warm it for his royal hinney. She gathered some sweets and cut up an apple. *The apples are sweet and crisp this year*, she thought. *That little tree I put in is finally making yield.* She filled a tankard with the mellow ale and Sydney reappeared clean apron and all.

"You look beautiful, my Love. Put a cap over them curls and take this up to the peer in the second room back. Tell him I'll bring his wine and a warm pie shortly."

"Yes, Ma, I need a clean serviette, and should I put a rose on the tray?"

"Ye be a good child, Love. Whatever ye wishes to do, just hurry with it."

Sydney ran outside. Morvyn was on her way into the kitchen with her sack full of the herbs. "I'm getting a flower for the tray. There is a fine man at the inn this eve. Ma be in a tizzy over it." Sydney told her Aunt.

"Just do what ye are told and help yer Ma." Morvyn bustled by the child muttering to herself, "Tildy should always be full with her cooking and Evan' stables. What happens here? They should be rollin' in the coin. Watch more, Morvyn, me girl. See as ye would see regular." Morvyn entered the kitchen and told Tildy, "Sydney be coming back with a rose for some tray. She be in a hurry and say ye be in a tizzy?"

Just a little extra business, first of the week. 'Tis hard to hold pies other than the icehouse and that is running a little low. Evan needs to cut more from the lake, but he never seems to have the time these days." Tildy sounded tired.

Take care, my girl. You seem to be restive. Are you worried?" Morvyn asked.

"Nay, just a little tired and I think something big is going to happen."

"Don't let it press on your mind, Love. Things have a way of straightening out. I am going to put these beautiful herbs away, and I'll be back to help you in a flash."

Sydney hastened inside with a rose bud for the tray just as the rains started. She folded the serviette and placed it with eating utensils on the tray along with the warm, fragrant meat pie and the rest that Tildy made ready. Tildy appeared with the wine and smiled her approval. *The girl has a knack for making things lovely,* she thought. Aloud she said, "Let's get this to the gent before he checks out and gives us bad tongue."

Sydney led the way with Tildy right behind. Tildy reached around Sydney and tapped on the door. The man answered, "Come. Make it quick." Sydney opened the door and stepped in.

He sat in a chair, covered in fine fur, resplendent in a velvet robe and great leather bedshoes. His boots stood guard at the foot of the bed.

"My man will be back shortly. You have fed my horsemen?" He snapped these words not even looking up at the two females.

"Aye, sir, your Highness, and your food and drink be here. Do you need a tray for your man, too?"

"No, my good woman, he will be down after he takes care of me. Treat him well." He glanced up as Sydney set down the tray. He gave her a long look. She looked to be seven or eight but carried the tray with the ease of a much older child. He drew his chair over to the table and took a long breath in through his nose. Surprised, he said, "This smells wonderful. I hope it tastes as good as it smells." He sipped the ale. "This is a good sweet ale, better than any I have had on my journey; better than I have had anywhere in this great country, Ireland, Scotland or even England." He looked at Sydney, "Aye, and ye brought me a Tudor rose. How did ye...who told ye...? He looked directly at Tildy, who was standing in the doorway. "Did someone herald my coming? Do you know who I am?"

"Nay, my good sir, my girl just does these things. There was no foul intent, Sir, really, Sir, she just like things to be pretty and neat." Tildy was nervous now. This man was upset. "Ye needn't fear. This be one of many roses what grow in my gardens. I have three bushes of roses. Please, what did we do that we shouldn't have?" Tildy was scared and nervous now. She put Sydney behind her.

"Nothing, good woman, and is this girl your daughter? She has bonny red hair like my...our Queen

Bess." He pulled on one of Sydney's curls. "Aye, a bonny lass."

Tildy blanched. He knew the Queen. She grabbed Sydney's shoulder and hissed, "Bow, curtsy, this man be royal. Then back away and we will deal wi' his man." Mother and daughter dropped deep curtsies to the gentleman and backed out the door. Tildy took Sydney's hand and they hurried back to the kitchen. "God preserve us. He be royalty. He knows the Queen. Peek in the dining room. If his man be there, find out what he wants and git back in here. Draw him some ale first. Go, GO!" Tildy was beside herself with worry. Sydney left the kitchen to do her mother's bidding.

Evan clumped into the kitchen. "Do ye have a spot of stew for a hungry man, Love?"

"Who be that gent what be in the back second, Evan? What mark be on his coach?"

"Tildy, the stew and a piece a' bread! He be a Queen's man—Dudley or something like that. He's going to East o' the Sun for a spell and then to Ireland. There be trouble there, and he takes care of trouble for the Queen. Why be ye so upset?"

Tildy related the conversation in the room. Evan laughed at her. "Oh, Love, ye worry about too many things that you shouldn't. Take care. Just don't let your cousin cook for him. She may poison him as not. Best not to let her know who's here." Evan dug into his dinner.

Northwest Wales

Georgie's father and Evan's twin brother, Euan Lewis, died in the winter of 1568. The winter was one of the coldest yet with more snow than usual. It snowed for three days and nights, and Euan's family was out of food. Euan had slaughtered the last pig for the winter. Its carcass hung at the rear of the now empty barn, which stood far from the cottage.

Sarah, Georgie's mother, sniveled at Euan, "My children are hungry. We have a small fire, but no food. Even the porridge is gone. What will ye do?"

"I will go and cut a haunch of that pig." Euan said and gave her a small pat. "I wish I hung it closer to the house. Here is a line. Hold it so I can get to the barn. Do not let it go, lest I be lost on the way."

The small light from the cottage window lit part of the way to the barn. The snow was a medium fall when Euan departed. "I shall be back in an instant with some meat. Best to get a pot going for the dinner." Euan said. "Remember do not let go of the line."

"No Euan. Just get on yer way. Come spring we will change our ways and have a cowshed next to the house for just such winters." Sarah said. "Safe journey, husband." Sarah tied a loose knot to the door.

The snow picked up during the time Euan was in the barn. Hacking off a haunch was more work that he thought, since the meat was solid with the freezing weather and the barn had no other life in it anymore to keep it warm. Even the pests had fled. By the time he was to come back to the house the wind was howling through the trees and the snow was a blinding blizzard. The light from the house was erased by the snowfall. He grabbed the line from the house and started on his way back, blinded and cold. A little more than halfway there the line went slack. Euan never made it back to the hovel. Sarah boiled the three potatoes in snow water and fed the children the weak soup. She sent the children to bed and sat up keeping the fire alive with what wood was available.

Sarah's children Georgie's two older sisters and his older brother still lived at home. Georgie's brother, James, was a bit simple and could do only the easiest of chores. One of the girl's was to be married in a year's time to a local farmer's son. The other helped her mother with the making of delicate lace.

Sarah slept fitfully and when the dark gray of morning appeared, she wondered why Euan had not. He did not return the next morning nor the next. The snow continued to fall, and the wind carried the light flakes into deep drifts that covered the entire farmyard. The snow stopped on the fourth day of Euan's disappearance. Everyone was hungry, the potato soup being gone for a day and only snow water to drink.

The morning came clear and very cold. The sun came out and the snow dazzled and glittered the trees and the yard area around the hovel. Lelah, the oldest daughter, claimed that she would go out to the barn to help her father. Sarah helped her bundle up and opened the door. There was no rope attached. Sarah cautioned Lelah to look for her father on the way.

Lelah left and halfway to the barn she saw a foot above the drifted snow clad in her father's work boot. She ran to the drift and clawed the snow off the frozen dead body of her father, clutching a haunch of pork also frozen. Lelah tried to free her father's body, but it was frozen fast in the mud of the pigsty.

"Oh Ma, I found Da. He be frozen in the sty, and I canna move him. He must have lost his way and wandered into the pigsty although he had a line. Did we let go of it while we ate? Oh, Mam, did we kill him?" Lelah was distraught.

"No, my darling, the weight of the snow must have undid the knot I tied to the door. We must get him out of there before the spring thaws, or we might lose him for good." Sarah wrapped her body in a warm shawl and went out to survey the scene. She didn't shed a tear. All business, Sarah was. She helped free as much as possible from around the body. A few days later there was a short thaw and Sarah started a fire and boiled some water to loosen the earth around her dead husband's body. The two girls and the boy with Sarah's help pulled the still frozen body from the sty and dragged it to a more secure place away from any hungry animals. Sarah and Lelah pried the haunch away from his body. The family held a small service to wish him goodbye until the spring and a full thaw could make a proper burial and blessing possible.

Lelah wrapped well against the cold and walked the five miles to The Cock and the Sow to tell Evan of his brother's demise. The weather held. It was cold, but the sky was blue, and the sun shone warm and bright. She rested a few times, but in all, the trip was within the day. She was to bring Georgie back to help around the farm when the weather allowed. At thirteen he was a strapping young man, and more than capable of the work.

Lelah arrived at the inn. Tildy saw her and ran to embrace her. "How be your family, niece?"

"There is sad news Auntie. Da is gone. He lies frozen behind the cottage. We canna' do a thing, until the thaw melts him a little, he bein' all curled up and such. Mam wanted me to come tell ya that we need young Georgie ta come back and run the farm, build it up. We canna do all the plowing and planting ourselves. I be married soon and Brannie be not far behind. That will leave James and Mam. And James don't do nothing without bein' watched. So, I come for Georgie."

"My dear, what makes you think Georgie will go?" asked Tildy.

"Auntie, he be the only man in the family what can do the work," Lelah said.

"I will fetch Evan and Georgie. They need to know about Euan's untimely death. Froze to death, you say?" Tildy remarked. Tildy went and got the men from the stables. Both were glad for the break. "Your niece, Lelah, is in the kitchen. I gave her some drink and some food. She looks thin, Evan. She brings sad news as well." Tildy told Evan as they hurried back to the inn.

"Uncle Evan, it is like lookin' Da in the face, to look at you. I miss him sadly," Lelah cried.

"Miss him, why do ye miss him niece? Why are ye here?" Evan asked.

"Did not Tildy tell you? Da is dead. Froze to death goin' for a haunch to feed us after three days of boiled water with a turnip and potato. We were down to the last. The cow died, so there was no milk, the flour ran out. Our crops was so poor last harvest there was naught to store. Mam thought there would be might enough for the winter with some meat, so Da slaughtered the last pig. It were hung in the barn, and he went after it. The storm turned into a blizzard, and he were lost on his way back to the house. Ma wants Georgie to come home and do for us." Lelah told the story again.

"I don't want Georgie to leave, Evan," said Tildy. "He is part of the family and earns a good income here."

"Aunt, I am thirteen and can do as I will. My family needs me. I can do this."

Tildy replied, "There must be a better way. Let your uncle and me talk, and we will decide. You are very valuable to us. You are like our own child, and if this happened here, I would never let you come from where you were to help me here."

Lelah chimed in. "Auntie, Georgie is the only man available to us. I will be married in the late spring, but there is still Ma, Brannie and James. James is useless for all but the simplest work and even then, he fergits."

"Lelah, I understand. Evan knows what is best," said Tildy.

"Tildy, they live in a crofter house. Their lord only collects and cares not for them. We can't let Georgie go to Sarah. She will overuse him, and he will wind up like Euan. I loved my brother, but he never learned how to farm, insisted on keeping his livestock far from the house, because Sarah said that the smell would be too much close by the house. Let us go to Sarah and make other proposals," Evan said. To Lelah he stated, "Lelah, we cannalet Georgie go with you. He knows much, but he does not know how to run a successful farm. The four of us will go with you We will talk with your mam and see if we cannot find a better solution to all of these problems."

"I am sure Ma will appreciate any help you can give her. We have very little seed and no more livestock. We even had to eat the seed potatoes Ma was saving."

"We will leave in the morning," Evan said. He took Georgie, who was glowering at all, by the arm and led him back to the barn.

"I am thinking that your mam and sibs will be much happier here with us than there, trying to rely on you and your brother. What say you, George?"

"I didn't think of that Uncle. I would much rather stay here, but me mam needs me. I could help them better here than there. You are right, Uncle. How can I repay you?" George knew that the wonderful life with Evan, Tildy and Sydney might end. He did not even remember life at his parents' home and was shocked to hear the conditions there now. He had little knowledge how to help that desperate situation. Thank goodness his uncle was coming to help his Ma and sibs.

They went together, this patchwork family, to Sarah's. Evan packed the cart with warm blankets and food. Sydney made a sign with a burned stick 'Closed'. They nailed it to the door and made their way to Sarah's home.

Once there, Evan looked at his own death mask, frozen on his brother's body. He looked at Tildy and whispered, "Love, this be me, but I am still in the flesh. We be born the same day. We look the same, but we be so different. I be scart of the future now. What would ye do without me?"

"Evan, my love, Sydney and I would survive. We are strong females. You are a smart man. You will not be caught in the snow and mud, frozen until spring thaws your bones. You keep too neat a place, and we are well supplied close to the house. You have the guide wires to lead you when the snow blinds all else."

"But what will they do, Tildy? They are three women and a half wit. Our Georgie is really theirs, but...." Evan gave up.

Tildy came to his rescue. "Evan, the stables, they could live in the stables. Sarah says Lelah is to be married this spring, and she will not hold it up for Euan's burial. Branwen will be married within the year and if not, she makes lace as Sarah does and has a fine eye with the needle. James may be useless for the big jobs, but he can sweep and mop and shovel, can he not?" Tildy made this as a suggestion.

"You would have my sister-in-law live in a stable?" Evan looked at Tildy.

"Nay, you big ninny," Tildy laughed. "The upper parts of the stable where you store the tack and supplies is clean and warm. Those rooms are quite large and there is a fireplace within. They are cool in the summers. There is enough room for the four of them. Georgie can stay with us, and we will be a real family."

Sydney tugged at Tildy's arm. "Ma, you cannot let them take my Georgie. He is my friend. He teaches me things and helps with the goats and the gardens. What would I do without him?"

"My darling girl, your da and I are figuring how we can keep both Georgie and the rest of the family. I think it will work. You will only be without Georgie for a week or so." To Evan, Tildy said, "I think we need to talk to Sarah and the girls. James will do what he is told."

Evan and Tildy unpacked the food stuff that they brought for the trip. Sarah gaped at the amount of food they had. "This could keep you for a week or so, could it not, Sarah?" asked Evan. "Tildy and I have an idea. It will take a few days for us to get done, but it may be a solution to all the problems. We do not want to part with Georgie. He is an important part of the inn. He runs the stables and makes a good living with the livestock.

"Lelah is married with the first bloom. Sarah, you be a good-looking woman with a heart of gold. You will marry again. In the meantime, you make the best lace in all the isle. There must be a market for that, once it is seen in the village market or by some of the passers-by. Branwen will be married soon, probably within the year, so it will be you, James and Georgie. George is well employed. Sarah, you could help Tildy with the inn as well. Sydney is eight years and she speaks well and can do her sums. She can teach young James some tasks, so he has something to take away. So, Sarah, what say ye? Will ye come and be part of our family?" Evan had never made such a long speech in his life. He looked winded. He blushed a bit and had a pleading look in his eyes.

"Aye, but to keep this place, the lord of the manor wants complete families with at least one able-bodied male to work the land." Sarah commented. The idea of leaving all tugged at her heart. *This is my home. Life is not easy here, but with Georgie it could become so,* she thought.

Tildy chimed in, "That is true. We are offering a way for your family to stay together and have all you need and no lord to satisfy, if ye can wait a week or so. This food will last you. The weather should last. Why not take Georgie, if he be willing, and get together your household for a move? We will leave the cart. We can deal with Euan when we come back to get you. We will have an extra horse and a goat cart. That should take care of what ye need to move, Sarah. This is sudden, but we need to make decisions for all of us. What say ye, sister?"

Sarah said, "And how would I pay for the rooms? I canna' live for free."

"Do I not get a say in this?" Georgie asked. "I am thirteen years and some months. You are my family, too, Mam. I can't say I don't miss you. How much livestock do you have? None from what I can see. Is there anything in the ground? The place does not even look farmed. Mam, I say you do what Uncle suggests. I can help support you as well. Uncle told you I make good wages and more so from the farmers whose livestock I help birth.

"We go to market once a week. You could really help with that, too—you and the girls. James will be fine in Sydney's hands. What will you to do Mam?"

"I need to bury my husband. That will not be until the ground is thawed. Euan were a good man. We have said our goodbyes and our prayers for a safe journey in the next life. It will take only a priest to pronounce it so. I will not hold up Lelah's wedding for the burial. Georgie, ye make a good point. We have no seed, no livestock and the cottage needs major repair. The manor has not been good to us in this way. Our fealty is paid for the year. Stay the night. We will sup together. I need to think. It is too much right now, and I want a clear head to make such a decision.

"Tildy, help me with the dinner. I see you have brought your fine bread and a sweet. Thank you. I will get the rest going, and the girls will do the chopping." Between Tildy and the three girls, a very nice pork stew and bread with Tildy's butter were served in a short time.

The sweet and some tea were a fine end to the best meal this household had eaten in a long time. Tildy and Sarah slept in her bed, and the three girls slept together, which left Evan, Georgie and James to bed down next to the fire.

Morning came and with it a breakfast of bread and eggs, also from Tildy. "We needs to be moving on, Tildy. Sydney, eat your breakfast and get ready. Sarah, I suppose you have made up your mind?" asked Evan.

"Yes, Evan, I accept your offer. You are right. With help around the inn and my lace and Brannie's stitching, we can pay for safe warm rooms and regular food." She waved a hand at the bare rooms and broken patched windows. "This is no way for a family to live. Can you give me a week to close and make all secure? If so, would you bring another cart if ye have one? Anything! I can send some chests home with you today. They have all the hopes, memories and linens. That is what is most important. I will pack sufficient clothing, though we haven't much." Sarah smiled. "'Tis so kind of you.

George, will you help James to put the furniture on the cart? Get on with ya now. Ya never know when the weather will turn. They have a long trip to do in a short time."

Evan said, "Syd, Tildy, get on with you. We needs be on the road. The sun is up. We will hit some frozen muddy ruts on these back paths, if we wait much longer. Syd, you will get your Georgie back in a week. You can live that long. You will also have another playmate and student. And you may finally learn to lay an even stitch." He moved outside to hitch the horse to the loaded cart. "I hope this be not too heavy for you, Margaret." Evan spoke kindly to the dray horse, elderly but with much work left in her. "We will get you home to a pail of oats and nice warm straw as quickly as you can draw this wagon to them." To himself he thought, *what a fool Euan was. No head for farming, but his woodwork was something to behold. All the furniture in the house was of fine wood and made to last. Each of the girls has a hope chest hand made by Euan. His fortune was not in the farm, but in the wood and his tools to work it. His family could have lived well in the village, where his talent was known. Damn fool!* "Tildy, Sydney get out here at once. We need to get a start, or we will be traveling in the dark and cold of night. Who knows what the weather will be by the end of the day?"

Tildy wrapped Sydney in a cloak and a blanket and put her in the cart out of the wind. "But I want to walk with Da," Sydney whined.

"Hush daughter," Tildy said. "Your da wants to go with speed and your wailing will just hold us up."

Evan frustrated, every nerve on edge from watching his nieces packing more and more linens and household items in their chests. They ran from the inside to the cart sometimes carrying only one item. Finally, by the grace of God and a hearty "No more" from Evan they left mid-morning, Evan walking, guiding the old mare by the lead.

By the late afternoon Tildy was stiff from riding the horse and Sydney was grumpy from being curled up in the cart. The fading light on the pathway made the trip a little harder. "Evan, I will walk with you a bit. I am stiff from the horse. I will keep apace. Sit on the horse, Sydney, and we will keep going. I am glad we won't be losing Georgie. I would miss him sorely." Tildy laughed as the feeling came back to her legs and feet.

"Ye know he will be marrying. Maybe not today, maybe not tomorrow, but some day. He is almost fourteen. I were on my own by that age. Even so he may not want to stay with us at the inn. There is a whole new world waiting for the young. There really is nothing holding him here, if he wants to leave." Evan put his arm around his wife's shoulders. "And ye ken that we all leave this earth sometime. Look at Euan. He be gone before his time, some might say, but

I say he went when he were supposed to. We was the same age, born on the same day." Evan gave Tildy an extra hug and kissed her on her head. "Aye and look at yon horse. The wee girl is asleep from the motion. And she is about to fall off." Evan left his wife and went to the horse. He grabbed his sleeping daughter as she slid sideways. Sydney woke up in Evan's arms. "Why don't ye walk with yer Ma for a little time, Syd. Give the horse a rest. We can have a bit to eat as we walk."

And so, the family munched on some cheese and a bit of bread, walking and laughing. By the time they were home the sun had disappeared from the sky. The moon was full and lit the road upon which they walked. Except for the loss of his twin, Evan was as happy as he ever had been. Tildy felt the joy of having another woman help around the inn and the possibility of two, maybe three weddings and gatherings in the next few years. Ah, the inn was a grand place to hold a wedding gathering.

***

The winters were different from the sowing, growing, reaping months. The land lay frozen and men stood close to their holdings, caring for their families and livestock and protecting all from the cold and hunger. Winter was the time for carving furniture, spinning, weaving and knitting and for women to make delicate lace that trimmed the clothes of the landowners and at times, the royalty and peerage. This was the time of year when men stayed to home and did not venture to the inn for ale. The only business was from travelers going to the coast or coming from the coast. It was always very sparse. It could be very lonely without family.

1568 The Cock and the Sow: The Week of Sarah

Georgie was almost fourteen. His Da was dead. How stupid of him. His family was safely ensconced upstairs in the barn. He knew that giving up that week to help his real mother interrupted his participation in the nefarious doings of his smuggler friends. He heard that a ship was due loaded with spirits and gold. That was the word. He wanted to go once more and hoped he could get home in time to not be missed by all.

By now he knew he did not like the idea of sailing on a ship. He got sick just watching the waves, but he worked to stow the booty the lads brought back to the caves facing the sea. These caves were inaccessible during the high tides, but if one went far enough back, one could store and hide the illegal take, so that was what the smugglers did: spirits from Spain, valuable spices from the east as well as the silk cloth woven with gold and silver threads and tobacco from the New World. These stories and more filled Georgie's head. He lived each adventure with its telling and enjoyed the glory of victory with each hoe kick and each horse rubdown.

The Crown of England encouraged the privateers to rob the Spanish ships coming from the New World. Most were not above robbing ships of all nations. Some said the pirates were employed by the Queen herself. They certainly had free rein from the soldiers and private ships that patrolled the Irish Sea for the Crown.

The swag was sold further inland, the tax money eventually reaching London, but not before many more were made rich. Sometimes it was brought further east to Birmingham. Georgie had no part in this. He had no idea how much any of this was worth. He knew he couldn't spend the coin and had no idea what to do with the gems. He hoped that someday all of the coin he had could possibly pay for his own inn, or perhaps give him a way to prove to Evan he could take care of Sydney if they married.

Sydney was the light of his life, his shining red-haired star of the future. He knew he was six years her senior, but he would never hurt her. He could see Evan keeping them apart more and more and those games they used to play in the barn stopped when Sydney made her announcement in the barn one morning last week.

Sydney marched down the center of the barn, her head held high wreathed in dried oregano and a stick in one hand, wrapped up against the cold. "Georgie, bow down to your Queen," she said imperiously.

George looked at the girl and laughed. "No, lass, there is but one Queen of the land and that is good Queen Bess."

"Oh, but Georgie, I am your queen. You can have no other until I am gone, so bow down to me now," and with that she whacked George on the head with her stick.

"That is enough, girl, when I catch you, I'll use more than that stick on you. It's you who should be bowing to me, your king. What gives you these ideas,

Syd? You, a queen? You are too dirty to be a queen. Straw in your hair and mud on your feet. If you are going to be a queen, you can't play with the pigs."

The cows were used to these shenanigans. The chickens just flapped their wings and squawked and forgot to lay that day. The children pretended they were the captives from the ship and chased them around the stable until Evan heard the ruckus and made Sydney go into the inn to help Tildy.

1569 The Cock and the Sow

Georgie finished up with the night's activities. He stowed all in the small cave and made it out before the tide came in. He had a gold coin in his pocket, Spanish, he thought and a sapphire the size of a robin's egg, but much, much bluer. He started for the inn roughly two miles from this place. He should be back by sunrise. No one should miss him. Late fall and early winters as well as early springs discouraged all but the most necessary of coach travel. Morvyn the Witch was at the end of her stay and would go back to London for another six months. His Da was in the ground and his sibs and Ma cozily ensconced over the stables. Lelah's wedding was postponed to the late spring.

Ma and Branwen wanted to go to the village, having tasted life at the inn and having more people around liked this new life. They made the delicate lace indicative of this area and Lelah was a wonderful seamstress. They would do well until one or all were married. Life was good.

He was halfway home. The sky in the East was gray and there was damp cold drizzle wetting his cap and clothing. It was the postlude to the downpour of last night, most of which he did not feel, being in the caves the whole time. He trudged on looking forward to a bowl of porridge and a steaming cup of tea before he started his work for the day. There would be time for a nap after doing the chores.

Evan was concerned. There was no Georgie last night and none this morning. He hesitated to ask Sarah about her son, since he didn't live in the same rooms. Georgie was supposed to be in the stable quarters. Ah well, business was slow as usual for this time of year, thought Evan. This drizzle could be good for a bout of the lung disease, but his family was strong. His mind was at ease about sickness. All he really feared was the pox and the plague. No one survived the plague, and the pox could close them down with equal ease. Morvyn did her arm scraping, but there was no proof that it would keep them from the pox. He didn't want to see his beautiful wife and lovely daughter scarred forever. Then, too, they would be horrified if it happened to them. Now this Dudley was here from London. None of the entourage seemed sick but how was one to know. Evan got back to the kitchen to tell Tildy that Georgie was gone, and who was sitting at the table with a big bowl of porridge and a steaming cup of tea but that young man!

"Where ha' ye been, son? I bin worried sick about ye. We ha' a customer with a lot of cattle, and I needs ya in the stables now. I really could a' used you here last night, bedding all them mounts and carriage people and makin' the animals feel safe and comfortable. Where were ye, lad. A queen's man came in an him in his coach and four and his men with supplies and all. Ye were needed. This be the second time ye ha' missed him."

"Uh, Uncle, I...I...I were wi' a lass in the village." Georgie's brain quickened the lie and sent it straight to his tongue.

This story did not ring true to Evan. Georgie was about fourteen as they reckoned. The village girls were knowledgeable and even the loose ones would not make hay with a young lad, they didn't know unless he were with an older man that they did. Besides Georgie had deep circles under his red-rimmed eyes. "Aye, I hears ye, but ye be here early. Were she nay as bonny as ye want, lad? Beware, git her with child and ye be gone forever. 'Sides, ye don't have that look about ye, lad, but as ye wish. Finish up here and tend to the stables. Be quick wi' ye now."

Sydney came into the kitchen. She'd been up for about a half an hour. She heard her parents talking and now here was Georgie eating, late in the day for him. "Georgie, how...?"

"Nay, girl, leave 'im be. He must get to work. Ye need to eat and then do as yer Ma bids. We got the peerage here today and with the rain last night, he might stay another day rather than push on. The castle be a long trip in the mud. It be gray today, but clear tomorra'. Someday, lad, ye will tell of yer midnight adventure. I hope ye be rewarded well." Silently, Evan prayed that Georgie would live through it and not see the knotted end of a rope early on. Evan clapped Georgie on the shoulder feeling the muscle that was early on the lad. Georgie up tipped his bowl and swallowed down the rest of his porridge. He'd had no supper the night before and had the hunger of an active fourteen-year-old. He hurried to finish his tea before Evan kicked him out the door to work.

Georgie was not happy. His pouch of gold and jewels grew by the months, but in the end what good was it? "I canna spend the gold. None will take it or if they do, I will swing. No one can know, for if they talk, I will swing. There has got to be a way to turn this swag into a farm or a pub or transport. There is the New World. Some must want to go," he said to the unfortunate cow he was milking. She bawled. "Sorry, Sally, I dinna mean to squeeze so hard. But ye need ta give me some good ideas. There is so much ta do. I canna stay here the rest of me life. What, be a pub owner or run an inn? I will ne'er be good enough with people to take their gaff and let it wash over me. And what about Sydney?" The cow swung her head around and gave him the brown eyed bovine stare of a bored cow who'd heard Sydney's name. Sally raised her back leg to kick the bucket at another word.

Sydney had a gentle hand with the milking, but she was very good at teasing the cows to distraction. She was loud and raucous, especially when she and Georgie played pirate. "Aye, ye like that one, dinna ya' Cynthia, me girl?" said Georgie to the cow next to Sally. "She named ya and raised ya and her only a little one then, but I ken Uncle expects me to take this place over. He won't let me own it though. Syd will own it and all with it. The only way I get a part is to marry the hoyden and I canna marry my first cousin no matter how much I love 'er." Cynthia nodded her head.

Evan kept them apart more and more. Georgie pulled the last few drops from Sally's teats and moved over to Cynthia. One bucket would be enough for today, but Cynthia needed the relief as well. More butter for Sydney to churn. *Keep her out of trouble and out of my way*, thought Georgie. *Them goats need milking, too*. Today was different. Georgie kenned that the Queen's man was the reason. He hoped that Sydney would not become besotted with the man. He finished Cynthia and brought the two pails of cow milk to the kitchen. "Where be the goat's milk, lad?" Tildy asked as she got some bread and cheese for Georgie and put it on the table. "Sit down, George, and have a cup of coffee and the snack. It might do you well for the rest of the day."

Georgie liked coffee better than tea. It was seldom served except to guests. Not many knew of the exotic drink and the power of wakefulness it brought to the drinker. It was rare in these parts. If it were not for Morvyn and her London trades, he would never have tasted this wonderful beverage with the powers it held in its dark, smoky brew. *Something is up*, thought Georgie, *a mid-day snack and coffee? Coffee ain't an easy to get.*

Morvyn also brought cocoa beans from Italian trader. Those two products helped make The Cock and the Sow what it was. Well, that and Tildy's fine cooking, if the customer could pay the price. If not, they got tea with their bread and cheese.

Tildy said not a word to the boy, but Evan talked to him later that day, when there was a lull in the work. "George," he started, "I think it be time to call ye by yer grown name, don't ye, George? George, we must be serious about what ye be doin' at night. I have an inklin' and if ye want ta stay free, ye must do something to keep the bairn away. I love yer Aunt Tildy, but Sydney be the only bairn we ever had. All the rest died, but yer mum were fertile and had ye four wot lived and several others wot didn't. Ye be careful, lad, lessen ye wind up wi' a bairn and a wife afore yer time."

"Uncle, Sydney's the only girl I love and I ain't touched her, she bein' too young and me cousin and all. I only go onct a month ta' town and meet some fellas. Oh, Uncle, I needs stop that afore it becomes a big part of me life. But Uncle what be here fer me? Sydney gets the pub and the land, and all that goes with it. I needs make my own way in this world, and I only know animals, stablin' and tinkerin'. I ain't no gypsy wanderin' the countryside wi' a wee cart and broke down horse, sellin' an' repairin' tin ware and stools and such. Wot see ye fer me?"

"Son, I hear the tales the travelers bring. Ye must, too, from their men. There be a whole wide world to the east across a great sea, beyond England and France. Mysterious lands where folk don't look or do as we do. An' then I heard tell of a New World full of savages and beautiful land. The voyage is dangerous. Wot be wrong wi' a nice pub and a little farmland; a day ending in a soft bed wi' a nice lass?"

"Uncle, you and Aunt Tildy ha' been very kind to me an' my family. Me Ma lives over the stables. James 'll be with her where ere she be. Lelah and Branwen ha' men of their own. I be worried about Ma though. She don't go to the dances and church since Pa died. She say it be her fault fer sendin' 'im out, and she don't want to kill another wi' such foolish ways. She say she worry about bein' a murderess. She sits that room and makes lace and stitch. Branwen takes all to market. Brannie does all the cookin' and the cleanin', but she'll go soon, and then who'll take care of Ma? Evan, there be much to worry about, an all I do here is with the animals and the repairin'. I canna take care of Ma very good, now can I? There ain't no one gonna pay me to do these things. These are things a man does on his own farm. Is this not so?"

"George, ye be right. I should be payin' ya direct low these many years. Ye ha' been faithful and truth be known, people stop here because of yer animal skills and Tildy's cookin'. Wi'out the two of you, I would not be living the life I got. There would be no garden kept as well as it is, and animals as happy and healthy as they be, except maybe fer them damn goats. I want another kuhe, but yer aunt say nay, we must keep the goats fer their milk." Evan's voice went singsong like a woman's nagging.

Georgie laughed out loud at the caricature. "I don't like them too much myself. T'is time I grew up. I am 'most sixteen now and yes, 'tis time."

"Thank ye lad. I have been wantin' to have a serious talk with ye fer a while and I will stop callin ye 'lad' and use yer proper name, man to man. I don't

know if I can stop Sydney and yer aunt from callin ye
Georgie, but I'll talk to 'em firm like and lay down the
law about it. Let's get back to work when you're done.
We got some carriage repairs for this Lord what be
stayin' here the next few nights. The wheel axle be
broke and the leathers need tending. Find a good bit,
George." This last Evan said loud enough for Tildy to
hear.

George Lewis still went to the village once a
month. He had an 'in' when it came to information
about the Queen's men at the inn. He also had a girl,
the baker's daughter, whose company he enjoyed. Her
father kept an eye for him as well. There were times
when the area was crawling with soldiers, and so his
'friends' scheduled no activities for this north shore
area. Things would shift to Ireland and those blokes
got all the riches. George didn't care. The villagers
knew when the army was in town. George would know
from the inn. Most stayed out of trouble. George
always did.

1574 The Cock and the Sow

It was late in August that Evan and Tildy took
stock of the children and how they felt about each
other. "Evan, we must tell her. She loves him and I
think more than a brother. She really needs to know.
George should know as well. They both think they are
first cousins and I think George thinks that he can
marry her no matter what. He were so young when
Sydney came that he didn't really know from whence
babies came. We just have to tell. If we really love
them, we will."

"Tildy, she ain't even fourteen."

"Aye, but she's seen first blood. If it ain't George, who is it ta be? Your little girl is grown to a woman. I was only fifteen when we first met. Georgie, bless his heart is nineteen almost twenty and should be thinking of getting wed and getting a place of his own as well."

"You were older than she be. She has only been to the village and to my brother's. When does she get out to experience life? You at least went to the big house to cook and bake for parties and such. You saw peer and gentry. Syd has seen none of that. How will she get along in the great world without any experience? We have sheltered her and made her a country mouse. Even the lads in town have not seen her at socials or at church."

"She has seen animals and it is a natural thing. You know she be doing it eventually," Tildy argued back.

"Aye, Tildy, ye should be a barrister. You make good arguments. We will do, but let us find a good time to tell both children at the same time," said Evan.

"Aye, you can tell the girl and I will tell the boy. What do ye think of that?" countered Tildy.

"Not much. I think we should do it together with both in the room. Then we can see if what we think is true." Evan made a good argument that Tildy could not counter.

"Both what, Da, Ma? Are ye getting rid of the goats like Georgie wants. Please don't. Jane and Anne are so happy here, and they have plenty to eat, and they give such good milk, and you make the best cheese from them. They just need to be mated again.

Oh, please keep them. Let them stay. I love them both so much." Sydney was close to tears at the thought of losing two of her friends.

"Oh, darling we aren't talking about the goats. We...we... need to ask two of the lodgers to leave on account they haven't paid their bill." Tildy covered the conversation.

"Oh, that be fine, Ma. They be no friends of mine. They get a little grabby when they drink, if you ask me. Do you want me to gather some apples for ye?" Sydney asked.

"Go get a dozen or so; get the ones on the ground. I'll make the sauce you like. Oh, and tell Georgie to come in for dinner tonight." Tildy was back in her comfortable self now.

"Aye, I will, Ma. I'll get those apples right away." Sydney almost fourteen was a luscious combination of womanly wiles and childish innocence. Her red curls flowed down her back when she wasn't working at the inn. The inn was all business; curls were pinned up and jammed into a mob cap and a large wide apron covered the curves so attractive to men.

George Lewis at nineteen was picture handsome. He was taller than Evan, his body was sculpted by the hard work of the farm and from the caves. Many a village maiden sighed as he walked by them in the market place. Sydney had taught him to read and write and do numbers long ago when she was learning. Both children were bright and both longed for adventure and a chance at the big wide world that was out there waiting for them.

Tildy and Evan never seemed to find time for this most important conversation. Either the children were busy with their work or Tildy and Evan were busy with theirs. Customers came and went. Not too many noticed that Sydney was growing to a fine young woman.

1575—The Cock and the Sow

"Mother, if I am to take a husband, why can't it be Georgie?" Sydney was not happy about the thought of mating with the fat son of the fat farmer to the north. In her head she knew that the fat boy was the only other person her parents might sanction. There was land to be had. She had to fight for what she wanted. "I like the inn, Mother. You taught me to cook, bake and garden. I can do all of the things you said the Queen of England liked at her visit so many years ago. We have prospered without extra land. And Mother," her voice dropped to a whisper, "I saw first blood at thirteen." In a firm voice once again Sydney said, "And if I must marry now, let it be Georgie. I know we are cousins, but we are great friends and know each other's minds.

"Because you sent me to the tutor at the manor, I am quite the lady for a pub owner's daughter. Do you really want this 'lady' to marry a fat farmer and slop hogs and have fat children? Oh, Mother please...."

Tildy looked at her as though Sydney were touched. Where did she get such ideas? Now Sydney never cried even when she gashed her knee on a rock at age seven. She did not cry when they ate her favorite ram, Harry. Today at the ripe old age of fifteen, she cried real tears, but still she argued her case. "How could you, Mother? Do you not want me to be happy?" she sobbed. "You know I know my poisonous plants well and I know how to use them. Fear not, I will hang fer a witch afore I bear bairn to that pig to the north. Ye ken our garden be much better than his whole farm—love apples be big, red and sweet and our horses and other livestock prosper on our oats and corn." Sydney rushed on. She could not let her mother get in a word. This woman who bore her, nurtured her, made sure her sharp mind was trained, would win her over, if she were allowed to talk. Sydney plowed on until Evan popped into the kitchen.

"Our lunch?' he asked.

"'Tis time to get the noonday meal for Da, Georgie and James. I will attend to that if you approve, Ma." Sydney turned away and scrambled for bowls and a knife.

"Aye, child, tend to the farmhands. I will tend to the paying customers." Tildy was almost in tears. She was losing Sydney. She only wanted a couple of grandchildren and Evan would have liked access to the northern fields, but nothing was worth an angry perhaps murderous daughter to get these things. She could wait for the former and Evan could buy the latter. "Oh, Sydney, poison if ye must, but you are smart enough not to hang for it, I pray. And child, where did you come up with the idea that you must marry 'a fat farmer from the north'?" Tildy murmured to the air as she went to the pub, drying her eyes on her apron before breaching the door.

"Oh, mother, ye be good enough to be a jester in the Queen's court, but for the funny hat and..." she paused, "Ye be not a man."

Tildy turned back, "Sydney, my darling child, ye be a little young to marry yet. Perhaps we shall wait a year or so until ye are too long in the tooth to marry anyone. I were nineteen before I married yer Da. Enough blather. We have work to do." Tildy turned back and marched through the door with a determined smile n her lips.

Sydney made three bowls of stew and hacked off some bread. She spread it with butter and rammed it together. She brought the bowls to the stable and gave one to each of the men, James, who did the least, ate greedily.

"I just had a big fight with me Ma, Georgie." Sydney said.

Georgie ate his meal. Between bites he asked, "What about now, Syd?"

"Oh, Georgie, I want ta marry ye. Why canna we not marry?"

"Syd, we be cousins. Ye know that. We be first cousins. Only gentry and royalty marry first cousins." Georgie continued to eat.

"Georgie, they be thinking that I be thinkin' of marry Athelos the Fat. He thinks he is the King—Elect of Wales. He be not even the Crown Prince of Bryn an Mohr. He don't even honor that Elizabeth be Queen of England and Ireland." She paused and then blurted, "He don't even read letters like we do. Georgie."

Georgie was through with his meal. "How do you know what Athelos say? Do ye spend yer other off hours with him? Ah, Syd, ye know I love ya. Where will I ever find a friend like you?"

"Ach, Georgie, ye be my best friend, too. Ma wants grandbabies. I told her the sow be with young soon come along and she laughed and said what a joker I be. She said she wanted real bairn of me."

"Syd, yer Ma be joking. She wants for you what she and yer Da have. And besides, do ye always do what yer Ma wants? Come now. Ye be my best friend. Ye ken we spend so much time with each other. We could make five babies fer yer Ma."

Sydney looked at Georgie shocked that he even thought that way and then shocked that she didn't.

"Sydney, *Sydne-e-e-y*" The call rang out from the inn. It was more effective than a bell. It was also the way Sydney heard her name when her Ma wanted something. "I gotta go, Georgie. We'll talk later. I don't think anything be happening today. See ya later." Sydney brushed the straw from her skirts. Georgie looked at her.

"Ye be the prettiest thing I ever seen, and I been ta the town on market days."

"Well, I been there, too, and ye ain't the prettiest thing I seen, but ye are the dearest. Ye have straw on yer trous. Brush up!" She checked her hair quickly with her hands—no straw. She was presentable. It was time to get to the dining room and start serving the farmers who came for a break from the close fields.

Northwest Wales

More and more military invaded the area. Piracy was a dangerous occupation and the Crown knew that locals helped the villains by stashing the loot. Much of it sold on the black market in England, so taxes never got charged, never reached the Court coffers, which were at an all-time low. Tax money was needed to fund the military to maintain the peace and fight a growing threat of war with Spain.

Georgie said to Evan one night, "Have you noticed a lot of military coming through here? I wonder what is going on."

"You are right lad. There seem to be more and more. I wonder if the Queen is leaving the city and coming to East o' the Sun for a stay."

"Nay, Uncle, I have heard some of the horsemen talk of smuggling and taxes. I wonder if they come to stop the smuggling I have heard of in town?" Georgie had been reporting the arrival of the military for a month now and the smuggling was at a nadir. Only the foolish would go out now. Georgie stayed at home. He learned more at the inn caring for the livestock than he could in town.

Two officers came to the inn that afternoon shortly after Evan and Georgie spoke. They were of a higher rank than mere lieutenants and captains. They talked of the inn as though it was their own establishment. "This will be a fine place to use as a headquarters, if there is enough room and sufficient staff to keep us." General Donald Cookson said to Major Charles Moore. "You know. Charlie, this room is big enough to seat forty or fifty people. It would be an excellent place for a spy to ply his trade. News travels fast in circles where there is whiskey, wine and wenches." The two of them enjoyed this quiet time at

The Cock and the Sow. It was August and the weather was chancy. Some days it rained and others the sun shone. In another month it would be going from comfortable to a chilling cold as the as fall brought the rain and oft times snow.

"General Cookson, Sir, let us see to the rooms. I hate being a dirty place for long periods of time. Don't you find it strange, Sir, that there is no one here to wait on us? I thought this was an inn. We should lunch here. If the food is not good, then we will have to bring in cooks. That means that we commandeer this place and put the owners out to pasture for our stay. We will still have to have supplies brought in. It could be too much for a place like this in the middle of nowhere. And yet it has a clean air about it. None of that greasy smell you find in city pubs."

"Charlie, relax. The lad that took our horses was very good with them. This place is clean and has a wholesome smell about it. Order us some dinner, and we will talk more over food. Quick, I am hungry," Cookson ordered.

Major Moore made his way in the direction of the doors that led to the kitchen. "Is there anyone here to help us?"

Tildy looked up briefly from her dough. "I canna help you right now, sir, but if you can wait a few minutes my daughter will be in to lend a hand."

Major Moore surveyed the room. The kitchen was spotless. A big cauldron of something savory bubbled, the scent of savory wafted to the Major's nose. "I am sorry ma'am. Could you dish us up some of that stew at your earliest convenience? A bit of bread would be nice as well...."

At that moment a red-headed whirlwind burst through the door. "Here you go, Ma, three bunches of savory, one each of parsley, rosemary and thyme. Just like ye ordered. The apples be on the bench outside. I couldn't handle it all at once without dropping something."

Major Moore's jaw dropped as he gaped at the red head. Sydney turned as she felt someone's eyes on her. Charles Moore gawked at the goddess in front of him. "Get ready, Sydney, we have hungry guests in the dining room. Change yer apron and cover yer head and make it quick, girl." Tildy barked out the orders without looking up.

"I'll be right out to take your order, sir," Sydney said after her bout of gaping at the young officer in front of her. She dropped a quick curtsey and headed for the larder.

She put on a clean mob cap and snowy white apron, smoothed her skirts and caught her breath. *No, I must be a lady.* Straightening up and raising her head she proceeded in haughty splendor to the dining room.

The major to his credit went back to the dining room and bade his commander to pick a place for them both to sit. Sydney appeared just as they seated themselves. "What will you have, good sirs?" she asked.

"Two tankards of your best ale and whatever you may have ready for luncheon." Sydney never heard of 'luncheon' before. There was breakfast, tea and supper. In between there was work. *Eat luncheon,* she thought, *what a boon to have a break in the day.* "Sir, we have pork or beef pie what heats in a jiffy, and a stew that is o'er the fire as we speak. We have fresh brown or white bread and fresh fruits or a bit of cake. Ye may have tea or coffee for both be on hand."

"How big are the pies? Will they feed two men such as we?" Major Moore asked.

"Aye, the pies will serve two or more, sir. Many a night we all share one and with a bit of bread we are suffice." Sydney held up her hands in a large roundish circle to show the size. "Neither my Da or my cousin can eat a whole one after a hard day' work in the fields moving rocks. They both be big men and they eat hearty."

"I'll have the stew. What about you, Major, what will you have?" Cookson asked.

Charlie looked hungrily at Sydney but contained himself. "I'll have a slice, a generous slice, of the pork pie. It has been a long time since I had a good pork pie. We used to eat them in the plains when I was young. We raised the pigs and sold them to market."

Sydney dropped a small curtsy. She drew two tankards of ale and brought them to the table along with utensils and snowy serviettes. It was noon and the sun was shining without, but windows with glass were a luxury. There were only three small ones in the pub, and even though Tildy and Sydney washed them regularly, the three windows did not give much light. Each table and private booth had at least one candle.

Sydney went to the fire and lit a twig. She brought it back to light the candle at their places.

"Thank you miss. I always like to see what I am eating." Cookson was sarcastic.

"It is only a bit of light. I can bring more if you wish, good sirs." Sydney said.

"That would be fine—one more should do it." To Moore he said, "A fine looking filly. Is she for sale do you think?"

"I think she is the daughter of the house. I doubt this is that sort of establishment." Moore said with a wistful turn to his voice. "Sir, we are not in London anymore."

"Tis a shame! It would be a nice roll in the hay with that one," commented Cookson.

Sydney appeared with the order. "Your pie and your bowl." She set the servings in front of the men. "Please enjoy." She turned to leave.

"Girl is there not bread with this meal. I thought you mentioned bread." Cookson was disappointed.

"Sydney turned and said, "I am bringing it now, sir. What do you prefer, brown or white?"

"Can we have a little of each?" Moore asked through a mouthful of pie.

"Of course. Give me a chance to cut some of each for you both. The stew wants of a good piece of bread." Sydney turned back and went to the kitchen.

"Cookson tasted his stew. The men looked at each other as they chewed. They were amazed at the flavor. "This is better food than I have in my own home, and I pay a cook to prepare it. Got him from

France last time I was there," Cookson said over a mouthful of stew. To Sydney who was back with bread and a liberal serving of fresh butter he said, "Girl, who is the chef here? I want a word with him."

Moore interjected, "It is the good wife, sir. She was making bread when I went to inquire as to the whereabouts of some service. There were no men about. Something of this flavor reminds me of a time when I was a child." Moore took another bite of his pie. "You know I was brought up north of here, closer to the bay. There was a woman my mother would call for balls and fetes. She baked and cooked but would never become part of the staff. She said she and her cousin had other things to do and they had to help their parents. Strange group of people they were, those crofters. They always stayed away from us. They never seemed to trust us. I remember my father used to have the small children in for lessons. He thought everyone should know how to read and write and do simple mathematics. We seldom saw children of nine or ten. Most learned quickly or not at all and went back to the farms to work at home. If there was a very special child, who learned quickly and well and asked the correct kind of questions, Father would request that child to continue and work to get him to university. Few of the crofters ever became staff at the estate house. My mother brought in French or Irish for those positions.

"Enough of your memories. Eat your food, Moore. Eat up and let's be gone, rather you be gone, I will talk to the owner. This will make a fine billet indeed. Good food, a soft bed, beautiful women; just the kinds of things an officer needs."

"Yes, Sir, and shall I get the rest of the unit, Sir?"

"Not quite yet. Check the stables for room and take a look at the lay of the land. If there is enough room to make camp, I will be happy, and if not, we must move on."

"Yes Sir," Moore finished his pie and his ale.

Cookson said, "Oh, I long for a sweet to finish off this meal. Girl," he paused and then said louder, "Girl, come here."

Sydney rose from the hearth and came to the table. "Yes, sir, be ye needing anything?" *If they weren't happy with the food or the drink or, heaven help me, the service,* Sydney thought, *I could be in trouble.* "Be there more I can get you?"

"Aye, girl, your name and..." there was a break in the order, "do you have a sweet? I don't want fruit. I want a real sweet."

"We have a bit of cake or some biscuits. Which do you want?" Sydney asked.

"Ah, I would like a bit of cake and your name." Cookson said as he leered at the pretty girl.

Sydney turned and disappeared without a word. They seemed nice before dinner, but she was a little scared. The locals would not dare talk to her that way. Ma would know what to do. Mayhaps she could serve the sweet and the tea.

Back in the pub Cookson said to Moore, "Captain, you must eat up and get moving. I am going to find the owner and negotiate some sort of an arrangement, if only for tonight."

Sydney reappeared with a generous slice of cake and a cup of tea. She set it down in front of Cookson. "My mother said this tea is perfect with the cake. She grows her own herbs, so this be one of her combinations. I will get you a drop of honey if you wish." Sydney did as her mother told her. Put the food and drink on the table and back away.

"Who owns this place? "Cookson demanded.

"Me Da and Ma own this place. Do ye wish one of them?" Sydney replied.

"Get your father in here on the double. Go, girl, go," Cookson demanded.

"Yes, sir." Sydney gave a quick curtsy and left the room on the run.

A few minutes later Evan clumped into the kitchen. "Tildy, what be with you? Why be ye pulling me away from the chores?"

"I did not call ye, Evan." Tildy was pulling the first batch of bread from the oven. She had a sink full of hops soaking in water she was working on for Evan.

"Woman, Syd came racing down and said ye wanted to talk with me."

"Nay, Evan, we have two guests what be military. Mayhaps they want ye, but I never sent out the word that I wanted you. Just go to the dining room. I'll clean the floor later after they leave." Tildy went back to her bread and the hops.

Evan went to the dining room. He didn't know what to expect. There had been more and more military around the area. He heard tales of them taking whole establishments and throwing the owners out for the length of their occupancy. Evan walked over to the only man in the room.

"Are you the owner of this property?" Cookson said in a commanding tone.

"Indeed, I am and the proprietor of this inn. What do ye want? 'Twas the service bad? Was the food not to your liking?" Evan was on the defensive, not one to take kindly to imperious tones and orders from outside the household.

"How many rooms do you have to let? Quick, man, I don't have that much time."

"Give me reason for telling ya. Ye haven't seen them. Mayhaps ye had best give them an inspection first. Are ye taking this place from me on the Queen's orders?" Evan was getting angry.

"Do not talk back to me! You are addressing General Donald Cookson of Her Majesty's Royal Army. If you do not have enough rooms, we cannot begin to do business. Do not be an ass about this," Cookson shouted.

Evan shouted right back, "If we canna meet on equal terms, we will nay do any business. If ye agree to that, we will carry on. If not, there be no business transacted here today."

Furious, Cookson said in a low threatening voice, "We can just claim this property as Queen's lands as you have pointed out, and have no more truck with you. You will lose all and be wandering about the land homeless and friendless, unless we bring charges against you for sedition and rebellion. What say you?"

Evan shouted, "Get out of this inn. It be....

Tildy came running into the room. "What be the matter here? Why be you two yelling at one another? Was the service not to your liking or the food? Perhaps you needed more light than just two candles. My husband is not easily upset or often. He only throws out those what are making a disturbance after too much drink. What be the problem? Answer me one of ye and do it now!"

Both men stopped mid-yell and looked at her. This slender little red head with her hands on her hips now had control of the situation.

The Cookson recovered first. "Excuse me, Mrs. ...?"

"Lewis, the name is Matilda Lewis, wife of Evan Lewis. As I asked before, what is going on here? My husband is not quick to anger. What did ye say?"

"Mrs. Lewis, I am from Her Majesty's Royal Army...." the Cookson started out.

"I can see that. I am a busy woman. What is your business?"

"I have four officers who need billeting. I am ready to pay for it. We will need to make an encampment around the inn. You would feed us and take care of our animals and help with transport. We will supply the food for the camp, and they will cook their own. You will cook for the four of us, nothing fancy, just stews and pies and porridge and tea. Oh, do you ever get coffee? I can get you coffee if...if you decide to have us here. The pay will be good, better than you usually get, I'll wager. We need to be here at least three weeks, possibly more if necessary. Can you do it?" Cookson spluttered the words as fast as his tongue would form them.

"Did he say all this to you, Evan?" Tildy was a step away from tapping her toe with impatience.

"Nay, me love, but I did not give him much of a chance, all things being equal. I got angry because he was ordering me to do what he wanted. He never asked nor did he give any information such as we just heard. I am sorry my love." Evan was abashed and blushing in the aftermath of the argument. "You can handle it my love. You fare much better with men the likes of these. It must be your magic touch. This is your inn. Do as ye please.

"I am sorry my darling. You can go back to your chores. This is my job. I will handle it. Tell Sydney to get back up here, please." To Cookson she said, "You never give my husband an order on his own property. Please forgive us. You and I can talk."

Evan said, "There be room for about 100 tents on the other side of the road. If that is enough then the unit can stay. If that is not enough, it is all the land you can use that is not in fallow."

"Evan, I can take care of this, I always do. Go back to your chores and worry not." Tildy was adamant.

"Mr. Cookson follow me. Have a look at our public rooms. There are four of them and the rooms are very generous. Follow me. I do not have someone to black boots, except if I hire some boy from the village. I would ne'er trust our nephew James with the job. Our Georgie is the full-time stable boy. He is a wonder with the livestock and should be left in place. I do have my sister-in-law to help with the additional work. She lives right here over the stables.

"But should we do this, you will have to take potluck. The garden only produces so much. The rest I have to deal with other farmers. I always purchase my flour to order after Evan does the harvest. I will have to stock some bread. How soon do ye want to be here?"

Cookson replied, "If we do this, we will start tomorrow night for two of us and on the next night for all. Now, the rooms, please."

Tildy opened the door of the room closest to the stairs. "They are all the same," she said.

Cookson walked into the room. It smelled of lavender and breezy summer days. The bed coverings gleamed white. There was not a speck of dust anywhere. "You have three more like this one?" he asked amazed.

"We have six rooms in all with two being smaller servants' quarters. We should be renting one for overnight guests that come through should the occasion arise. It would be good to carry on business as usual, Major General." Tildy was polite but firm.

"The servant quarters, you said you had two. May I see one?"

"Of course." Tildy went to the end of the hall and opened a door on a smaller room. "I keep two rooms like this, one for valets and one for ladies' maids." The room had three beds, neatly made with homespun bedding covering each one. Again, the air smelled of lavender and the outdoors, not musty and dusty as other inns did. "They are not large, but the beds are comfortable, and we change sheets every week when in use or if the customer leaves. All is boiled. I will have no lice or fleas in my inn. We dust every day and refresh the herbs every other day to keep the rooms fragrant. We also open windows on the days the weather allows. Would ye be able to use one of these for one of yer men?"

Cookson, surprised that such a gem lay in such an outland as Wales, said. "Mrs. Lewis, these rooms are probably the best I have ever seen, better than most houses, better than in my own home. You have the touch, Mrs. Lewis, you have the touch. Let us go downstairs and make the arrangements."

Once in the pub, Cookson said, "I would like to take three of your regular rooms and one servant room. The leftenent can use the smaller room with my valet, don't you think Moore? We will be here for about three weeks, possibly more, as I said before. We patrol the coast looking to stop the smugglers and bring down Smuggler's Cove. If the billeting and the camp arrangements are considered acceptable, we would like to start tomorrow night. We would like the rooms at the far end of the hall. That would leave you the one at the head of the stairway and another servant room. Will that be acceptable?" Cookson handed a purse of gold sovereigns to Tildy. "This should pay for the first week. If not let me know."

"Yes, Major General, it does. I hope the meal was acceptable." Tildy took the purse. "I will return this after counting."

"Mrs. Evans, your cooking is some of the best I have found outside France. You have a delicate hand with the herbs, and you use spices. I am personally looking forward to supping here. You must be the best cook in all of Britain."

Tildy blushed at these words. She excused herself, satisfied that all was well. She knew she was going to have to keep a close eye on Sydney, who was all girl and beautiful to boot. This would be some good income if they didn't have to wait too long for the Crown to pay them.

"This was a most fortunate choice, Moore," Cookson said when Moore returned. "The Queen will be pleased with a bill this small, and we will grow fat on the delectables that woman cooks.

"'Twas a happy circumstance that brought those fellow here," Evan said to Tildy that night as they prepared for bed. "We will grow rich on their rentals what with the fields and the barns. That coin was for one week, you say. That is more than we get in a month. I hope the Crown will be happy with the arrangement and pay us regular.

The next day Tildy went to Sarah. "We have four new guests at the inn, possibly permanent, and I will need some extra help besides Sydney. I will pay you. Are you willing?

Sarah replied, "James can sweep. I can help. Branwen can finish the lace order for the estate. It is almost done. This is good. My eyes need a rest."

The two women had a short embrace. Sarah thought of the extra income and was glad for Branwen's wedding. The priest would be a happier man for it.

***

Georgie panicked as the soldiers came in droves and set up camp. Line after line of tents in formations, just like the soldiers formed every day, when they answered call and marched away to the North, to the West and to the East to search for smugglers. Every night those same troops came home tired, wet and empty-handed. George knew all they had to do was talk to the right villagers and all would be lost. He would finally get his dream to travel— straight to the gallows. He thought about running away, but didn't know how he could escape for long since he was tending the officers' horses while they billeted at the inn. "I just need to keep my own counsel and do what is necessary," he whispered to Bess, one of the milk cows. "You just stand here and keep watch and moo twice if you hear or see a military man approach. Then we need to stop talking aloud. Thank you, Bess, for this beautiful milk. Auntie will love it."

The dinner supposed to happen a week ago was forgotten. Tildy and Sydney prepared the inn for the billeting. Georgie and Sydney would have to stay ignorant of their relationship a while longer.

Evan had George clean the already clean stable into a spotless horse palace, each stall strewn with new hay. George bade James to strew the old hay around Tildy's gardens. This was important to Uncle, so George complied with the request. He knew he had to get to the village to notify all about the billeting and invasion of Her Majesty's troops. He wondered if the famous English 'navy' sailed the bay during the day as well.

That night George took off and made for the pub in Bryn a Cywd. He walked in to a few soldiers and maids but none of his companions. He paid for an ale and the keep nodded to him to get out after he was done. George took the advice. None stopped him. They were too involved in drink and women to pay attention to the local lad.

The 'local lad' did not want to be seen. He disappeared down an alley and went to his friend and fellow loader's house. He arrived and looked through an unshaded window before he knocked. There was a soldier with the man's sister. His friend, dressed to the nines, was there with a neighbor wench, and his parents sat around as chaperones, broad smiles wreathing their faces. Every once in a while, one would get up and wave his arms about. Then they would all laugh, and the process would repeat. *They must be playing a game,* George thought.

***

George took his own very good advice and went back to the inn. He sneaked in through the pig sty unseen by the soldiers on guard on the other side of the barn. Once home and cleaned up, he stewed in his own juices. *Sydney isn't here to talk to. I want to share my life with someone. Why do you have to be my first cousin? What if some soldier, handsome in his uniform, wins yer heart? Ye be just a girl with little experience in life and none in love. Oh why? Why?*

***

Days ran into nights ran into days. Tildy baked, Sydney cleaned and served. Both tended the gardens in off hours. The harvest was plentiful. Tildy and Sydney preserved what they could and dried the rest. Somewhere in this busy life Tildy thought of Morvyn and that she was due. Tildy had not heard from her cousin for quite a while. The herbs were ready as were the more successful spices. *Morvyn should be here now,* Tildy thought as she kneaded yet more dough for raised buns.

Evan and George took care of the stables. At night Evan served as pub master pulling tankards of ale. This last brewing season was good, so the ale flowed plentiful. There were many more barrels in storage, enough to see them through this plethora of business. The inn had never done so well. Tildy and Evan talked in the wee hours of the night about retiring and leaving the whole thing to George and Sydney and watching them marry and have a family. They fell asleep in these dreams many nights during the billeting.

There was one fly in the ale! George and Sydney were not privy to these plans or that they were a possibility. As far as the youngsters knew, they were first cousins, and so forbidden to marry in the eyes of any church.

1575 London—Go West

The weeks went on. Morvyn was now just over forty years old, if time be kept. Her knees hurt constantly. She had horrendous headaches, some bad enough to keep her abed a little longer in the morning. But none of this kept her down, just grouchy and not much fun to be with. Jack hired a girl for the pub so Morvyn could continue her work in the kitchen and to keep her away from the customers when she felt ill and out of sorts. He loved her in his own way, and knew she was a necessary part of his life.

Morvyn thought about Sydney. She never got another call to destroy a child as she had with Sydney. Many came to her to end pregnancies. She did those and made a goodly amount of money. Her potions and rubs earned her a little less but were still worth making. She felt better about those than the abortions. Because of some of her mixtures the rat population around the pub stayed down and neither bed bugs nor lice entered the beds above the pub. Used as they were, her rooms were still the cleanest in the area.

Morvyn knew it was time to see Tildy. She dreaded the trip but welcomed the warmth and love of family. The preparation for this trip took longer than the last. Each trip was slower and slower. She could only stay for a couple of weeks instead of a month, because of the length of the trip itself. The headaches were more frequent these days and sometimes she did not feel like getting up in the morning. She did prepare some draughts that helped the pain, but they made her fuzzy headed. This did not bode well for a four-day journey on horseback.

Finally, she was packed and ready to go. Jack kissed her goodbye and thumped the nag on the rump. "Come back soon, Morvyn. I need you here. I miss you so when you are gone."

Morvyn looked back and smiled. He was so full of himself. She knew that he amused himself in her absence, but she was his lifeline until she died. Perhaps he prayed for that day. She waved and turned toward her trip.

Two days out, she took an extra day at a country inn. Her head pain was great, so she took an extra dose of her draught and slept for sixteen hours straight. It was too late in the day to leave so she stayed another night, careful not to overdose.

Her arrival at The Cock and the Sow was a tearful joyful greeting. "What took you so long, Morvyn? You are so late. Did Jack give you a hard time about coming? The last time you sent word." Tildy hugged her cousin and led her into the pub. "Evan will get your gear and Georgie will take the mount. I was so worried about you." The words spilled out of Tildy as she sat Morvyn down and went to the kitchen to make tea and a bite. Tildy came back with cake and a pot of tea.

"Aye, I remember the last time I was late. It was when I brought you the babe." Morvyn nibbled on the cake while Tildy fetched some cups. "Where is that child?" Tildy poured and Morvyn breathed in the aroma of the tea.

"She be well, Morvyn, and she be slim and straight, not like most of the young around this place. She is not the usual farm girl, overfed and made ready for marriage." Tildy took a sip of her tea. "What is the problem, Morvyn? You are just rattling on and going nowhere, or is that me? What took so long, cousin?"

"Ach, Tildy, I get these headaches. The sun blinds me. I have to stay dark until they pass. I feel so useless on those days. I see a halo—the light changes and the pain pounds in my brain. It has been getting worse this last year, going from every few months to once or twice in one month. My joints hurt and my fingers and knees swell. It is hard to walk some mornings, but as the day goes on, it gets better. But enough about me, how does your garden grow? I am in need of some of those new herbs I brought you last time. Did they catch?" Morvyn took another sip of the tea. Her headache went to slumber, and she felt so much better.

"Those new plants are beautiful and lush. I need one of each to go to seed, so I can continue growing them for you. You take the rest. I use them not. How about another slice of cake or some more tea? We don't have much time for talk this visit. The Queen's men are here for at least another week at last word.

They told Evan they were going to stay for three weeks. It has been five. They just told him they were close to their goal and when they were done, they would pull out. I have only a servant's room for you this time or you can sleep with Sydney."

"How is young Sydney faring through all this?" Morvyn asked.

"She is well and very busy. I try to keep her out of the dining room when all the soldiers come for a tankard or two, late in the evening. I am afraid one will try to get fresh, and she will knock him to the ground. She did it once a few years ago. Evan had to talk to the man and explain that his daughter was not for sale and how would he like it if someone did it to his daughter? He gave the gent a free meal and a tankard on the house and all was forgotten. Syd does have a temper to go with her hair. I wonder where she got it. Neither Evan nor I have tempers and Georgie boy neither. We be pretty calm around here."

Morvyn laughed. "I have seen you in temper, my love, and I can imagine the girl does just like you. Slow to anger and a raging storm when it is too much. I know, it must be her gypsy stock. I always thought it was the girl who brought us the babe was the babe's mother I don't know why. It was just a feeling. . She said she worked for a peer, but she looked like a Romany. I understand those Romanies can be pretty violent when they get upset. I could be wrong."

Morvyn changed the subject, "I understand our good Queen Bess is sending troops out here to capture smugglers and pirates. How can men on the ground catch out men on the sea? I wonder about this. Word in London is she desperately needs the money to pay for the military and the new fleet of ships she is building to keep the Spanish out."

"Morvyn, this is men's talk. We have those troops here now or at least some of them. We need to get out to the garden. I have to tend to the meals and the washing up. Tomorrow is linens day. It is a lot of work, but your wondrous herbs keep things fresh. We wouldn't have this business now, if it weren't for them. Let's get to the garden. I have tea on the fire. I hope you like the cake. I used some of that Indian spice, that cardamom, we got to grow. What a wonderful flavor to cake and fruit alike. Thank you for that."

The women walked out to the gardens. Morvyn exclaimed over the herbs. She looked at the small enclosed spice garden. The whole building was perhaps fifty meters square. Evan and George built this small house with a glass roof to bring in the sun and the warmth during the winter months and the cold snaps. There was a small oven to make heat in the winter. Buckets surrounded the outside to collect water for the garden during the colder months. The roof lifted off during the warmer months to let the sun do its business and to let the rain fall , watering plants naturally. Tildy had a sample of every spice known to man including nutmeg and cinnamon. There was a clove plant and several peppers.

Tildy had learned much about growing exotics. One had to carefully harvest the cinnamon, since the spice was in the bark of the plant. She experimented with it and cut it back like her roses. The yield was huge from just one plant. This little house was the result of losing several delicate plants to the cold of this Northwest coast and those goats Sydney insisted on making pets.

There was nothing like this on this coast. Morvyn was thrilled. She breathed in the aroma in the small building and said, "I want to have some of everything. You know when a potion smells good it works good. Smell is powerful, Tildy. If something smells bad, it can cause illness, even if it is a cure.

Sometimes I ken this is caused by how people think, not how they feel."

"Morvyn Hoggins, you mean you don't work magic with those mixtures and poultices?"

"Not magic, cousin just medicine. Thoughts cause other results. My pain draughts are medicine. My love potions are 'magic.'"

The cousins laughed. "Where is that girl of yours? I haven't seen her at all. She is usually the first to greet me."

"She should be making beds or dusting. I will call her when we go in. You will need her to help harvest." The two women continued their walk in the now extensive gardens behind the inn. "I must be getting in soon, Morvyn, so enjoy a little time out here. I will find the girl and send her to you." Tildy gave her cousin another squeeze and went back to the kitchen.

Bryn a Cywd—The Same Day

Evan and George went to town. George asked Evan to go to the two pubs in Bryn a Cywd so he could see how the soldiers off duty flocked to them because of the women. "Uncle, maybe you should consider hiring other women besides Auntie and Sydney to work the inn in the evenings. It could prove profitable for all. You will see the business the Queen's End does now that the soldiers are in the area." The Queen's End was the name of one of the pubs in Bryn a Cywd.

"George, I don't need any more business and besides where would I put them?

"You have the two extra rooms at the inn, the servants rooms," said George

"And how do you suppose your aunt would feel about that? There is so much work for her now," Evan argued.

"Just see, Uncle. We will be there soon. It will only cost a tankard of ale, which by the way is not as good as yours." George and Evan were almost there. Evan knew the pub master by name.

"Good day to you Maurice." Evan reached even before they got to the bar area to shake the man's hand.

"Evan Lewis! 'Tis been a long time passing since you were here." Maurice greeted Evan with a heartfelt welcome. The Cock and the Sow was well thought of in the village since the shopkeepers profited from his new business with the military.

Maurice drew Evan a tankard on the house. From the looks of it, he could draw many on the house and still break even. George ordered a tankard as well but had to lay down coin for the privilege. "Thank you, Maurice," Evan said.

Neither George nor Evan noticed Robert Bourne leave the pub at the nod of the pub master's head. Good fortune rained unexpected down on Smuggler's Cove. George and Evan finished their brew and wished Maurice a goodbye. On the road George said, "Well, Uncle, the middle of the day and he is full. The ale is not as good as your brew and I doubt the food as good as Auntie's. 'Tis the women that bring them in. What do you think? Is it a good idea for the inn?"

"George, I think your mother, your aunt and your cousin would be horrified with such goings on. I don't think the gentry would stop, either. Reputation is very important. We are not in London. We are three miles hence of Bryn a Cywd, in the middle of the country. Most of our clientele is looking for a good night's rest not a roll in the hay. I think we shall stay as we are. When you and Sydney take over then you two can decide what kind of establishment you want."

"Sydney and me take over?" George looked at Evan in surprise. "Sydney and me? Uncle, we are first cousins. We cannot be married, and I would be sore put to keep my hands off her, if you two were not around. She is feisty and can throw a mean punch. She kicks like a mule and I shouldn't tell you, but she swears like a sailor when you are not around. She is always mad at me and I love her like a sister. She were me first love until I met Gladys. That baker's lass is good for my animal lust and she be easier to take than Syd. That is one of the reasons I want you to consider women at the inn. I have been thinking of making transport to the New World. I don't know how much longer I can live in this place."

"Oh, my lad, I have something to tell you. What with this military billet and all, it went right out of your aunt's and my mind. We never got around to that dinner we talked about. Then with them staying so much longer—it has been hard work. We just didn't get around to it. We should have a long time ago." Evan stopped in the middle of the road. He grabbed George by the shoulders and turned him to face him. "George Lewis, I must tell you this. Please do not be angry or upset. Now, listen and do not interrupt— Sydney Lewis is not your first cousin. In fact, the two of you are not related in any way at all." George opened his mouth to interrupt. Evan held up his hand. "Just listen, then you may do what needs to doing.

When you were six and were just with us a few months, Tildy's cousin Morvyn brought us a wee babe. A young girl came to Morvyn with a newborn babe and asked her to get rid of it. Morvyn could not kill the child. She thought of us and made a trip to bring her to us so we could have a child of our own. The child was swaddled in fine linen and the name Sydney was stitched on it in fine hand—as fine a hand as your sister Lelah's. We wanted to tell you both at the same time at that dinner like I said."

George looked at Evan. Surprise, followed by joy and then by worry crossed his face that fast. Then anger took over and that look stayed. "Do you mean that you were just going to let us go on believing we were unholy related and not fit to marry one another? Oh, Uncle, I loved her for so long but now I have Gladys. I ken ye want Syd and me to marry. Ye have been kind to me over the years and I owe you fer that. Does she know?"

"Not that I know of, but you cannot be the one to tell her. Her Ma and I need to do that. Please be patient a while longer, son."

Several mounted soldiers came at them, galloping fast. Evan and George leaped out of the way to avoid a trampling death. More horsemen followed and a few minutes later foot soldiers appeared.

Evan pulled one of the foot soldiers off the road. "What is happening?"

"I don't know for sure, sir, but a ship be washed up on shore, beached, and all aboard was dead or dyin'. The dyin' say it were pirates. We are ta meet the ship on patrol, and become sea borne. I dunna like the water in the least. Please let me go. I must catch up."

The men passed and George and Evan met again in the middle of the road. "I guess we will be getting some time to have that dinner, hey Uncle?" and the two men walked in the direction opposite to the soldiers.

"Them soldiers were from our inn, Uncle. They were packed and on the march. Why did we not know about that?" Georgie asked.

"They were to be gone long ago. Mayhaps their orders finally came. Good riddance, I say. We need some peace and rest." Evan replied. The two walked on towards home.

Bagging It

The goats were loud, bleating an almost a goaty whine. *They need me,* thought Sydney. *Where is Georgie? This is his job not mine.* Sydney went into the barn. Georgie wasn't in the stable nor was he at his ma's rooms. *He must be working with Da somewhere, cutting wood.* Sydney continued to ponder since she could find neither of the men. She grabbed the pail and called the girls. Jane came right away, so she sat down and milked her first. "Annie, Annie, come along," Sydney called. Where is that sister of yours, Janie, me good girl?" She heard Annie's voice bleating from the cabbage patch behind the barn.

Cabbage and onions were grown separately from the rest of the vegetables. The smell could be overpowering. Da sold the vegetables when ripe at the market in town. The problem was that sometimes the animals got into the patches unseen and made quite a mess, eating the tender cabbage leaves. When that happened, the goat milk would have a funny taste and couldn't be used for cheese or baking, so it was used as slop for the pigs.

"I had better get this pail to Ma, Janie. But I also have to get that damn goat out of Da's patch before she ruins all. Maybe there are some onions ready for digging, too." Sydney left the pail of milk by the stable door and proceeded to go around the outside of the building. When she got to the rear, she saw Annie in the middle of the cabbage patch, straddled by a large burly man, her head pulled back. He had a knife and was ready to slit her throat. She was bawling and jumping about as much as she could. If she hit his privates, he would be in a great deal of pain. Sydney shouted. The man dropped the knife. Sydney ran pell mell and whooping loudly straight for him. His look of surprise turned to a satisfied grin. He relaxed his hold on the goat. The goat, feeling the slack back away in time and ran to her sister in the stable.

Sydney hit the man full on with all her fifteen-plus- year- old power. Sydney thought she'd run into a stone wall. The man wrapped his arms about her and lifted her from the ground.

"Jest what I come after. I weren't going to kill the goat but to shut it up, but you done that for me, you fine little missy. They said you'd be a spitfire, but you are much smaller than they said." Sydney started to yell and felt a large hand effectively over her mouth. Since her mouth was already open, she bit hard when the hand covered her. All she encountered was a well calloused palm, the calluses of a working man. He laughed and holding the flailing girl in one arm, he tied the kerchief from around his neck around her mouth. He maneuvered the coarse sack he'd brought for the purpose over her head and shoulders and up ending her, shook her so that her legs were covered. He lowered his sack of child to the ground and bound the open end with a leather thong. He picked it up and flung it over his shoulder. He looked around for witnesses. Satisfied that there were none, he strode off toward the cover of the trees that bordered this piece of land. Sydney never stopped kicking.

***

"Sydne.e.e.y, *Syd.d.d.ne.e.e.ey*, bring that milk in now! Ye have had long enough to milk those benighted animals, God rest their souls when they go." Tildy was yelling for her daughter when she found that the girl was not dusting in the rooms. The bedding was on the lines and the rooms spotless and airing. Tildy looked at Morvyn. "How can it take an hour to get the milk? Even if she slopped the pigs, she should be done by now.

"Evan said Georgie wanted him to go to town today. Mayhaps that blasted girl is doing George's chores. Morvyn, go down and check, please. I need her here more than they need her there." Tildy did not stop working as she spoke aloud.

"Aye, cousin, I will go for her. I haven't seen her since I got here, near to sleep last night I was and then, this morning up so late. I want to see her even in these busy days. I need some time in the open air. I feel so much better now and have not had even a glimpse of a halo since I arrived." Morvyn stood up and left the kitchen, her cup still half full.

Morvyn felt in her bones that something was not right. *Evan and the lad gone together off the property and the girl disappearing—in the middle of the day.* "Hold, cousin, I will look behind the stable, while you get nuncheon ready." Morvyn thought a little more. *Behind the stables, hmmmm!* She walked out looking for signs. The pig sties were on one side. No one went that way unless it was time to slop the animals. She passed the stable door and noted the pail of milk by the door. She went down the other side. There were little signs of disturbance, but those goats could cause that. Nasty little beasts they were. She knew the only reason they were here was for their milk. They ate anything and Sydney loved them. Morvyn got closer to the field behind the stable. The smell of cabbage filled her nostrils. A goat looked up briefly from her culinary delight, then got back to it. Morvyn stepped into the garden. She had never seen it before. Tildy told her that she had demanded it be apart from her gardens so room windows could be opened in good weather without gassing out the residents with the smell of ripe cabbages and the pungent smell of onions. *A wise woman is that cousin of mine,* she thought.

As she walked, Morvyn looked at the ground. Little hoof prints were rife, but when she got to the middle of the patch, she saw a half-eaten cabbage and trampled plants and soil with human footprints, some large some small. *Something has happened,* she theorized. She looked toward the inn. It was not visible from this field. She looked in the opposite direction—a small copse of trees stood behind a fallow field. The stable blocked the sight of the road. There were grain fields opposite the stable. The ripening grain tall and green waved in the gentle breeze. Morvyn looked down again. A glint of gold caught her eye. She reached down and dug it from the trampled ground—an ear ornament! It was the same as Morvyn gave to Sydney a couple of years ago. Tildy was so upset that her beautiful daughter had any sort of adornment. Morvyn's thought *Tildy protects that child too much. Something did happen here. This earring is proof unless the child was careless and lost it working out here in the garden. It would be difficult to lose one of these earbobs* with a French clasp to prevent that kind of a loss. *No, this earring snagged and dropped in a struggle. The child was out here today.* Morvyn palmed the earring and made her way back to the inn.

"Where is she?" Tildy cried.

"I couldna find her," replied Morvyn.

"Morvyn, where can that scamp be? She must be somewhere with those benighted goats. Did ye check the barn?" Tildy's face was getting pink and her eyes were wide. "There is naught at the inn. There were no one at the stable?"

"There were a pail of milk by the stable door. It were only one goat's worth," said Morvyn. "And there were only one goat around. It were in the cabbage patch, eating."

"Ach, that is it, the girl has gone to hide the goats, so Evan cannot get rid of them, but we told her they were safe from us." Tildy was busy with the kitchen, preparing meat for a stew. "She'll be back soon enough when she thinks the girls are safe. I must tend to tea and to the nightly meals. The money is good, but I hope those soldiers are away soon."

Morvyn stared at her cousin. She knew there was more to the story than goat-napping. The girl was gone. She had seen the goat in the cabbage patch.

"Tildy, I did find something, one of those ear bobs I gave Sydney. I found it buried in your cabbage patch, the ground in the middle of the patch trampled down and several of the plants stepped on by a man not a goat. I chased the goats out of there by the way. They were having a grand meal. I guess you won't be making cheese for a few days. Oh well, the pigs will fare pretty well, instead." Tildy started to cry into her stew. "Tildy, come here and stop your bawling. Tell me why anyone would want Sydney?"

"She is beautiful and ripe for the picking."

"She is a hoyden, feisty and mean when upset," Morvyn said. *Something else is going on,* Morvyn thought. Aloud she blurted, "The smugglers! Tell me true Matilda, was Evan involved in the smuggling? You know the Queen is down on all, because she can't collect the taxes for the goods sold on the black market. I have heard tell that she is planning an all-out invasion on Wales northwest coast and Ireland's Northern Sea to stop these goings on. Now, has Evan been involved?"

"Morvyn Hoggins, I love you, but you should know my husband is honest and hardworking, and we have nothing more than the income from this inn. He would never get involved. He could hang if caught. Why would he want to risk that?" But it was too late. The seed of doubt was planted the in the twenty-two-year marriage. Tildy now had a wisp of a reason to distrust Evan and her heart broke anew.

"Then what about the boy?"

On the Road—The Same Day

Sydney stayed very limp and quiet listening to the sounds of a person preparing a fire. *We must be stopped for the night. Will he share some food with me? Does he snore? How will I know he sleeps? We haven't gone that far. How can he set up a camp without someone seeing us? There only be that little copse of trees, and it don't hide much. Smoke from a fire can be seen easily from the road. Mayhaps he is not making a fire. Where are we that he is this confident of his hiding place? What did he use this sack for,* she thought, *transporting chickens, very scared chickens? This thing smells bad.*

She felt his presence near her and heard him mutter, "Right'o, me girly girl, time to have some dinner."

Ah, she thought *I can stick him when he lets me out to eat.*

He picked up the sack and felt for her head. "You can breathe now lass. I know you are not dead in there." He hoisted her dead weight to a sitting position and took some twine and bound her legs together still inside the sack. Then he wrapped a goodly length of cord around her upper body to keep her arms at her side. He leaned her against something sturdy, so she was at least head up and only her bum and legs touched the dampness. "Don't worry, my peach, I will make sure you are comfortable for the discomfort you are in." He laughed, "You may go hungry for a few days, but I cannot chance your screaming and us being caught. You are here for a reason. You were my part of the job and I have accomplished it." Sydney heard his words. This was the intent the whole time. Why would they want her?

Sydney stopped wiggling. There was a gag in her mouth and screaming was not possible. So was eating, and Sydney was hungry. It was time for thinking and listening. She looked around for the man. He was gone. *Am I alone, dumped on this wet ground to rot in this bag?* She sat still and thought, *I have my pig sticker. How could I forget it? Ma told me to strap it to my leg or keep it in my skirt waist , but I used it in the garden and stuck it in my bodice for easy use.*

All women carried knives. They concealed them somewhere on their bodies. They were not just for protection. Women used these knives for a multitude of duties, cutting fruit, harvesting leafy vegetables, poking holes in a too loose bodice or a belt for a man. Anything could happen to a woman at home or away from home, and now it had. Sydney had hers close to her breast in a leather sheath. The problem was that the bag she was in was so tightly bound that she couldn't reach it.

Sydney lay very still, and she heard nothing. She decided to take a chance and so worked her right arm across her body. It was a very tight fit. She tried wiggling about and pumping her arm away from her body to get some room, much like one does in a voluminous chemise that has wrapped itself around one in one's sleep. That wasn't the case. The sack was very narrow. She tried moving her arm upward and over. She just had to get the hilt and draw it very carefully out of the sheath. A noise stopped her motion. Wherever she was there were leaves on the ground. A great thump, thump, thump sounded and then a man's voice swore. Sydney sat very still and held her breath. *Maybe if he thinks I am dead, he will loosen the sack. Then I can stab him.* Her blade was a halb dagger; not long enough to kill but sharp enough to leave a bloody wound. *Oh! Wait until Da hears about this,* she thought. *He will kill this man and they will send Da to the gallows. Better I should do it. They burn witches and behead traitors. I am neither, so I will never hang for the murder of a kidnapping knave like this one.*

She listened and heard rustling sounds then the unmistaken sound of a flint. The bloke was making a fire*! Pull me closer. I am cold and where is my food? I have not had tea and it certainly must be dinner time by now. Why did this happen to me? Why?*

The Cock and the Sow— The Same Day Evening

Evan and George came into the kitchen of the inn only to be greeted by a weeping Tildy and an angry Morvyn. Evan went to Tildy's side. "Why are you crying so my love? What has happened beside all the soldier left and we have some peace now to go back and live our lives like normal people."

"Sydney!" Tildy cried, "Sydney is gone, kidnapped we think. Look at this." She nodded to Morvyn, who fished the earbob out of her apron pocket and showed it to Evan on the palm of her hand.

"Somehow the French clasp broke and she lost the bauble." Morvyn said with anger- tinged sorrow in her voice. "Just where have you two been?"

"We went to the village to look in at the Queen's End during the day. We've only been gone a few of hours, enough to get us there, have a tankard and come home. We met the soldiers from here headed for the village. They almost mowed us down in their haste. I pulled one aside, and he said a ship beached in the cove and some of the sorely wounded said it were pirates. Most 're dead. Just a few lived to give those words." Evan explained.

"So how long is she gone?" George and Evan asked in chorus.

"A few hours, I think. She left half a pail of goat's milk. Morvyn found the trampled place and the earring in the cabbage field. Oh Evan, where can my babe be?" Tildy collapsed into his arms in tears once more.

Into the Wood—The Same Night

Sydney, still ensacked and gagged, tried to free that right arm. The man missed her lower arm when wrapping her. Slowly, slowly she moved those fingers across her chest. She sucked in her breath to allow passage of that lower arm across her burgeoning breasts. Her fingers felt the hilt. She moved the halbdagger slowly up the sheath and then past the sheath up the outside of her chemise.

He cooked a rabbit over a small fire. Sydney was offered naught but the smell. Juices formed in her mouth. A muted voice asked, "Are ye thirsty, lass?" Sydney grunted her affirmative.

She felt clumsy fingers force a reed into her gagged mouth. "Suck and ye will lose your thirst. There is fresh water come through. Drink all ye want until it is gone. I have no way to give ya food through the reed. Ye have to be happy with the drink."

A parched Sydney sipped when the reed came through the hole. She sucked and sucked and then there was no more. The reed left the hole.

"I'm so hungry." She shouted her words, but they were muted by the gag. She still could not see anything. *There were no bogs around so where did he get the reed?* She couldn't guess. Musty cool air came through the small hole. *We must be near water, but where?* Sydney's eyes started to get heavy. She felt her body relax and her fingers slip from the halbdagger. *He must have mixed me a sleeping draught in my water, the bastard,* was her last thought until sleep took her. During the time someone threw a blanket over her for warmth. Sydney slept on. The draught did not wear off for many hours. When she awoke, she was on a soft bed that was rocking rhythmically back and forth like a cradle. She was still in the sack, but her fingers were no longer around her pig sticker. She knew it was somewhere in the sack and she started feeling around for it.

The Cock and the Sow—The Days After

The next day life at the Lewis abode was much subdued. Tildy broke into tears with no known provocation. "Tildy, love, you are weeping as though she is dead. We have no such word. Please believe me, love, with the army gone, Sydney will return.

"I have talked to Cookson and Moore and told them what happened. They said their mission was at an end and their orders were to pull out today or tomorrow. They knew nothing of the child being gone. They said they had no time to investigate either."

"Evan I never in my whole life expected anything like to happen. She is my only one. I want to kill whoever took her and for those feelings I feel guilty. I don't care if I fry in Hell for all eternity for that. I just want my babe back safe and sound."

"Auntie, I must find out what happened. Uncle told me about her and me. I will to marry her as soon as we return. I will pack and go today, if that be all right with all of you. Aunt Morvyn, may I have the earbob? Someone may recognize it along the way."

"Son, I know you think you must go, but we need you here. Can you not wait until morning when the officers leave the inn?" Evan asked. "There will be fewer questions and it gives you time to put together a kit for a trip."

"Uncle, there is no guarantee that they will do as they said. They may be laying a trap for those who would bring Sydney home. Is that what you would wait for? I think if that happened, they would kill Sydney on the spot. Might as well hang for murder as well as kidnapping," exclaimed George.

"I will do what needs doing to get the girl back. She won't even be fifteen for another few months. I won't have her married so young. Too many young ones die having bairns so young. So it is with kuhe as well. You never breed at first blood." Evan said, angry fear coloring his words. In a calmer voice he said, "Patience, lad, have patience. She will be back and soon I warrant. We must get back to work. We have missed many hours to keep the inn going and the dining room will be opening soon. I know you want to go, but at least wait for a day. I will give you travel money. If you do find her, do not tell her our secret. She will never truly believe you. I know she loves you with all her heart. Is that not right, Tildy?"

Tildy burst into new tears and nodded. "Go and get my babe back, Georgie, and take care of yourself. I couldn't bear to lose both of you. And be sure to say goodbye to your Ma. She needs to know you are going. Come and give us a hug and a kiss goodbye."

"Tildy, he isn't leaving right now. Pull together girl. We need all our wits about us," Evan said. "George, we need some way to communicate. How can we do that? I would like to hear from you as often as possible. Do not endanger yourself trying to get news to me. Do you think you can do that?"

George thought a while and said, "I can send you messages by whatever way I go. If I have to sail, I will let you know. If I go by land that will be easier, and I can send you word as I go along. Would it not be nice to have a shouting contraption that lets people talk over distances? I think of these things once in a while. It pays to have chores you know how to do.

"I will not wait for the morrow before departing. Janes can help with the simple chores, but he is not good with the greetings."

George left the inn and went to the stable. He finished his chores in record time. He set James to clean the stalls and polish the leathers as he was taught. Then he packed a small kit. In his room he burrowed under the hay and lifted the floorboard. The sack was still there. *I have travel money without Evan,* he thought. *The rest I will keep buried until I get back. No one could find it in this mess.* He then went to the kitchen and got some bread and cheese and was on his way.

***

They forgot Morvyn in all the drama. She knew she should be going but hated leaving Tildy in such a tizzy. She took her leather sack and went to the herb garden. She cut and tied as she did on every trip. As she worked, she turned the last two days' events over in her mind.

She hid in a dark corner of the pub the night before and listened. She helped Evan by bringing tankards to the tables as needed. She was listening for a hint of who or where the smugglers were. The foot soldiers knew little more than Evan had learned on the road. Several farmers, local men, were in the pub and they were no more help than the foot soldiers. Late that night a cloaked man came in. Morvyn was close to the tap when she heard a rasp say, "get rid of the soldiers, if you want to see your daughter alive again."

Evan grasped at the man but to no avail. He twisted away and was gone into the night. Morvyn went to Evan and put her arm around his waist. "How can you answer to that sort of thing cousin, how?"

Evan looked at her. "I don't know why they picked us except that I took the billet order. It was that or Her Majesty would take over the inn and we would be out until they finished with it. Even then we could lose it as they would give it to one of the officers as a reward for duty done. If they are responsible for taking my daughter, I curse them to their dying day and that be the sooner the better. If it is the smugglers the same curse for them in addition to burning in Hell. What do you think is going on, Morvyn? Ye seem to ken these things. Who would have gone to the cabbage patch?"

"Evan, I have done you wrong with your wife. I have laid a doubt in her mind about your involvement in this smuggling ring. I suggested by asking if you were part of the ring. She denied it, but I am sure it put doubt where no doubt was before. I also asked about the boy. I am sorry about all this, but my mind does work differently. You know I have to get back to London. I will start to ask around in the Witch's Brew.

I may even have a connection to the Queen. Be easy. I will do some work in my area.

"I must start to get ready to go back tomorrow. I will leave on the following day. I must go. I will set things straight with Tildy, too. I love you both too much to let this stand between you." Morvyn left the inn and went to her small chamber off the kitchen. She was not feeling well. Her knees hurt. She took a pain draught and prayed for a good sleep.

On A Ship in A Cove

Sydney felt her pig sticker. It was close to her bum and was sticking into her. She tried rolling on her side and working her left hand to her right side to get the knife. She wound up lying on the knife. She worked that left arm behind her and rolled onto her left side. Her fingers touched the blade. She worked them up to the hilt. There was no use cutting herself and revealing her weapon. Her fingers wrapped around the hilt and she rolled onto her stomach and started to work that arm over her back to her left side. That accomplished, she rolled on to her back and brought the knife straight up through the sack. Her limited motion made a hole in the sack, but there was no relief from the thing.

She dropped the knife on her belly and used that left arm to pull on the threads of the sack in an effort to loosen them and make the hole bigger. If she could only get a hand out, she might loosen the rope around her arms and with them freed, make a bigger hole in the sack and get free. She worked. An hour went by then two and finally she reached the knot on the rope. She'd rubbed her fingers raw and only freed one twist of the knot. Whoever tied it knew what he was doing. She thought about working the knife back and forth against the rope, thus cutting it and getting herself free. It could work. She rested a few minutes then reached for the knife on her belly. She worked it out the hole in the sack and started to saw at the rope. She felt one strand break and then another. Then the whole thing let loose. Her arms were free. She grasped the knife with both hands and dragged it up the hole. The hole became a slit and soon she could get her arms out of the sack. She started cutting sideways to allow more of her body to get free.

    The door rattled. Sydney stopped cutting and drew the knife into the sack. She turned on her side hoping her back was to the door. The door opened. Someone clunked across the room. Whoever it was wore boots. She would never know their presence if they were barefoot. She heard a tray hit the table. "Decided to take a wee nap did ya? Well, I ain't gonna waste this food on a sleeping sack." Sydney drooled. She was hungry and now she was thirsty as well. "This be fine grub. Perhaps tomorra ye 'll be ready to eat." A chair scraped back, and she heard the boots clump to the door. "Sweet dreams, lassie. They'll be your last fer a long time." The door closed, and the key turned the lock.

    Sydney had to get loose. She rolled back onto her back and kept cutting. *I'm lucky the man did not check on me before leaving,* she thought. *He would have caught me, and the knife would be gone, but perhaps I would be free of the sack and able to eat. Stop wool gathering. Do what you have to do to get free.* She pulled that knife against the coarse fabric of the bag until the hole was big enough for her to work her head and shoulders out. She untied the rope around her legs and shed the sack. She could smell the odor of it on her skin and clothes.

She took off her shoes so no one could hear her walking about and got up to look around the room. The room swayed. There was a round window that looked out at the water. The man had left a tray on a desk. Did they expect her to get free of the sack? She smelled the food. It smelled wonderful and she jammed a piece of bread into her mouth. She wolfed down the rest of the meal and looked for something to drink. There was no water, but there were some bottles of wine on a shelf behind the desk. This was not good. Sydney did not drink spirits. The water at the inn was fresh and clean. She was missing home already, and she was only gone a short while.

***

There was no word of Sydney. The officers left the day after her kidnapping. The soldiers had left several days before to be located closer still to the beach heads of the Irish Sea. Life at the inn went back to normal, or as normal as it could be without their daughter.

Morvyn was packed and ready to leave. Tildy packed a hamper for her to take with for the trip home. To be sure, she did not miss Jack anymore on this trip as the others. She had to get back, so Jack did not think he now owned the Witch's Brew.

Morvyn knew things were not right with her. She was starting a headache—the halo formed, and the colors of the earth were very strange like oil on water in the sunlight. Morvyn took her headache draught and lay down in the dark alcove. Tildy found her there several hours later. She looked at the peaceful look on Morvyn's face and let her rest.

Tildy looked around her kitchen. She missed Sydney to distraction. Georgie must have left at dawn. She noticed some bread and cheese was gone. He had not said goodbye.

Sarah was taking a few days respite to catch up on her lace making. She had been a comfort the day Sydney was taken but felt out of place with Georgie going to look for her and the news that Tildy had not birthed the girl.

Tildy was glad Georgie knew their secret. That knowledge seemed to give him a determination to go after her Syd. She fetched down her bread bowl and put some yeast into it. She added a touch of honey and some warm water. Covering it with a towel, she put it aside. There was not much to do today. The stew from yesterday would heat up and only a small pot of porridge was necessary for today's breakfast. Tildy sat down at the table, put her head on her arms and wept again for her lost child.

***

Sydney was full. She was tired and needed some sleep, but this was dangerous. Loathsome as it was, she knew she had to have the filthy sack as a cover. Maybe the clumping man would not remember how much food he left on the tray, if he remembered leaving the tray at all. Sydney slit the sack to form a blanket and made sure when she lay down that it covered her head and feet. She was soon asleep.

***

The situation at Smuggler's Cove is heating up, and someone is bound to talk to get his freedom or at least keep his life. The talker would finger George, since they took Sydney as bait, George thought as he trudged along.

Her Majesty's Army gathered at the cove. The search would include the caves. The unsold treasure was only a few days away from discovery.

But George was wrong. He was the least of the smugglers' concern. The privateers, flying the Tudor flag, patrolled the shoreline in the bay between Ireland and Scotland on a daily basis. The two ships went back and forth like the changing of the guard. No one could go to the caves for fear of discovery. The pirates worked the sea north and west of Ireland. The Irish didn't care, and the Scots welcomed the extra loot. They were used to thumbing their noses at the Queen and her military.

George thought of his farewell to Evan. The conversation had been short. "I must be going. If I stay, either the army or the smugglers will conscript me. No matter which, I am in for trouble." George told Evan.

"Lad, ye must do what ye will. I appreciate yer going to search for Sydney. Ye will make your aunt a very happy woman should you find her. What idea do you have for her whereabouts?"

"You know, Uncle, I figure she must have been taken by the smugglers. They seem to be the ones angry with you giving billet to the officers and allowing the camp. I heard the boats were on patrol in the bay and that most of the smuggling cannot happen while the soldiers are rife in the village. I think she must be some place in the village. I fear for her. No matter what I still love her and will have her for my wife if you wish."

"Just be careful, lad. Too much nosing and you might end up in the same situation. I just don't trust anybody any more. Be careful!"

"Goodbye, Uncle. Have my Ma help you at the inn. She needs to be around people and so does Auntie. I said my farewells to Auntie yesterday. I can't bear to see her cry. Thank you for all you have done for me, Uncle. I hope I am back soon. Wish me luck."

"Good fortune to you, my son. I told you that I would give you some traveling money. Here are a few coins. I will not give you gold. It is too traceable. I looked over some of the coin I got over the weeks and there is a surprising amount of Spanish gold amongst it. Some of these soldiers didn't know what they had, and I wonder how they came by it. That is another little clue you might follow. Good journey, ye." Evan gave the boy a quick hug and then shook his hand.

George hoisted his pack and pocketed the money. "Thank you, Uncle, and goodbye." He headed up the stable stairs to the rooms his mother kept. He was down in just a few minutes. Evan never saw him leave.

***

George walked straight to the village. When he got there, he hid his pack and went directly to the

Queen's End. He paid for a tankard, and when Maurice asked him why he was in town, he told him that Evan sent him in to get some goods for Tildy. He pulled the pub master to him over the bar. George leaned over close to Maurice's ear and whispered to him that his cousin was gone from the inn under nefarious conditions and he, George, was searching for her. "Do you know anything, or have you heard anything of this, Maurice?"

"Nay, young George, I have heard nothing. Why would anyone want that little spitfire? I heard tell she was nothing but trouble." Maurice whispered back.

"I tell ya, her ma is in a fit over it and they have been so good to me and my family over the years that I just have to find her. Spitfire you say. She always seemed so sweet and nice at the inn." George lied through his teeth, grinning inside at his little ruse.

"Boy, I don't know nothing. Never heard tell of this at all. The last time I seen you was earlier this week, were it not? Then the soldiers invaded this town and the shoreline, and the ships started passing every few hours, two of them, back and forth. That started the day after the beached ship showed up. Only two lived from it and one is in danger of death even today. The other I understand wasn't as badly hurt as they thought. That's all I know, George. Another tankard?"

"Nay, you know my capacity be only one at a time. I needs get on my task for Evan. See you soon Maurice."

George left the pub. Not much information there. He retrieved his pack and started through town towards the harbor. He didn't get far. There was a blockade closing off the street.

"Halt! What willst thou with this street? Know ye not it is closed to all traffic but the military?"

"Nay, I know not. I can go a different direction. I need to be getting to the next town and I usually follow the coast. I do not like the sea and its rocking. It makes me sick."

"Do I not know you?" The guard looked more closely at George.

"Have we met? I go occasionally to the Queen's End and I work at The Cock and the Sow. I am on a task now for the owner. I suppose I will have to go over the mountains now since I canna take the easy route."

"The Cock and the Sow you say? We were camped there until a few days ago. You were on the road from the village with an older man. He owns the inn. That is where I seen you. Well, you can't pass, but if you go around, you can take some of the back alleys and avoid the rest of the blockades. The coast is clear about three miles up. We have no reason to be there."

George thanked the guard and thought about three miles up. They didn't know about the caves that dotted the coastline! A couple were that far up and the last that George had worked in. That told him the military spies hadn't done a good job and no one had talked. Perhaps they were even in on it. He was safe for a while and getting out of town was paramount.

George followed the guard's advice. He came to the edge of town and there was no blockade. He continued down the path to the shore and walked north. Every so often he looked out to sea. There were no ships moored this far up. There wouldn't be. He looked behind and saw a ship in full flag sailing this way. A few more miles and he saw another ship sailing in the opposite direction. The privateers was patrolling far better than the Army was searching. Best hie away and find Sydney. There were plenty of places for hiding her. *Oh Sydney, I am so sorry for this. I hope I am in time,* he thought. He trudged on.

The Cock and the Sow

"Evan, why are you bringing the milk? Where is Georgie?" Tildy was beyond remembering all but the present.

"George is gone away to look for Sydney, my love. It is you and me for a while, I am afraid. Since there will be so much more to do without the lad's help and I am so much older now, I had best be getting back to my chores. I will see you at tea."

"He left without saying goodbye?" Tildy started to cry again. Her eyes were in danger of becoming permanently red from the crying.

"He said he couldn't bear to see you crying and that you said goodbye the eve before and that would have to be good enough. He asked me to drop a kiss on your cheek for him."

"Why that ungrateful wretch!" For the first time in two days Tildy smiled. To Evan it was as though the sun shone through to light the whole kitchen. He reached for her and wrapped his arms about her and held her for what seemed forever.

"Morvyn is still here. She got one of her headaches and had to rest until it left her. I told her it was because she had to go home to Jack. She looked thoughtful after that. She is packed and ready to leave today. She needs to be going soon. Would you get her horse ready, please?"

Morvyn came into the kitchen shortly after Evan left. "I am ready cousin. I really must be going today. I will keep my ears open to see what the word is in London. We get to hear the strangest things at the Witch's Brew. I love you Tildy and Evan too. It has been an interesting visit. Your herbs are very special this time. I took some spice, cinnamon bark especially. It will flavor many a warmed hard cider during the winter."

Evan appeared in the kitchen. He said "Morvyn your horse is saddled and ready. I have been riding her to keep her from being too frisky for you. Take care; the roads are dangerous these days. Keep awake and stay only where you are known. Tildy told me you had one of your headaches. Make sure you dismount when one sets to strike. That could be dangerous. We will wait for a message of your safe arrival. Here is some coin for that." Evan wrapped his arm around her shoulder as a comfort and a goodbye.

"Thank you for everything, Evan. Tildy packed me a nice basket for eating on the way home. I hope I do not have to stay too often because of the headaches. I will be gone as soon as I say goodbye to Tildy." She gave Evan a hug and a kiss on the cheek and he responded with the same. He had an eerie feeling about Morvyn this time. He shrugged it off.

"Goodbye, Tildy, see you in about six months when the winter crop is ready. Thank you for everything. As I told Evan, I will keep my ears peeled for information from the big city. You never know what tidbits you can gather in a place like the Witch's Brew." She and Tildy hugged and kissed and said their goodbyes again and again. Morvyn took up her basket and went to the saddled horse with the sacks of good herbs already strapped on its sides. Evan hoisted her onto the animal. She wore stout trousers under her skirt because she rode astride like a man. "Goodbye. Take care. Listen carefully. You never know what you may hear. Goodbye, goodbye." Morvyn was on her way home.

***

As Morvyn rode east a stranger rode in from the north. He looked at the couple waving goodbye to a woman. He noticed the pub sign, The Cock and the Sow. Gilpin shouted. "Take my horse and grain him. Wipe him down. Hurry, I am on the Queen's business."

Evan looked at the man dressed in dusty black clothes, pale as a shadow, slender as a weasel, his face thin and narrow, eyes small and close together. "Aye, Sir, and welcome to The Cock and the Sow. Go on in. My missus will serve you up a nice stew or pastie. The ale be fine according to others and the beds be soft and clean." Evan took the horse and led him towards the stables. "Connie, take this horse and do him the honors. I needs to the kitchens."

Evan waited until the pale man entered the inn and ran back to the kitchen. "Love, something be afoot! There be a man in black in our dining room. He says he be on the Queen's business. Git you the best for him. Let Sarah serve him. I will wash and go draw a draught." He pecked Tildy on the cheek, delighted with this new turn. *Queen's business, hmmmm. Wonder what that could be,* thought Evan. He finished his splash and dried on one of the fragrant towels Tildy always had for him. Pulling his blouse back on, he hurried to the bar. He looked at Sarah taking the order and drew the pint. Sarah left the room and Evan brought the pint to the table.

"How many are in the inn today?" Gilpin asked.

"Naught but you, Sir. All left yesterday."

"What know you of the pirating at the coast?"

"The army have been stayin' here and campin' on the lay across the way for more than three months. The troops pulled out a week ago, the brass three days later. We have had an occasional visitor, but they stay a night and move on. Nothin' what I noticed bein' suspicious. Just nice people, traveling in these hard times."

"Were you contracted by the Queen for the military stay?"

"The Colonel in charge said he was to put up here until further orders came through. They must have for all the soldiers and officers left, like I said. Nice lot of lads most of them. We don't serve hard spirits here, just the ale, so they would have to go to the town a few miles down the road for some of that. We had a couple a children here until just after the soldiers left. My daughter were taken from my field in back o' the barn and my nephew left to see if he could find 'er. That be why we have Connie on the horses and Sarah on the dining room. My nephew be her son."

"No one coming in late at night just going through?"

"Nay, Sir. Most what come in stay in and leave with the sun."

Gilpin concentrated on his pint. Evan waited a few more moments and then went back to the kitchen.

"What did that man want , Evan?"

"Don't know, Tildy. I think he is looking for smugglers, same as the army was. Didn't get much from him. Sarah, do you think he will talk to you? I must find our daughter. I think that he might be the reason she were kidnapped or, oh hell, I don't know what I speak of."

"Brother, I will listen to whatever that man has to say. I don't like his manner or his looks. He is a spectre. I don't even know if he be truly on the Queen's business. He seems to have a mean piece about him, not that he used it on me, but just his manner. He be so cold. Nary an extra word in his order, just which be better the stew or the pastie? I answered that they were both the same for flavor, but that the stew came wi' some bread and butter, so he ordered that. He doesn't seem to be in a big hurry or nothing."

Sarah served Gilpin with a smile and said "Sir, I hopes you enjoy the meal. The bread be fresh today, and the stew were started just this morning. More ale?"

Gilpin took up his spoon and took a small taste of the savory stew. Whatever could be said to be a smile started across his lips. He took a bite of the bread and chewed. Soon he was gobbling the stew and the bread as though it was his last dinner. "More ale," he ordered between bites and some of your cook's sweet to finish the meal. This be the best I had, perhaps ever. Where be the cook?"

"I will fetch the ale and check on the sweet."

"What takes it to make the night here?"

"If you wish a room, I will make it ready in anon." Sarah returned with the ale. "Let me check on the sweet first, that you be not waiting. Would you like a cup of tea or," she paused, "we do have some coffee if that be your drink of choice."

"Coffee? What is this coffee?" Gilpin heard of the drink, but never had it, since his travels did not take him to the parts of the world that served it regularly. He was anxious for a taste of it and then he wondered where these people could get such an exotic drink this far into the wilderness of the coastal plains of Northwestern Wales. Smuggling was the only answer that fit. "Yes, I will have some of your coffee. Does it go well with the sweet?"

Sarah bit her lip for mentioning the coffee. She liked it with the sweet cream, but she knew that the only source was from the plants that Tildy grew in her little glass house where her strange flowers and herbs grew. Tildy grew them for Morvyn as an experiment to see if such things could survive in the harsh weather of this area. So far with the protection the little house offered, they could. Sarah ran back to the kitchen almost sobbing. "Oh, Tildy, I might have done something really bad."

"What could you do that was so bad?"

"I offered that man some of your coffee to go with his sweet. He did not know what I was talking about. Do you think there will be trouble?"

"Oh, Sarah, do not think so much. I can always show him my little glass house and the plants I grow there. Perhaps he would like to take one to the Queen to win her favor."

"Tildy, you are the kindest person I know. What have we ready for a sweet? He wants a sweet."

"He had the stew so the berry tart would be a nice finisher to his meal. It also tastes goodly with coffee or tea. Take some sweet cream with the coffee as well. There is a small pot on the fire. It should taste fine." Tildy took a tart from the plate and gave it to Sarah, who wrapped it in a snowy napkin. Sarah poured the coffee into one of the mugs that she had in the kitchen for their tea. She filled it with enough room for the sweet cream. "Sarah, just show him how to add the cream so it stirs itself into the drink. Then watch him to see what he does, if he likes it."

Sarah brought the sweet and the coffee and set it down in front of Gilpin. "Just a moment, Sir, I have to bring the sweet cream." She ran back to the kitchen and brought the small pitcher of cream to the table. "The cook says to add it for you to show you how to let it stir itself into the drink."

Gilpin looked at her. "You drink this beverage every day or is it a treat?"

"It is a treat, Sir, on account of we don't get too many berries from the trees."

"You mean you grow trees with berries for this beverage?"

"Yes, Sir, that is what I just told you. My sister-in-law grows many strange plants. Her cousin provides the seed or the root, and Tildy plants and tends and sees what happens. Tildy's thumbs are very green, you know."

"Where does this cousin live?"

"Oh, Sir, you needs talk to Tildy. She can tell all."

Gilpin finally bit into the sweet tart. He ate it all. "Do you have another? I have tasted nothing like this since...I have never tasted anything like this. Does your sister-in-law grow these berries, too?"

"Nay, Sir, they grow wild. We gather what is available during the year. I will get the mistress of the house. You may ask her." Sarah left Gilpin crunching his way through the tart.

"Tildy, you must go and see this person right now. He be askin' too many questions of me and bring him another tart when you go."

"Sarah, you are afraid of too many people. What harm can this man do? Worst, we will charm him with good food and drink. Is he to stay the night?"

"Aye, and I gave him the best room. That is taken care of. Evan can get him upstairs if need be. You have naught to put in his food or drink that will loosen his tongue and put him to gentle sleep?"

"Sarah, where do you get these ideas? My herbs and spices are for the flavors, not the questioning. La, the Queen would be on hand for something like that.

Now, I must go and serve this tart. It is just berry, nothing fancy."

"He liked the last. He should like this one, too. Go sister make haste and find out what he wants. I am afraid for George. I oft wondered what he did at night when he went to the town."

Tildy gasped and thought, *Went to the town? Our Georgie? I must talk to Evan about this. Did he know that Georgie was out and about? Is that why he left?* "Sarah, for how long was Georgie leaving for the town? What time? At night or in the afternoon?"

"Tildy, just go with the tart afore it cools. We can talk later. I thought you knew. Go and be quick." The two women looked at each other, thoughts flashing through their minds and a tiny bit of trust lost because of the secrets each held.

Gilpin looked up from his glass and saw the slender but voluptuous Tildy approaching with a tart and a bowl of something. "Good woman, are you the cook here?"

Aye, and the owner, too. My girl says you like the tart, so I brung you another wi' some cream whipped to a froth for to dip it in. Just give it a try and let me know how you like it."

"Mistress, have you anyone else around that helps with this establishment?"

"Aye, we have the stable boy and my husband and my sister-in-law. That is all. We manage quite well since the soldiers left. Then it was busy, and my daughter helped out as well. But..." Tildy started to cry. "But then she were taken from the field behind the barn. We heard nary a thing. My Sydney be gone.

And then her cousin left to find her. He be Sarah's boy. Now there be no children around this place but the stable boy who comes here from the village. I wish my girl would come back. I have much to tell her." The words flowed in a torrent from her lips as did the tears from her eyes.

"So, your girl was kidnapped?"

"Aye, Sir, just taken wi'out a sound. She were there and then just a...just a..." Tildy could hold back no more. She ran back to the kitchen.

Sarah looked at her aghast. "What happened out there? Why be you crying your eyes out? Did he say or do somethin' to ya?"

"Nay, he asked about Sydney and I couldn't get through past the takin' o her. Oh, Sarah, I miss her so."

Sarah held Tildy for a moment. "Excuse me, my dear. I have to do something." Sarah left the kitchen through the back door and ran to fetch Evan. "You must come back in, brother. Your wife is crying on account of somethin' that man said. You must find out what is happening. I be worried."

Evan made his way to the kitchen. He took her in his arms and said, "Tildy, what have you done? Why are you tellin' a complete stranger about our daughter? You didna tell him how we got her, did ya"?"

"Nay, my love, only we know the truth of that. Nay, I told of the takin' and couldna' help myself no longer. He still be out there. He took a room for tonight. He likes the food, though I can't for the life of me see where he puts it, he be so thin. But a man must eat sometime. I will go and talk with him. Sit, and dry those tears before you do anything more. Our girl is alive and probably being a stitch in the side of whoever has her. Be comforted by that." Evan wiped his hands and went into the tavern. Gilpin looked up munching on the second tart.

"Good day. A man could get fat with food like this always at hand."

"A man who has food like that always at hand has to work for it."

"Do you know the owner here?"

"Aye, my wife and me have this place. What be your excuse fer being here? My wife say you be from the Queen or perhaps a spy."

"Nay, I be not a spy. She was telling me of her daughter and how she was taken right from your field, without anyone knowing. Perhaps it was, the heavens forbid, some of the soldiers that were camped by here that took a liking to her."

"I dunno. She was there and then she were gone. We miss her vitally. She were our light and our life, and something in us is dead with her gone."

Gilpin had the grace to look abashed, but just for a moment. He raised his head and looked full on at Evan. "Your daughter is precious to you. I understand that. I had an idea that maybe pirates or smugglers took her for ransom. Have you received any requests for coin or...or, oh, I don't know, what would smugglers want or need from someone like you?"

Evan looked sharply at this man seated at his table. "You have the nerve to question me? It is my daughter that has gone missing. She is a good girl. She is bright. Yes, she is our light and we want our light back. I am not a common criminal. I am a man who has had his precious jewel stolen from him for some reason, I hope. I have not found her body. I can only hope that she is still alive. She will fight with her brains and her brawn until her dying breath. Now did you take her or have her taken? Why are you questioning me? I have the loss, not you."

Gilpin, taken back by this verbal onslaught, burst out, "Who are you to question the Queen's man? I could have you arrested and jailed for the rest of your natural life should I choose to. You need to answer me. Now, where are the smugglers. The Queen wants a stop to this ravaging of the Irish Sea. She needs the money from the trades and with it being taken, she gets nothing to protect this fine country of ours. Speak, now!"

"Dear Sir, I know nothing. Truly I don't. The soldiers—the Queen's soldiers—camped here for several months. They left to search on the coast for pirates and smugglers. After they left my daughter was taken. I heard nothing until you came here. That is the truth. I love our Queen. She visited here and took some lunch many years ago when my child was but a few years old. I have heard that she has a castle not too far from here, but we have never seen her since that day."

Gilpin listened to Evan, staring straight at him, and dropped his eyes to his half empty glass. He knew in his heart that Evan was telling the truth. He was simple country folk and probably couldn't lie to save his soul. "Another pint of your wonderful brew and then I am off to bed. I did not mean to upset you further. I will ask about your daughter on my travels. If I get any information, I will let you know."

He looked deeper into his glass. Harold, Bardsley, Second Marquis of Craegelon, better known by his assumed name of Mr. Gilpin, sipped the ale. Repleat with the food and drink, he was the happiest he had been since the death of his wife.

Gilpin stayed true to his promise of one more ale and then to his rest. He napped the rest of the afternoon. After the sun set, he rose and dressed in his habitual black. He walked back down the hall to look for alternate excape routes and discovered the back stairs to the kitchen. That would do when he left tonight, but he needed to hear what was happening in this area. He managed to come downstairs and sit in a dark corner of the pub. He signaled the girl that Evan hired came and she took his order of ale and brought it back to him. He sipped and listened to the talk in the pub. Not much was said that interested him. The room was warm, and one ale led to another. Bored he started to doze until two men came in. They were loud and boisterous and clapped some of the patrons on the back as they sat down to have a glass themselves. "How be ye? Hain't seen no of ya fer a long time. Pickens getting' slim?"

This could be what he needed some information. One of the men at the table said, "Leave it alone. There be too many ears to talk in public and too many soldiers out on the paths to risk anything. Let the Irish take the brunt. They're used to it. Ain't you tired o' takin' their leavin's for all of the risk?"

"Ach, ye jest be scairt. Hae' ye seen the pile o' rocks she's got on ycr coast. It ain't very far from here. She got so'jers and guards and all kinds of riches goin' in an' out o' there. There be riches galore and we might jest as well take 'em as the Queen, God rest her soul."

Another of the men spoke up, "Quiet, there are too many ears ..." He stopped talking as the serving girl approached with the ales.

"Jest drop 'em here, lass, and get ya goin' fer our food. Some stew if there be anything left."

Gilpin thought *these men are locals, and they are involved in the smuggling and perhaps the pirating that has been going on. I can ask no questions here.* He took some sips of the ale and tried to edge closer without being obvious.

"I'll be back with your order, sir, how many do you wish?"

"All around, lass, and make it quick. Walking gives an appetite." He waited until she left and continued, "There be boats that are floatin' up and down the sea, close to shore, but no one is there to takc 'cm. You know they be loaded wi' treasure."

"Don't be an ass, Harry, you know that it be treason if ye be caught and it ain't worth my life to join ya in the robbery. Let the Queen have her due. Mayhaps she will spend in Wales as well as England. 'Twould be nice to see some o' the realm's money spent in these parts. We won't get rich, but we can survive and maybe even have a nice little business, if she buy our goods. My boy, John be as good a silversmith as any in London but hasn't a chance lest he go there an' show his wares. Then he stay there because there be no business fer 'im here.

"We wouldna have ta' do the night work if the day work paid enough to live on. I don't want to go to the prison isle, if I can do an honest day's work fer an honest day's pay. Look at Evan here. He got a lovely wife, what can cook like an angel and he brews the finest ale in all of the kingdom, but do the Queen buy his goods? No, she ships from London. What be the point? It be closer, better and cheaper I dare say. She should be shipping in the other direction if ya asks me."

"Well, nobody asked ya. I'll continue to do the night work until me coffers is filled enough to go back to my day work and not starve half the winter." The man quaffed his ale. The rest sat silent. Sarah herself brought the food out and the men ate the hot stew and warm fresh bread.

After dinner the men had a few more pints and then left, most just going to their homes. Gilpin had the luck of the Irish in that the one night a week when the men had dinner out was this night. He heard enough to follow the two late comers on foot and find out more of their secrets. He managed to track the two. It was almost like they waited for him to come out. They walked down the road toward town loud and laughing. Gilpin followed, at a discreet distance, and tried to hear their conversation. There was not much to hear.

Gilpin, no longer heavy with food and drink and on foot, turned back to the inn. He entered the pub at the front door. No one noticed him. He repaired to his room and packed his sparse belongings. Then he left down the back passageway that he had found. He went to the stable and found his mount, saddled him and rode away in the direction of the two men. He caught sight of them and dismounted, following discreetly on foot just outside their purview.

The Captain

Sydney lay on the bed covered by the cut-up sack. She awoke when she heard the door open.

"Ah, my beauty, you are still asleep? I hope you are not dead. Let's see."

Sydney had her fingers wrapped tightly around the hilt of her sticker. She would aim for the throat if he uncovered her. She heard his steps come toward the bed. She tightened all of her muscles, ready to strike. He touched the sack. She did not move. He ripped the sack from her and held up in astonishment. It was whole and tied when he put her here. The snip must have ripped it somehow. The man hesitated too long. Sydney was at him with a wild screech and sticker raised. She struck like a snake going for the most vulnerable spot—his neck and she landed her strike not on his neck but in his shoulder. He screamed in pain and shot out the door still screaming.

Sydney was up in that instant. She looked for a hiding place. She spotted the porthole and tried to open it. It was locked. She fussed with the lock and her fingers hit the right combination and got it opened. The hole was large enough for her to crawl out of. She looked out and down. Nothing but seawater met her eyes. *This would never do.* She looked for hand holds but there were none. She heard the thunder of feet on the deck coming toward the room. *My God, I didna kill the man* she thought as she cast around the room for a suitable hiding place. The porthole stayed open. There was a small cupboard behind the desk. She was small and just barely fit. It was none too soon, either, for a passel of men rushed into the room.

"Where she be?" one yelled.

"Where kin she go?" shouted another.

"The porthole! Tis op'n," yelled the first.

"My God, you men test me to my limits. Get out of my chambers immediately and look to John. He has a scratch and a little blood. What children I have on this ship. Go, go all of you!" The door slammed shut and the pounding of feet sounded on the deck while they ran to find their mate. "What fools I have to man this ship," he muttered. "I have to do it all myself. If that urchin jumped into the sea, she is braver than any of us. I will miss seeing what she looked like. They said she was a spitfire, a redheaded spitfire with the temper of a demon straight from Hell. I like my women like that. Ha!" William gave a humorless laugh. Sir William James, Captain of the Sea Witch, pirate of the northern seas sat down at his desk. He reached around and grabbed the bottle of spirits he kept in his cabin. This called for a wee dram. Here he was with a girl gone missing, privateers patrolling the bay in the name of the Queen of England and him sitting here in a cove with a ship full of 'treasure' to be traded away. He was here for days now and so far, had no chance of escape nor had he been seen, 'captured' and robbed. He sipped from his glass and leaned back in his chair.

For a pirate he was not bad looking. He had longish blond hair. His eyes were blue and his features regular. He had been one of the Queen's faithful, a Captain of his own ship, until she called him to special duty. That was what Walsingham said as he gave the orders. *I am now in secret service as a pirate of the North and Irish Seas. No one knows but me, Walsingham and my own few men. I am to spy and capture those pirates that threaten the Crown and its safety. I am be the first to be hanged if I am caught. Now I have an innocent, possibly dead and if not dead a ransom for the smugglers. How did things go so wrong?* Captain William James had some decisions to make. He laid his heavy head on his folded arms. The desk held the weight.

Sydney had a decision to make as well. She was cramped in this cupboard, and she was thirsty. She opened the door and stuck her leg out the door. She breathed a sigh of relief.

The Captain sat up right. *What was that?* he thought. He lifted his head from his arms; nothing in the room. *It must be a shift in the rigging or a lap of the ocean against the ship.* He dropped his head once more.

Sydney shifted her other leg out the door and scrunched her bum to the soft carpet underneath. She looked closer. The carpet was beautiful; much too nice for a ship, even if it was the Captain's quarters. She looked up. His chair was inches from her face. She had to move away to give herself a chance at escape.

The captain sighed and sat up. He took another sip of the spirits and looked around the room. It was a comfortable room, much nicer than his chambers in London. He sat back in his chair and tried to rock it back on its back legs. Something impeded his progress, a cabinet door. He looked down and saw two legs. He crashed the chair to the floor and made a move. Sydney was faster. She tumbled away from the desk and stood up. All that play at pirates had taught her a few moves.

"A'vast ye hearty! Who are ya and just where do ya think yer goin'?" William had a huge smile on his face. A right proper beauty stood before him; her dagger raised in self- defense.

"Your grammar is terrible, Sir Captain." Sydney said, on her guard.

"Oh, give it up, girl. I will not hurt you," William laughed as he reached for the tiny dagger. "And isn't that the way a pirate is supposed to talk, grammar be damned?"

"Um, I suppose so, but, but you are the first pirate I've met face to face; the first real pirate that is, and, and you are nothing what I supposed you'd be. You are fine of face and fairly clean, although with all the water around, I think you should be. Where I am from there is no problem about bathing, at least in the summer, and we wash a lot in the winter in the kitchen." Sydney was babbling now. This man was more handsome than Georgie and much better spoken. "You won't give me up to the others, will you?"

"Nay, lass, I will keep you a secret. Let them think you jumped overboard. That was a smart move leaving the port open. You have a head on your shoulders. Can you read? I have some books you might enjoy. And, no, they are not the Bible. I got them as a child."

"Aye, Sir, I can read and speak the Frenchy language as well. I would love a book to read. I am also very thirsty. Can you get me some water or buttermilk, if you have it?"

"Of course, I will have a carafe of water in this room at all times. I will call for a tray of food if you wish. Just keep out of sight when they deliver it. By the by, I promise I will not touch you." *Without your permission,* was his afterthought.

"Thank you, Sir, I have a love to whom I am true. I canna marry him, though and this is the tragedy. He is my first cousin. I have loved him dearly all my life. He is my best friend in the world after Jane. As I have grown to be a woman..."

At this the captain laughed again. Indignant, she started again, "As I have grown to be a woman, I love him more than a brother or cousin. I miss him sorely, and I am afraid he will do something stupid, like try to find me for my Ma and Da. Please do not kill him, should he find you."

A broad grin broke on William's face. *Should he find them,* he thought, *they would all be in the drink and he would hang. If only he could be free of this cove and this ship and this duty.* "Should he find us, and I doubt that he will, I promise not to kill him. Should he find us though, it could be the end of all of us. The Queen's army or the privateers will fire upon us and we should sink."

"Oh, Sir, thank you, thank you with all my heart. I will pray for you and your crew even though they did bring me here and away from my home and my goats and kuhe and the gardens. I can forgive them for they were only under orders from someone. Was it you?"

"Nay, how could you think that I would want an albatross on board my ship? Fie on you."

The Captain was laughing at her. Sydney got indignant again. "Where is my water? Oh, and where can I hide that doesn't cramp my body into small pieces?"

William glanced at the empty tray and smiled again. He rose and showed her his clothes cupboard. There she could stand or sit, whatever she desired. She waited until the captain called for some food. Then she got in and stayed very quiet.

On the Road

George walked several miles to the north past the village. The area was desolate with scrub and sea grasses. The hills got steeper the further he walked. He scanned the coast below for any ships. All he saw were the patrol ships every so often. He stopped for a bite around three o'clock in the afternoon. He wished he had some tea or coffee, just something to warm him inside. The wind was picking up and it looked like a storm was on the way. There should be some caves nearby where he could at least get out of the rain. He went to the edge of the pathway toward the water. The water was far below him, but there was an outcropping of rock that should suffice as cover until the storm passed.

He could have his wish for a warm drink, too. He scrambled over the rock and landed on the shelf below him. There was a nice little alcove protected from the wind and perfect for a small fire.

There wasn't much for a fire around this area, but a short climb and he found some sticks and dry brush. It would do as likely as not. He took his load and nestled into the alcove. He built a small fire and put his tin cup with some clean water from his skin onto the flame. He added a few leaves of Tildy's tea and waited. The water warmed. George pulled out some biscuit.

The tea and biscuit sufficed for a meal. He leaned back against the rock and closed his eyes. This was as far as he would get today. The rains came and poured down, but George was warm and dry. Tomorrow was another day and he would go on to find Sydney.

***

Life at the inn was sodden with Tildy's tears. She burst with a new flood every few hours. Now Morvyn was gone as well as Georgie. She walked over to the stable and went to the rooms above.

"Sarah, I hate to bother, but would you like to come for a spot of tea and some talk? It is lonely over at the inn now that all are gone. I miss your presence. Why don't you come and take a room there? Of course, there is no charge and it is warmer. It looks like rain soon so, just bring some night clothes and stay for a while. I need company. Evan is out tending the stable and will be in shortly. I doubt we will have much business tonight what with the rain and all."

Sarah came to the door and opened it wider. "Come in Tildy. You are always welcome. I would like some company, too. I worked the day your Sydney went missing. My Georgie is gone now on a journey to find her. God bless him, I hope he does. He loves you all so.

"Let me get a few things and I have some lace I am working. I won't be empty handed. Take some of these biscuits I baked yesterday. I made them for Georgie, but he did not say goodbye. We might just as well enjoy them with a bit of your jam. Here, take this basket and I will see you in just a few minutes."

Sarah thrust the basket into Tildy's hands. Tildy made her way down the stairs and back to the kitchen. The kettle was already on the flame for the afternoon tea. Today she would have the Sarah's company. It wasn't the same, but it was better than being alone.

***

Morvyn saw the storm clouds gathering. She had a mile to go to get to her first inn. A good soft clean bed and a hot meal would be welcome tonight. It was late afternoon, but she didn't want to get caught in the rain. It came down hard and cold this time of year. She urged the horse on.

There was no use getting excited about the newfound spices from Tildy. There was no use getting excited about the child. Sydney was grown. It was up to Tildy and Evan to tell her of her origins. That was not her worry. She knew the love George and Sydney shared was as brother and sister. After all they shared a life of being together in a family. Nay, t'were not her problem anymore.

The first wave of nausea swept over her. She urged the horse with renewed effort. The inn could not be that far away. *This upset ain't the pox. I canna' get it thanks to that sailor. This is something else,* Morvyn thought. *It is a headache that is upon me. My guts tell me so.* Sitting a horse was difficult with the nausea and the headache was not far behind. *There are the fairy lights—stop waving. Ye make me faint.* The horse plodded on.

A half hour later the horse came to the inn. Morvyn was slumped over in the saddle. The horse whinnied and stomped. A boy came out and ran back in. The owner and his woman came out and eased Morvyn from the saddle. Her breathing was shallow. She was very pale.

They carried her up to her usual room. The boy brought her saddle bags, and then went back down to put the horse in the stable.

"Madame, Madame, are ye wi' us yet?" the innkeeper asked. His wife patted Morvyn's cheeks to try to wake her. "Git a bowl of broth and some cool towels, woman. We canna ha'e this woman a'dying here on us. I'll be sending the lad back to her relative. Mayhaps they kin come an' git 'er."

"Ach, Julius, you be unkind. We kin work 'er an' bring 'er around. She ain't dead yet."

Morvyn retched. The vomit was full of bile.

"She be sick wi' the liver ills. Mayhaps she drunk too much o' the spirits. I'll bring some hot tea and a few biscuits fer her."

The wife left the room, her husband trailing behind her. She went to the kitchen and fetched a pot of tea and a small plate of edibles. This woman would be hungry when she woke. The good wife soaked some rags in hot water and brought them with her. The woman in the bed seemed cold and in need of some care.

The innkeeper's wife trudged back up the stairs to the room. She set the food and drink down and started applying the hot rags to the woman's feet and hands. As the rags cooled, she placed them on the woman's face and neck. Morvyn stirred, giving a sign of life.

"Where am I?" Morvyn whispered. "My head is so tired, and I am so cold. Get not too close to me. The plague was in London when I left. I go to visit my cousin and her household. No, no, this is not the plague. I know that well." Her voice growing louder, Morvyn said, "A sip of tea, please. Twas the headache that got me down. Thank the horse for getting me here. This was my stopping place tonight. Ye know me, Madame. My name is Morvyn. Do ye ken?" The woman held the mug of tea to Morvyn's lips and she sipped a large bit from the cup. "'Tis not my time yet, Madame. I have other tasks to complete before I go. I must get back to London. Let me sleep. Leave the tea and some edibles. You have done enough for me now. Sleep and we will square in the morning."

"As ye wish, good woman and I do remember ya. Ye have helped with the herbs and mayhaps you will have some to sell to me afore you leave this place? Sleep well. Should ye need of anything, call. This place is nay so large that I canna hear ya."

"Thank you," and Morvyn slid into a deep sleep, and as she slept, her headache and nausea disappeared.

The next morning, Morvyn felt refreshed and rested. *There are not too many more journeys left in this old body*, she thought as she wiped her face with the damp cold cloths. *I will dress and get on the road with the sun, if any there be. The good woman here is deserving of some of the best. I will pull some good tansy and basil and see if she be right with that and her payment. 'Tis the least I can do.* With these thoughts Morvyn dressed and made herself ready for departure.

Morvyn came into the keep hungry. The good woman of the night before greeted her, "How be ye this morning? The sun is trying to peek through, but clouds keep coming. It still be chill out there. I will pack ya some meat pie and some tea. I have porridge with fresh cream and some dried fruit or some eggs and sausage from the farm. Which will ye have?"

"I'll have the eggs and meat and a cup of hot tea. Sit with me, when you get it ready, and share some tea and a chat. I have some savory which you might like." Morvyn had her bag ready. "Please, my breakfast and hurry. I am anxious to get on the road and get back to London. Thank you for all you did, madam."

"Here is yer tea, ma'am. Yer eggs and meat are cooking. I brought ya a taste of the porridge. We had a plentiful crop this year and the fruits is good. We grow the oats as well, and me husband grinds them by hand."

"Thank you. I have some here that you may like. As I said, sit with me a spell and we can talk."

Within minutes the good wife appeared with the eggs, sausage and some bread, toasted and spread with butter. "Here ya go. You be the only one up yet, so I can sit wi' ya. Ye have somethin' ta say?"

"The sausage is savory and fresh. The eggs look delicious. How do you all learn to make the food edible. I canna cook to save me life. I have someone to do it for me in London at our pub. Enough, though, I have a cousin who is a master grower, and she have given me some o' her herbs and spice. I have some for you for the extra service if you wish."

The innkeeper's wife sat down at the table. "A master grower, ye say. What have ye? My garden yields only the regular necessities. I should be interested in purchasing some more exotic tastes."

"Use your nose and see if you like any of what I ha' here." Morvyn revealed a small bunch of sage for the woman to smell.

"That be extraordinary strong, Mi'lady. That make my sausage very savory indeed. Could I have a few leaves and at what price?"

"This bunch I give you. All you sniff this morn are fer you. Here is some basil, Genovesie, I think. It be strong but sweet. You can use with love apples and the such and it be good wi' your chicken meat. And this be some cardamom my cousin grew from the seed I brung to her for experiment. Your scones and cakes can use it. What say you? Be this good?"

"Madam, I hae' ne'er smelled the like. How much do you want?"

"Are you daft, woman? I told you this were all fer your service to me last night. You gave me bed wi'out question or payment. You made me comfortable. I am quite recovered and thankful for your services. Take this wi' my blessing and the blessing of your Father in Heaven. Oh my, but you have the good breakfast here." Morvyn ate and asked that her horse be brought. She paid the woman for the night and the food. The woman pressed her hand and thanked her for her gifts. Morvyn mounted and rode off.

The Cock and the Sow—Several Days Later

Tildy was beyond weeping. "Evan, we be needing water for the washing. The linens are dirty and must be done before the evening. Have you heard from the travelers anything of our young'uns?"

"Tildy, my love, there ha' been nary a word from anybody on the road or for the stay. Please stop asking. I miss her as much as do you and I miss Georgie's help even more, for I am getting no younger."

"Evan, what did we do to be so wrought upon?"

"Nuthin', me love."

"I just know we will see her again, Evan. I just know. How could the God in Heaven take her, when she were so justly lovely and innocent? Nay, we will see her again." Tildy spoke with finality. "Now, the water, so's I kin heat it up and get the rest o' me chores done. Today is bread day as well." Tildy hiccupped and sighed. Tears still oozed from her eyes.

With the troops marching through the region in quest of pirates and Spaniards, the inn was never quiet. Every night was full up both in rooms and dining. The ale flowed freely, so freely that Evan wondered whether his stock would last until the next batch was aged enough. Tildy toiled from dawn to midnight to keep food on the tables and sheets on the beds. Every room was purified with the smoke of smoldering sage. Lavender pomanders hung in every room. When possible, she flung windows wide to air out rooms, where guests in need of bathing did not seek water to remedy the situation. The sheets were stored with lavender and rosemary in the folds to keep the fresh outdoor smell, when possible in a linen closet Evan had built early on. Randy bodies might lie on them at night, but come morn all beds were stripped and washed, and every room was swept. There was always fresh water in the ewers and the bowls were always cleaned after a guest left. Tildy's inn was one of the cleanest and freshest in all of England.

"It is tired I'm getting, Evan." Tildy said one day after a full house for both sleep and food.

"I know, my love. We're no spring chicks ourselves anymore and our help is gone, heaven knows where. Mayhaps there be a village girl in need of employment."

"Nay, Evan, I canna imagine any girl would work here with our reputation for kidnapping and an inability to protect our own daughter from harm. Oh, Evan, what happened to our girl? How could they just come up 'n grab 'er? How did we not see?"

"Matilda Lewis, what need I say to give you rest on this matter? The barn hid the child. None of us were within eyesight of the barn. Bah, woman, George and' me wern't even here. There were no more soldiers in residence that day. They all marched to the village. Whoever planned the abduction carried it out well. All we can do now is pray."

Tildy sucked up her tears and gave Evan a dirty look. "Ye can make do as you please. My girl is gone and I ha'e no other to help me. Yer boy is gone, and ye have no other to help you. We are in a fine fix. Too much of work and no one to help do it even with Sarah and James. And us gettin' on wi' our age and all." That speech fostered a new set of tears from Tildy. Evan stomped out of the kitchen. Tildy looked after him and felt deserted and sad. This was a low for her marriage. *If Evan left, who will I have to rely upon? I want my girl back,* she thought, *and I want everything to be as it was.* But nothing stays as it was.

On the Ship Several Days Later

Sydney sat in the closet for less than ten minutes before she heard the door to the cabin open and the sound of a tray dropped upon a table. *Tea and a biscuit would be nice,* she thought. She heard the words of the Captain to the mate and then the door slammed again. Sydney waited until she could wait no more. She opened the closet door with a great deal of caution. No one was in the room. A large tray with a pot of tea and table service for two lay on the captain's table. The captain was nowhere. Perhaps she'd missed a conversation. There was half a biscuit on a plate filled with dried fruit. Sydney's mouth watered. *I am hungry again,* she thought, *he won't miss a biscuit and a drop of tea. I'll just pour me a cup and taste this biscuit afore he comes back.*

She listened carefully for activity around the door. Hearing none, Sydney followed through with her plan. She poured the tea. There was no sugar. She would drink it black. She reached for the tempting biscuit and heard the sound of arguing growing closer to the cabin. Sydney grabbed the biscuit and fled back to the closet. She settled in, leaving the door open just a crack. The cabin door flew open and the captain and two mates were speaking loudly all at the same time. A third person, silent and grim looking, was held tightly between the two mates.

"We get you a major spy and you say nothing? What was the plan, anyway? This person was lurking about the grove beyond the ship. He seems to know nothing of how he got here. I called Sammy here who was cooking those rabbits we shot, and he helped me with him. So here we are, Captain. Throw him in the brig?"

"Aye, Sir, I needs get back to me rabbits."

William raised his hand for silence. "What is your name?" William was short with the man.

"Gilpin," the man said in a surprisingly strong authoritative voice. "I am under orders from the Queen's castle, sent to ascertain the situation here on the coast. Speak now, pirate, or I will have you hung, you and all your mangy crew." The derisive laughter of the men still echoed in his brain. "What the hell are you running here, whatever you are. Two of your men were at an inn, the Cock and the Sow looking for recruits for the smuggling ring or a pirate ship. What do you think you are doing?"

Sydney squinted through the crack of the door. The man facing the Captain looked like a weasel. *He looks dangerous What is this all about?* she thought.

He was medium height and very thin, dressed all in black. His clothing was of fine stuff. His face was sallow, and his eyes darted from person to person. He craned his neck to see more of the room. John yanked on his arms. "Yer a spy," he said, his voice hoarse and menacing.

William's back was to the desk where the food was set out. He had noticed the full cup of tea and the service for two and wanted to keep it hidden. There were forces at work here William didn't like. *This interruption is not a good sign.* The thoughts raced through William's mind. *Perhaps this man in black is a counterspy and saw the table before I did. If he is smart, he will draw some conclusions.* William silently screamed for identification. His second in command was still talking, albeit in a lower voice.

William interrupted John, the first mate. "Pray, how would you like your tea Mr. uh, Gilpin, did you say? We have no sugar since the embargo, but we have some lemon and some cow's milk to offer. John, you need to get up on deck and check on the nest. The activity seems to be picking up and I don't want to miss anything."

John and Sam acknowledged with a salute, turned smartly and left the room. William turned and picked up the now cool tea.

"Mr. Gilpin," he said. "You may address me as such. I am from the Queen, her special service. I will have that tea. " He nodded his assent to a cup and sat in the chair.

"Now, Gilpin, what do you really want? I do not believe for a minute that you are the Queen's man. I could have you thrown in the brig. I will let you go with escort, if you keep insisting on being the 'Queen's Man'. I will know which action to take...."

Gilpin interrupted William's statement. "There is a girl, newly taken this last week or so from an inn not two days from here. Turn the girl over to me. She must know what is going on at her parents' inn. She has information about the smugglers. How could she not? She works in that inn. Surely she has had sweet words with the regulars."

"I have no such orders. Bring me the proper authority in writing or desist," William ordered. "Is she a young girl? Would you wager she is not a virgin?"

"You would lose," Sydney said as she opened the closet door and stepped out. "I am the person you are looking for. I can guarantee I know nothing. I just want to get back to my parents. They must be missing me something awful and my Ma needs help running the inn. There is baking and washing and cleaning up to do as well as serving the guests their dinner and ale.

It seems I have been gone at least a week, so please let my parents know I am all right."

Gilpin stared. This red- headed little snippet with curls and curves was the girl they'd kidnapped? She could be the Queen twenty years ago. Even her features were like Elizabeth's, but no, Elizabeth had no children and no husband. This must be Harry's throw-back. In any case she should see this child or never know of her. Gilpin's thoughts were confused, and he was never confused about things. This was most unsettling. "What is your name, Missy?"

William cautioned Sydney, "Ye need not answer, Miss. We have not ascertained this man's credentials.

Sydney looked at William. This man was a threat. If she answered, he might leave them alone. "Sydney Lewis," she blurted out.

"Who are your parents?"

"Tildy and Evan Lewis, Sir."

"Where do you hail?"

"My parents own The Cock and the Sow, a fine inn near Bryn a Cywd with the best ale in the country. My father makes it. My mother is the best cook in all the land, too." Sydney withdrew her hand from behind her back, a biscuit half eaten in it. "This be good, but my Ma's is better. She uses the herbs and spices she grows, and we get the best flour from the mill. My Ma, she even uses her own honey for the sweets. The bees make such lovely honey, none can resist."

Mr. Gilpin stared once more. This child came from the same inn he'd supped at while on reconnaissance. It was a day's hard ride from the

Queen's Welsh castle, where he went trying to sum up the situation in this remote area. He was determined to impress his brother-in-law, Lord Walsingham, and the Queen that he could be useful in the secret service. This child had no idea of him and spilled out those things which were important to her. "Are there any others in your household, lass?"

"Yes, Sir, my Aunt Sarah and her sons, Georgie and James, you see, because my Uncle Euan Evans died and left his family to poverty and ruin on account that Georgie was the only boy left to do the farming and the animals because his older brother James is light in the head, but he was sent to be with my Da, because there was no money to feed him and the rest of the family, who got married after their da died. Georgie is the one I truly love and wish to marry. And he loves me right back. But we canna marry on account he is my first cousin. It is sad. He be my best friend as well. Please sir, get me back to my family so they can stop worrying. I am their only child. They will miss me."

"Do you know why you are here, child?"

"No, Sir. I were in a bag, a smelly old sack and a smelly old man carried me here and said I would be a good dessert for the crew. I don't know what that means, but I was scared. Then Captain William came in and I hid in the cupboard and then he discovered me and told me to hide in the clothes closet and then you came in and it sounded like the captain, who was kind to me, was in trouble and I am just so hungry that I came out. That is why I am here right now." Sydney raced on her words crashing from her mouth, the only way she knew to win an argument. William gaped. Gilpin glowered.

"No, you are here because you know something about the smuggling going on along this coast. We think your father might be part of it. We know you must have information and we will do what we need to get it out of you. That is why you were taken." Gilpin sputtered out his words.

"Nay, sir, my Da don't do that kind of thing. There were one rich man what stayed wi' us one night. He were dressed in fine woolens, leather and fur. He smelled clean. Me ma even said he was neat as a pin and didn't leave an odor on his sheets like other officers do. She says that being clean is like being like God or something like that."

"Miss Lewis, hush! Gilpin leave the girl alone. She hasn't had a bite to eat since she got here," William lied, "and I am convinced that she knows nothing. What have you? You may be a smuggler's ear to find out just what this ship is doing here. It is you I should lock in the brig!

"You will hang should you throw me in the brig. She stays here until she talks. If you don't like my methods, employ any of your own that you think will work. Just get the information. And as for you my dear, the sooner you talk, the sooner you can find your way home. It is all up to you." Gilpin turned to go. He knew he was on slippery ground, that he had no real cause to be here.

"Canna you not let me parents know that I am safeish? They be worried, I warrant, and I dinna want them to be short-handed or worried. I bet me Ma be cryin' her eyes out and addin' too much salt and water to the bread."

The captain laughed out loud on that statement. Gilpin stayed sour-faced and stern. He was beginning to have doubts as to the girl's knowledge and even her intelligence. "I say make her talk. Then release her. She is old enough to make her own way." Gilpin rose and strode out of the room.

Captain James called his first mate upon Gilpin's departure. " Let him go. Follow him. I do not like his looks," William ordered. "I will send Arthur to the castle to notify Walsingham about this Gilpin."

***

The night did not help Morvyn's headache. She was in for a long stay. The maid found her crammed under her pillow moaning in pain. "Wha' kin I do fer ya', ma'am?

"Water and my sack and no light, please no light. I have a pain draught in my leather sack. Bring it forthwith and fetch me some cool, clean water." Morvyn's words were slurred as if she were drunk. It was the result of the horrible headache. "Hurry, girl, hurry. I need to be on my way. Send your mistress to me as well."

The girl scurried from the room and within minutes the wife was present with water and a request for another piece of gold for the room. Morvyn reached for the water and put some of the powder in. Stirring, she said, "You will not go hungry for the money. I have paid for one night and food and have had no food. When I can eat, I will let you know. There will be gold on the table before the end of the day. Be satisfied with that. I own an inn myself and know what it is like to be cheated. Thank you for the water. I hope the pain in my head goes away quickly." Morvyn drank the draught and handed the mug back to the woman. "Go, leave the shutters drawn and the room dark and cool. It will help the healing." She lay down and covered her head again as she pushed against the hard surface of the wall to help the pressure. The good woman of the tavern turned as if to leave, and then started to go through Morvyn's things.

***

Georgie awoke cramped, cold and hungry. The fire was out leaving a small pile of ashes. The rain had stopped, so he gathered his scant belongings and stretched his legs before trying to stand up. The sound of feet on the ground above him made him draw his legs to his chest. He knew the ledge hid him, but he couldn't take a chance on getting caught.

"This be a waste of time, this be." One voice carried down to Georgie.

"This be our orders. Keep moving and keep looking or we don't get our grog tonight. There must be somethin' out here to find. Why else send us?" replied another.

Georgie was scared. He did not want to be the subject of the search nor conscripted into the military. He rued bringing the blue and red stones and the pin as well as the gold. They would convict and hang him for that alone. The remains of the fire would blow away in the wind. Under the cover of the sounds that the patrol was making, he reached into his sack and took the contraband that he had. He wrapped it in his kerchief and put it in his food pouch. He pushed it way back into the crevice of the overhang. It would not be seen, unless someone came in and felt around and even then....

He waited for the sounds of soldiers to disappear and took care as he climbed out onto his precarious perch. Feeling lighter in conscience and pack he walked up the path being careful to stay far enough behind the patrol as not to be seen.

The Cock and the Sow

Life goes on. Evan and Tildy made the inn work without joy and without ease, although Sarah pitched in and helped with the cleaning and the serving. Evan found another boy to help him with the stables, but this boy did not charm the livestock like Georgie. Tildy missed Sydney's cheery brightness. Life goes on.

Morvyn sent word that she might not do a spring visit. Tildy worried that her cousin was ill with more than headaches. Tildy swallowed that disappointment as well, not realizing that Morvyn was still on her way home.

The inn proved to be more profitable than before as more and more of the gentry stopped by on their way to the East o' the Sun. The land was changing, and the stench of war was in the air.

The Queen did not stop when she was on route. Once there she urged Walsingham with new and ingenious plans to conquer smugglers. The Spanish were amassing an armada and her coffers were lower than ever. There was no money to launch a fleet to sink the Spanish fleet.

***

Captain James looked at the door of his chamber and wondered. Sydney spoke his thoughts. "Does he think I canna hear or see him? What are you gonna' do with me? I canna' stay here. It be too dangerous for both of us. And did you see how he stared at me? Do I have three eyes in me forehead?"

"Nay, my girl. He looked like he knew you. Have you ever seen him before, perhaps your father's inn?"

"Never! He is the blackest person I ever seen. He looked at me like he saw a ghost. Am I that strange and pale?"

"Nay, and you are right. He did look at you right strange like. There is something going on. We need to get you away from this boat. It is not safe for you or my men." Captain James gnawed away at a fowl's leg. Sydney drooled.

"Would you please give me somethin' to eat?"

"Oh, sorry, my girl, help yourself. Have a pastie or a scone and some tea." He made a lazy motion with his hand, "What could he want? We are on assignment. Someone is getting nervous. I cannot sail under colors and will not sail until I feel sure about my quarry." Captain James mused aloud. "There is something going on.

"My girl, you need a disguise. It is a shame. You are so lovely, it is a shame to cover you in boys' clothes and hide that hair."

Sydney looked at the handsome Captain. She felt her insides stir. It was with effort that she held herself back from flinging herself upon him. "Can you not just sail out with the flag of another nation and head for open water? It seems to me that you could solve two problems doing that. If you are the master of disguise...."

"My dear girl, that would be dereliction of duty on my part. My orders are to stay here, until I make contact with the smugglers, then bring them to justice after questioning. What you are proposing is preposterous. Why I...."

"Can't you see?" Sydney interrupted, "If you sail under another country's flag, well then mayhaps the pirates or smugglers or whatever will attack you and try to steal your ship and you can then make your arrests when you turn on them."

"My God, a strategist with a red mop and a skirt; that plan is worthy of the Queen herself. Are you daft, my girl? They would shoot my boat to pieces and murder all aboard."

"Not if you shoot first!"

"How do you know so much about how this works? You do know more than you say. You had better tell me, girl, what you know or when Gilpin makes his way back here, you are in for the brig and some torture or worse."

"I don't know anythin'. I just thought how I would do it if I was a pirate. I don't know nothin' about smuggling. Don't pirates and smugglers do the same thing?"

"Nay, my girl, they don't, but they may work together. I do know that in the New World pirates keep what they take and sometimes take a whole ship rather than sink it. The merchant ships are well-built and sound, so it makes sense to take an armed ship and make it into a pirate ship with the change of a flag. Smugglers have an arrangement with other smugglers to take contraband and hide it and then sell it on the black market. That way they make the profit and the Queen gets nothing to put in her coffers."

All this while, in the back of Sydney's mind, a plan was hatching. Somehow, she would lure the captain into letting her stay on board and he could take her to the New World. The only hitch in this plan was leaving her Ma and Pa and all she knew and making her Ma cry. There was Georgie too, but Georgie was lost to her, him being her cousin.

The captain stirred her insides like Georgie never did just by looking upon him. He was handsome and kind and if he liked her, she would be happy with him.

She had to test the waters as it were. "Sir Captain, what would be wrong with goin' to the New World and stop worryin' about all this pirate and smugglin' stuff? You see I can cook and clean and grow food and make pictures and do other chores, if you show me what you want and mayhaps you could marry me if you were pleased with me. All we need do is let me sew you a flag and you can hoist it and we can go. You can take me now to see if you like me." Sydney launched herself at the surprised captain, who lost all from his hands to catch her. Her weight dropped the both of them to the floor with a resounding crash.

The door to the cabin flew open as John, Andrew and Sam shoved into the small space, mouths agape. Sydney rolled to the side and the captain and she sat up, red flushing their faces. All was silent for a few seconds and then "Get your arses out of my cabin." Captain James got to his feet, touching the slight bump on his head. He helped Sydney up. She brushed her skirts down. "You had better have something important to say, if you were that close to my hatch."

"Aye, Sir, we do. There is a military patrol marching across yon parapet. They seem to be goin' to the next town. If anyone saw...." spoke John.

"I am back from the castle, Sir, and Walsingham has sent a message for your ears only," said Arthur.

"Thank you, Arthur, in a moment. Now please leave. Say naught to the crew. You, John, stay close and help me with some of these maps when I call. The rest of you back to your stations. Keep me informed. Report to me and only me every half hour unless there is a change in their motion. We cannot be discovered here. Andrew, what is the message and how did you get back without that troop seeing you?"

"Sir, I have my ways as you have taught. Please the order so's I don't forget. There is to be no more paper that can be taken." Andrew whispered the order to William.

***

Georgie followed as closely as possible to the patrol. He could not be discovered, having no valid reason for his presence on this path. As he walked his stomach grumbled and he reached for the pocket that held his biscuit. A snag in in his kit stopped him and, as he looked around for the problem, from the corner of his eye he saw the ship nestled into the small cove and mostly hidden by trees. The image registered on his brain and he turned and looked more intently. *That is a dangerous place for a ship,* he thought. *There is no easy way out for sailing quickly if discovered.* His experience with emptying ships was that the ship had to be able to escape mooring with no impediments. Sometimes ships were unloaded under full sail for quick getaway. *That ship may be under the black flag,* Georgie wondered. *There are no colors flying! What is it doing there? Is it my business to investigate this? Nay, Sydney is more important. I must keep going.* Strap released and biscuit in hand, Georgie walked along the high embankment. With patrols coming through he couldn't tarry long. The next town was a few miles away and there was safety in crowds.

***

Morvyn stayed some extra days at the inn. The headache abated and she felt well enough to ride out with the sunrise the next morning. The woman who attended her thanked her for the extra coin in hand. The owner's wife thanked her for the generous gift of special herbs Morvyn gave her and for instructions on their medicinal use. She left some seed so that the woman could have her own lavender and basil near that kitchen. Morvyn showed her how to keep the seed and then loaded her waiting mount and got on her way.

The ride to the next inn was easy and Morvyn felt better than she had for months. Perhaps getting home would be the cure for her malady. Good as she was with the herbs, she had a hard time curing herself. The rest of the trip to London was quick and Morvyn greeted Jack with a hug and a kiss much to his surprise.

"You were longer this time. What kept you?" he asked once the greetings were done.

"I been gettin' these head pains with the blinding. Took me some extra nights at an inn on the way home to cure. Don't know if it be me age or if the evil spirits finally got me. Either way prepare for the worst Jack Hoggins. Either I be in bed fer the rest o' me life or I be dead in a fortnight. Then wot will you do?"

"Morvyn, don't you be talking that way. You know in me own way I love ya. I don't want ya dead. We got a lot a' good years left to us. We can sell this place and move away from the city. Your witchy ways could keep us for the rest a' our lives. I can turn my hand at other means. I got a feel fer tinkerin' and can build things from the bottom up. We be good out o' the city and the dirt and the crime. Wot say ye?"

"Jack, no big cat changes his spots. We be too old to start over."

"Lady, you wouldna start over. It'd be me wot finds a new way of livin'. No more pullin' the handles and tossin' the dregs. No more whores to put up fer 'n hour. No more…"

"No more ladies askin' fer your help. No more sots ta rob blind. No more of the only life you ever knew. So, wot makes you think you are gonna change?" Jack hauled back to swat Morvyn and she leveled the evilest stare she ever leveled at anyone. "Ya hit me, and it'll be the last thing you ever hit, ya miserable sod. I have me ways and ye are not gonna put them down. Now listen. We will git from this town, but the inn be mine and the money from it be mine. Make up yer mind. Ya either stay wi' me and do my biddin' or ya leaves wi' a payoff and we go our own ways. Either way ya makes out, ya duffer. Make up yer mind and do it fast. I ain't waitin' fer ever." With that , Morvyn turned and left the great room for her bed chamber. Jack stayed planted with his arm still drawn back and his mouth agape.

She's more of a witch than I thought, he mused.

***

A liveried messenger appeared in the doorway of The Cock and the Sow. The place was empty. He shouted, "Some help here. My horse is in need of stabling and I am in need of the master of the house. *Post haste* now."

Sarah came to the tavern room at the sound of the voice echoing through to the kitchen. She wiped her hands on her snowy apron and asked, "What have you need of, good sir?"

"I'll be needing a meeting with the master here. Summon him forthwith. Bring food and drink."

"Aye, good sir, which do you wish first? It'll take a few ta git Evan. Will I do?"

"Bring drink and hurry wench."

Sarah pulled the draught and gave it to the man. She excused herself and ran in search of Evan calling as she ran. "Evan, come quick. There be a man what wants you."

Evan came from the garden and caught his sister-in-law. "What is this? You come running and shouting? There may be people asleep in there. Hush, woman."

"Oh, Evan, there be a man what come and needs talk wi' you. He be dressed in finery, like he be some Lord or sumpin'"

"Sarah, take care. He will wait. You needs be goin' ta the kitchen and stay wi' Tildy. Both 'o you be ready ta run if you hear arguin'. Is that clear?"

"Aye, but hurry. He be dressed in finery and ..."

"I'll be right there."

Evan stuck his rake in the ground. He would be back later. Tildy would be glad not to have to do this today with the baking and the cooking. This person better have something to say to interrupt his day. Evan wiped his hands on his pants and took off his apron as he approached the kitchen. Tildy was working steadily at the bread dough, kneading it back and forth. "Who be in the tavern, Love?" he asked.

"I don't know, but you should wash your face and you smell a bit."

"I don't have time fer a dip. Take me or leave me, he has his business, I got mine. What's it about?"

"Go in and find out. I don't know. I'm elbow deep in bread dough and can't stop now. Tell Sarah to get back in here. We have a lunch and a dinner to get on the fire."

Evan gave her a hug and wiped his face on one of her towels. "I'll git on wi' it."

"What took so long, you lout? I need to be out of here and on my way to the castle to prepare."

"We all have our work to do. What is it that is so urgent?"

"Her Majesty will be by in a few days. Should be here by Friday. Keep this inn clear and be prepared for luncheon for her and her ladies. The men can eat in the stables. She wishes to see the girl who lives here as well. Have everyone ready to receive her. Ye will be paid fer yer time and isolation.

"Now I will have some lunch and another of this fine ale. Never tasted better. I must be gone by the high sun."

Evan drew him another pint and said, "Lunch will be out presently. What wish you? Stew or a pastie? Both are fine. I needs get back to my garden. We have no help here, just me, my wife and my sister-in-law."

"I'll have the stew and some bread if you don't mind and be quick about it."

"Sarah will bring it to you." And with that Evan left the room for the kitchen.

"Queen be comin' by Friday. Wants ta see the girl. Gonna need food for all both in and out. Headed fer the castle yonder. Been years since she been here."

"She wants to see the girl? Evan, that be Sydney! Sydney be gone. What shall we do?"

"You bake your bread and make sure that codpiece in the tavern gits his lunch. I'll go finish wi' the garden and tend to the stables. We'll talk later."

"Oh, Evan, I be worried. The lass be not here, and Her Majesty wants ta see her? This be not good. We may swing fer this."

"Quit yer worrin', love. I'll go ta the town tomorra...."

"And what makes you think you can do that? You didn't get any answers the last time. You spend your time working away. What makes you think that a miracle is gonna happen now?" Tildy started crying.

Evan wrapped his arms around her. "Darlin' girl, she gotta be somewhere. She be gone what seems like weeks now. Mayhaps now there be some loose tongues ready to wag for a sum. We can only hope. Swingin' ain't my idea of a way to end my life."

"Wait till this one leaves. Then we'll plan." Tildy tried to brush the flour from Evan's shirt. "You'll have to change your blouse afore you go, Love." And she kissed him out the door. Evan considered sticking around. It was the first smile she made in a week.

Caper

Georgie started down the escarpment. He was careful to place his feet so that there would be no slides. He dusted himself to blend with the dirt and rocks. Scrub foliage dotted the hillside. Hand holds were plentiful.

The descent was slow. Grab a bush and tug to make sure it wouldn't come loose, find a foothold, never look down. Every foot brought him closer to discovery and perhaps death. Thank goodness he'd ditched the booty. He could get it later, if there was a later. Grab, tug, step; the way was tedious as well as exposing. Georgie thought Syd, I'm coming for you. Nothing matters except you and me. I will fight for you and... Georgie's foot slipped.

***

"Captain James, I am ashamed of you. Is this how you treat an innocent young girl?" Sydney flirted. She was plopped herself down on his lap, a finger wrapped in a curl.

Captain James expelled her from his lap. "You needs behave yourself , young lady. This is serious business you know. There is more to this than you can see. We both need to be very careful. That Gilpin was after something and I am not sure what. I know he must be something to the Queen. I also know the Queen wants the smuggling and pirating stopped, unless she can profit from it. I explained all this before. Why am I wasting my breath?"

"But, Sir Captain, I only want to go home. My Ma and Pa are worried sick about me. I am their only one; the only chick in the nest. The inn will be mine in time, mine and Georgie's, and who is to take care of the parents when they get old and sick? Just let me go. What difference does it make to you? I don't know anything. I told you that afore." Sydney tried a come-hither look and an eyelash flutter.

"I can't let you go. If I let you go on your own, Gilpin may get his hands on you. You may not live through it. Do you ken? He is looking for answers. I understand that you know nothing that you know you know, but you may have heard something you didn't understand, or you may have seen something that was not important at the time. I am only afraid he will use methods that are painful. If you know anything just tell me. I don't think you want to be the plaything of this crew. They are exactly what they seem. And will you please stop that blinking immediately."

Sydney looked at him and asked. "Why can't the Queen just ask me? I met her once when I was little. I don't want to be a plaything for the crew. I do love Georgie. What if he comes and rescues me? I warrant he is on his way right now and angry and ferocious about his little Syd. He'll take on all them men what want me for a plaything." Her attitude changed, all business, as the words came. "You'll know a good hand when you see it. Georgie is the best. He is strong and smart. He might know something more than me for sure, Captain. And don't worry, he'll fight the whole bunch a yas. He'll save me for sure." Sydney's cheeks pinked. She looked down at the carpet and traced the design with her toe. "So, your gonna let me go afore my Georgie comes and blows everything to bits, right?"

"Oh Miss Sydney, you are just a pack of lies, aren't you? Met the Queen? Why, I haven't ever seen her, and I have been on her business for several years. Keep it up and you will be in the bag—again." William winced at his own lies.

Sydney peeked up at him, "You would'na do that would you?" She tried flirting again. " If I tell ya what I know, will you let me go immediately?

"I don't know anything, but I do know my Da' been keeping many officers for the patrols that pass through. Some of them stay a while longer than the patrols and get back reports from the patrols. They don't even go out with their men. That be in part because of my Ma. She is a terrible good cook and keeps the rooms clean and spotless. There is nary a mote of dust anywhere in her rooms. People seem to like that. They even wash daily, so they don't stink up the place. We have had many come in reeking with stench of the road and the city. Once they go to the rooms, they leave and find the creek and wash up so's they can stay in the inn proper-like.

"The patrols camp out around the inn, but they come and eat and drink as their money allows them. Sometimes Georgie and me bring them buckets of my Da's wonderful ale. It be the best in the land according to most. It be the water he uses, but there ain't gonna be enough if these patrols don't stop comin' by. They drink most hearty.

"And that's all I can tell ya' about the inn and what happens there. I help my Ma in the kitchen and the rooms, but I never get to serve in the tavern part in the evenings, only at the lunch time. Me Ma thinks the men are too rough at night. Oh, and I help with the gardens, the herbs for my Ma and the vegetables for my Da. They need the hoeing and the weeding, and I be good at that. I ain't much good at the stitching and the needlework. That be my Aunt Sarah and her girls. They be wizards with the needles and the shuttle. My one cousin makes the laces for the Queen's dresses, her lace be so fine. The Queen don't know where it comes from, but my cousin makes a nice piece of change by making the lace."

"That is the most you have talked about your family since you have been here. Sounds like I might like a glass of your Da's ale myself. I have heard my men talk of it, but thought it was just a story that drunks like to make up. If I can get you back to your family, might I get a meal and some sweets, do ya think?"

" You would take me home? Oh, Sir, I would be pleased to serve you myself; all that you would want."

"I can't make a promise, but if it can be done, you must be ready. Do you understand? And you can't say a word to anyone. Make me that promise now. Even if it doesn't work out, you can't talk."

"Sir William, I solemnly make...."

The door burst open and ...

***

Georgie slipped and slid down the steep side of the cliff. He reached for a branch, but it broke off before he could stop completely. The braking effect of that grab helped him to consider the end result. He looked down and saw the shelf. It was narrow, but if the rock and dirt held, he would be bruised but saved. He let go of the twig and twisted his body. He grabbed at any holds he could see to slow his descent. The landing knocked the wind out of him. Georgie checked his arms and legs. Nothing broken, but he would be sore later on. The big question now was how to get to the shore without being seen. *I am naked as a bird perched here on this shelf,* he thought. *All what need be is for someone on that ship to look up.* Georgie made himself as small as possible lying on that cliff. He looked through his bag and his pockets; no rope, nothing.

He looked at the long way down and then glanced at the long way up. No way to get to either place without some tools at least. Down was easier than up. Being a dirty mess and unseen was better than clean and seen. Georgie grabbed his only weapon, his knife. *So long sharp edge* he thought as he stabbed it into the soft rock of the cliff. The dirt moved, but the cliff rock allowed for a tiny slit and a secure hand hold. *It's gonna be slow goin' if this is what I have ta do,* he said to himself. *But down might be closer to Syd and that is what I want.* Georgie sat on the cliff ledge and rubbed the dirt into his hair and clothes. He moved his back against the wall and collected what color he could. Satisfied he moved himself over the cliff and started his slow descent.

Capture

Georgie's eyes stopped watching the world go round. He shook his head to clear it. The second fall was a long one, but again nothing seemed broken. He looked around and was surprised that all the noise he made attracted no one. The ship was a far piece down the beach. The brush and trees hid him rather well. Georgie made his way to an even less exposed position. He crept down the beach peeking every once in a while, to see the ship. *No colors, but a fine looking ship. How am I going to get on board without being seen?* he thought. *There was no word of this ship the last time he 'went to town to be with a lass'. What was this captain doing there? If a pirate, he would be gunned, when he left his cozy little inlet. If it was a spy ship, it would be gunned when it left the inlet. Was it a ship in distress? Couldn't be. They weren't that far from town and 'friendly' natives. Maybe it was Spanish and made its way in under cover of night to spy on the English and the pirates and report back to that Spanish king on how to defeat the English. I can't let that happen. I have to find out,* he thought and started his journey toward the ship once again. Come what may, Sydney was first and the Queen and country were second in his heart and until he found Sydney, his country came first.

Georgie worked his way to the small inlet and copse of trees that hid the ship. It started to drizzle, and now he was wet and muddy. The weather was getting colder as well. He had to dry off and get warm, but the ship looked enticing and his curiosity rose.

He looked around and saw no one on this side of the ship. *Where were the lookouts? Where was the guard? No one appeared on the sand around the ship. 'Tis a dead ship, a wash up? It is in too fine a shape for that. It is kind of ship that any self-respecting sea-goers would like to take over and make their own. Dreams, George, dreams and you get seasick on a rowboat, and who would leave a big ship like this unattended? Something is very wrong.* Georgie started to stand to find a pathway to the ship's hull. A noise in the thicket behind him made him freeze and hunker down. He peered through the thicket and a lovely rabbit hopped again. That reminded George how hungry he was. The footfall just behind his hiding place reminded him of the danger he was in and the possible danger Sydney was in. Georgie stayed very still and held his breath.

So, there were people around! The man passed by without a glance at Georgie. Georgie heard a snap and the plump rabbit he had seen flew up as if on wings and came down in a heap with an arrow in his gut. The man hunter was a very accurate shot with the crossbow. *Someone is going to have some rabbit stew today.* The hunter gathered his prey, cleaned it and strung it on some vine. He flung the vine over his shoulder and moved on down the thicket. *There are more than just this man about,* George thought. *He is looking for more game. There is the Irish Sea out there. Why isn't someone fishing the area? Too exposed,* was his next thought. *This boat is in hiding.* He peered upwards. *It is flying no color. It is a disabled pirate ship. This boat is stuck here until repairs got done. Hmmmm!* Georgie's imagination went wild. *Report it* one part of his mind said; *join up* said the other part, the wilder part, the adventuresome part. Georgie sat still and pondered. *What are my chances?*

Sydney the Captain

Sydney had William wrapped around her little finger, and all of the men hopped to her bidding. She was wined and dined in a royal manner. William went through some of the trunks and found her clean clothes. Sydney was queen of the ship, and she loved every minute of it, until she thought of home. William made sure that someone was with her at all times. He also made sure that she was not manhandled. He asked that she not go out on deck on the ocean side of the ship. The chance of her being spotted was greater here.

She loved breathing the sea air, but she missed her home and her parents. Every day she looked for an escape route. She had not one minute alone when she was free of the quarters that William provided for her. There had to be a way. Her plan was to get rid of the guards. Maybe she could fool Jack. He was simple minded and would do anything for her. She could ask him to fetch her a parasol or a hat or something. Convincing him to go was the hard part. He loved her but he loved and feared William more.

Looking out over the deck she saw the copse of trees. One of the men usually went hunting out there. He always came back with game. Perhaps there were berries in that copse or somewhere around it. Perhaps William would let her take a berry picking excursion to the copse—with Jack. She could send him in one direction and go in another. The bank was steep, but climbable. Why was no one looking for her? Sydney felt sad that no one would come after her. She understood Tildy and Sarah staying home, but Pa or Georgie? Where were they? Sadness fell on Sydney like a blanket. No smiles, no running, her shoulders slumped in depression at the thought that her family didn't care enough to come for her.

***

Timing is everything, and so it was with Georgie. From his cold little hiding hole, he saw the ship's deck. He saw a beautiful woman walking around—a woman with flaming red hair and a lilt to her step. Sydney; his heart stopped for a beat or two—

he found her. *Now all I have to do is board the ship, unseen, find her room, unseen, and spirit her away, unseen. A lot of unseens, George, me lad*, he thought. *Maybe the best plan is no plan at all.* He would do what he could and let the Devil take the hind-most. *What can happen? There seems to be no one on guard with Syd and I can scale the side of the ship.* Georgie's mind raced. He could not see what was in the portholes or who could see from the gun hatches. He knew from experience these pirates could be sneaky. He crept closer to the edge of the copse. He saw the smoke from a small fire on the sand. *Thank goodness the wind is in my favor. There might be a small chance that the smoke would cover me as I go to the ship.* There it was in his mind's eye, his body running for the cover of the hull of the ship with no one seeing him. He secured his pack and started to run. A high clear voice sounded, "Oh look, someone is coming to the ship."

*Oh, Sydney, why couldn't you...*A bullet whined over his head. He crouched in his run and started to zigzag like he did when tracking a deer or rabbit. Another bullet zinged past him. He never thought he would be the one to be dodging bullets like a bit of game in the forest.

Georgie just kept running like his life depended on it which it did. He reached the prow of the boat. Here at least he could not be seen by people on deck. He could hear Sydney yelling "Stop shooting, he's my cousin. Oh, please stop shooting!"

Shut yer gob, Syd. You're going to get me killed. Thoughts like these flew through Georgie's brain as well as the ones like *how do I get out of sight of these kidnappers and how do I get Sydney back again?* As he peered around the prow of the boat, he saw the source of the fire and smelled the spitted rabbit. He heard the sizzle of cooking flesh and his mouth watered. *What do I do now? I can't just rush them. They will shoot me or knife me or whatever pirates do. Maybe a stroll up and a request for a bite would just get me captured, but then I am on the boat. God, it smells good!*

Georgie ambled up like a wanderer who has just discovered civilization. His feet gave quiet crunches in the damp sand. No one looked in his direction until he was a few yards away. "Avast, who goes there?"

Georgie raised his hands in surrender. "I be who they was shootin' at, but I be just a weary wanderer, and I be very hungry. Could I have a bite?"

"Don't be a fool. Ye be our prisoner. How did ye find us, anyway?" The tallest and ugliest pirate was questioning him. Another shorter man held a pistol on him, and the third came around to his back and nudged him forward with the barrel of his pistol. Georgie recognized none of them.

One shot each, thought Georgie, just one shot and then reload or use the knife. He did not know what the man at his back had but the tall one had high boots on, very military-like boots. There was a knife in one of those boots. The one with the pistol in front had a sword belted at his waist. None of them looked stupid or incapable of doing him mortal harm. Georgie cooperated. As he drew closer to the fire and the food, he started to drool. *It smells so good,* he thought, *so what if they kill me, at least my belly will be full.* He took a step and fell to the ground. All three men surrounded him, weapons drawn. He felt the cool sand on his face and hands and was tempted to start weeping in frustration.

"Get up, you worthless piece of flotsam, get up or die." The lead pirate was talking again. He did not sound like the pirates with whom Georgie was acquainted. He was much better spoken. Something was not right. Georgie stood up. The lead man grabbed him by his sore shoulder and pushed him toward an opening in the ship. "You are a surprise. Get on board. I have needs to take you to the captain. We heard the yellin' o' the lass on board. You be her cousin?"

"Aye well," said Georgie blathered on. " I just found out a few days ago that we be not related. I am her Ma and Pa's nephew, but she be not my cousin at least by birth."

"Are you daft, my lad? If you be a nephew, how can she not be your cousin?"

Georgie paused and then said, "Me uncle told me afore I left that they got her as a babe only a few days old, and she were bereft of Ma or Pa 'til she got to them. Now she is to be my wife, but she don't know that yet, like I said afore."

"Git your ass in gear, lad, and git up the plank. The Captain needs hear of this."

Gilpin Returns

Gilpin walked the path away from the ship. His mood was black. He needed to get to Walsingham but knew that this upstart captain had orders from someone. He decided that going to the castle now was not an option. He needed to confront this captain and get the girl into his custody. Then he could do his will. He turned around and made his way back to the ship. Once on board he headed to the captain's quarters. Without knocking he burst into the room.

"You planted two men in The Cock and the Sow to recruit smugglers. What is the purpose of that?" Gilpin was raging again.

"What makes you think I did that? I admit to getting anxious about staying in this inlet. We are not going to stay hidden forever. Unless I can gather some information about this smuggling ring here in Wales, I will be assigned to another post. That would suit me fine, but now I have a hostage and that hostage connects me to The Cock and the Sow. Yes, I sent two men, my men not the common blokes, to see if they could drum up any business. I think it is interesting that since the patrol ships are more frequent, the activity has placed itself on the west coast of Ireland, with some on the southern shore, but none in the Irish Sea. Explain that if you can. And just who do you think you are trying to take command of this ship without any orders. I told you cease and desist until you show me orders in writing from an authorized officer."

Gilpin looked at William. "I just wanted to know if they were instructed to have anyone follow them."

"If someone were interested, I was hoping for a revelation. According to my men the only person to follow was you. They reported that no one was willing to expose cither the operation or the people involved. There were no admissions of participation or even knowledge of any smuggling or pirating.

"Here I have a young woman aboard who has basically taken command of this ship. She only wants to go home, and I am inclined to send her there, unless you think there is a reason to keep her." William stopped.

Gilpin said, "Why not slit her throat? She is smart and talks too much for an average girl. She will reveal you and this ship and ruin the whole surveillance. Are you sweet on her?"

"I am not going to 'slit the throat' of an innocent young woman. I may ship her to the colony, but I will not kill her. I do not think she will reveal anything. She could even be an asset and do some basic surveillance for us. I think you need to go back to The Cock and the Sow and listen some more. Stay a day or two. Dress down. Let them think you are their friend. Find out what is really happening. Also, what happened to the troops. They marched north of here and we have seen them no more. What do you say, Gilpin, what do you say to that?"

"Not a bad idea. It would be good to find out some of the local information. The Queen..." he broke off his statement and looked long and hard at William. "It is a good idea. I am on my way back as of this minute." Gilpin gathered his cloak about him and started to leave. "I don't want to use the girl for surveillance, at least not just yet. Is there any place else we can stow her for a few more days? Oh, and I don't want your men knowing anything of her whereabouts. This has to be on you alone. East o' the Sun is but a few miles from here. Her Majesty will be coming in a few days. I may have a use for the girl. Then you can recruit her all you want." Gilpin smiled. It was not a pretty sight. James was uneasy at his change in attitude.

"As you wish, Sir. I will sequester her for a few days. May I suggest the secret service of the Queen to her? It could help to make her more compliant to our wishes." William said, a sarcastic tone to his statement.

"Anything to make her cooperate. I do have plans for her in the next couple of days. Make sure she has a clean face and hands and make her do her hair. You know what they wear in Court."

William looked hard at Gilpin. He kept his expression neutral. Sydney was in trouble. The tone of Gilpin's and the look on his face gave away his plan. Unless he acted fast, Sydney was a dead woman. Strange at a time like this he thought of her as a woman.

After climbing up stairs and ladders the band of four stopped in front of a door and the lead man knocked loudly. "Captain, may we enter? We have another prisoner."

"Wait there. I have some work to finish and then I will see you," William answered. When done he addressed Gilpin in a whisper, "Get in that cupboard and don't say a word. My men have a prisoner, and they would just shoot him or her on the spot unless they thought it was important. I beg you just listen."

"Don't you address me like that again you...,"
and then the light dawned. *This could be the break I
was waiting for. A smuggler, the clue to the
smuggling rings and an end to my exile to this God-
forsaken country. Back to court? Dressed in my
finery? Oh, bliss!* Gilpin complied.

Once the cabin was in order, William invited
his men in. They entered pushing Georgie in front of
them. "Well, what have we here?" asked William.

"It is the prisoner that the girl labeled her
'cousin', Sir." The lead man answered.

"She what?" said William surprised.

"She begged the watch to stop shooting on
account of it was her cousin they was shootin' at. We
didn't see him until he approached the cook fire with
the rabbits spitted and asked for a bite of food. I
would imagine the poor lad is very hungry about
now." The lead man was very sarcastic.

William looked at the lad. "Who are you?"

"George Evans, Sir," Georgie stammered a little
afraid of the splendor of William's uniform.

"What are you doing sneaking around this
ship?"

"I-I-I was hungry. I fell down the cliff and after
I saw the ship and thought there might be..."

"Enough. We know that is not so. What do you
want here?" William got sterner as the questioning
went on. Georgie got more frightened. He stared at
William's uniform.

Who did he kill to get this uniform? Georgie
thought. *You didn't just tell somebody to strip to steal
their clothes. You got rid of them and stole their ship*

if you were a real pirate and this man must be a real pirate.

Georgie had never seen a real pirate, so his supposition was based on the stories the smugglers told him. *He's real handsome for a pirate* thought Georgie. *No scars or hooks or peg legs or nothin'*.

William asked, "And you are here because?"

"Okay, I am lookin' fer me cousin, who were taken from her Da's cabbage patch back at The Cock and the Sow by a smuggler, we think. It coulda bin a pirate, come to think. I been lookin' fer her now for a while. I run outta food and when I noticed the ship, I thought maybe I could hitch up or sumun would know where she be. Then when I were hid in the trees over there," Georgie pointed in what he thought was the general direction of the copse of trees, "I seen a girl. Well, ya see, I fell down the cliff from the road. There were a troop o' the military marchin' and I hid from them on account of I didn't want ta be caught and impressed. Then my pack fell and when I reached fer it, I fell and landed on the sand finally. I got the bruises. That's the truth!"

William eyed him with suspicion. "And you say you survived a fall down that cliff. You hit not one rock or tree?"

"I hit rocks an' grabbed at twigs as I went down, but the twigs didna' hold me weight, and the rocks hit me legs and me shoulder. Do ya want ta see the bruises?"

"Nay, good fellow. You are too ignorant to tell a lie and stick with it. Go on with your story."

"Yessir. When I saw the man track and shoot a rabbit with just a bow and arrow, I thought oh, there be food here. Just then I heard the girl and thought she be my cousin from the sound o' her voice. I thought this might be the pirate ship what had the man what kidnapped her, and her Ma and Da be very sad at not havin' her around." Georgie paused with his tale. "But I was too hungry to attack the ship. I thought if I could just get on board and look fer her meself..."

"Lad, I need not tell you that you are in a great deal of trouble. I could have you hanged right here, right now, but I won't do that. For the time being you are to be confined to the brig and fed a meal. Do you hear that, Cookie? A real meal, not just your bread and water. Throw in some of that rabbit you caught and make it snappy.

"First Mate take this boy to the brig and make sure he is secure. Then bring me the girl. Now all of you clear this cabin. I need to do some work."

The men left the cabin, Georgie securely restrained. As they left, William heard first mate say, "Ya be in much trouble, laddie. Better you never followed anyone at all. The Captain 'ull have yer head, 'e will." They kept walking.

William opened the closet door. "Gilpin get out of that closet. I hope you heard all you needed to hear and can carry your story back to the castle. I think it is time you left, and we got this ship back on duty. There has been enough excitement for all these past few days. Please go. Do not reveal any of this ship until we are through with our mission."

"Tis easier said than done, my boy," Gilpin replied, "You will have to finish very soon to have any veracity in this matter. Oh, and hang that boy. I think he may be a spy himself. Mark my words." With that Gilpin left the cabin as well. The Queen would be very unhappy with Sir William, if he had anything to say about it.

The Witch's Brew

I needs warn Tildy of the Queen's travel. Morvyn was agitated, since one of the men at the pub let drop the information that the Queen was moving to the coast of Wales for several months if not years. *Nay, she couldna move there for years, but the troops be afoot and there be a general nerviness in the city,* she thought, *but it would not hurt to go to Tildy and take a look at her gardens. I am about due or will be.* "Jack, I be going to see Tildy. I am in need of some more herbs and I would like to see if any more of her spices caught and can be harvested."

"Morvyn, my love, are ye sure that this trip is a good one fer ya? Remember how it was fer yer ta come home after the last one. Ye almost died. And that were but weeks ago. What would I do then? Your body ain't as strong as it were once," Jack whined

"I didna 'most die. Jest one o' my headaches kept me down for a day or two. It don't matter, Jack. I must be going. It be my last trip, and I needs to see my cousin once more. You'll do very fine after I'm gone. But you ain't seen the last o' me yet."

"I jes' don't wanna see the very lasts o' you, like yer dead body comin' home on a cart."

"That ain't gonna happen, Jack. Yer jest afraid ye can't sell this place on account of ye don't know whether I be dead in a ditch or alive and on me way home. Now get me a good carriage. We can afford it. I will make the trip easy this time and not use the horse. I will take a carriage to and from Tildy's. I promise"

Jack went out to the farrier and asked for his finest horse and covered carriage with driver. They haggled and Jack went back to Morvyn with the good news. She was going in style. Morvyn packed her bag and stuffed a couple of herb bags up her sleeves. There would be only one stop on this trip and that was Tildy's inn. They would get food and drink and drive day and night. She could rest in the coach. The driver could rest in short stretches. She would be there in two days and that suited her just fine.

The next morning fortified with some biscuits and some meat from the last night's roast, Morvyn walked over to the farrier's place and got her coach. Jack had not paid. She paid for the first half of the trip and told the driver the second half would have his tip if he could make the trip in triple time. His eyes glinted with greed. He knew Morvyn paid well for what she wanted and knew that she could afford far more that she looked like she could.

The trip was easy, the roads dry and passable with few bumps. The weather was pleasant and Morvyn kept the curtain up for most of the day's journey. She felt strong and healthy. Perhaps it was the London air that kept her feeling weak and old. She nibbled on the biscuit, then droused into a little nap.

She dreamed of idyllic pastures and cool breezy hillocks, dotted here and there with flocks of snowy sheep grazing from the emerald green grass. And so passed the morning. She shuddered awake when the coach came to a halt. "Time to take a quick break, Milady," shouted the coachman as he hied himself behind a tree for some relief.

Morvyn, too, felt the need and climbed from the coach to stretch her legs for a few minutes and then take care of nature's insistence. Both ready to resume the journey, Morvyn asked, "Where be we?"

"On the high road to the first inn. If ye want to stop. We are making good time and could be well past before dark. It is yours to name. The horses are fine. We have not pushed them today and with a couple more rests they can get us further down the road. If you are in a hurry, t'would be my choice."

"As you wish. I am anxious to get to my cousin's as quickly as possible. Thank you for taking me *post haste*. Let us go."

***

Georgie lolled in the brig. He had an ankle cuff chained to a beam. He had about three feet of wander room. *What will become of me* he wondered? The bread and meat William gave him was long gone. *Oh, Syd, what have I done to both of us. What will happen?* His thoughts went in circles.

It was certain death to try to escape or was it? Something was not right with this ship. Captain William did not look like a pirate. He was dressed too plain, and he had no scars or false hands or legs. He was very handsome. He spoke too well for a pirate;

at least the pirates in Georgie's experience. The first mate stood too straight. He had not worked at heavy labor nor kept fields or hoisted anchor. There was something of the military about them and several other crewmen.

Georgie's stomach rumbled. He was still hungry. Something scurried over his foot; rats! *Am I to eat rats or be eaten by rats? And why was a pirate ship pulled into an inlet out of sight, but with lookouts, scanning the Irish Sea. The only thing out there was...and there were no colors. Flags were signals and the signals were wrong! Heaven Bless me! What kind of ship be this one?*

***

I am to stay inside until further notice. Sydney laughed out loud. *And just how are they going to make me?* She tried the cabin door. *Damn, it's locked,* she thought. *I'll try that round window again. A dunk in the water is worth escaping from a trap.*

She went to the porthole and opened it. Hiking herself up on the rim, she looked down. *A jump would be fatal. There were too many rocks. Rocks and the boat was moored here? Did that make sense? What was this anyway?*

She looked from side to side for footholds and handholds. There was a rope along the side. *But if I miss when I drop, I will die, and where did the rope lead?*

***

Gilpin approached the castle. He looked up. Edward II had a mighty fortress, most defendable so high upon this hill. *The queen would be very safe here unless....* The less Gilpin thought about that the better. His stay on William's boat should earn him credibility. Now it was just a matter of getting the information about the girl, the boy and the spy ship to Francis Walsingham. *I am his brother-in-law,* Gilpin thought.

He walked to the first watch gate, "Let me pass. I am Harold Lord Bardsley, Second Marquis of Craegelon, Queen's Intelligence. I have to report to Lord Walsingham immediately."

"There is no Lord Walsingham here, my lord. No one is in residence."

"That is not true. The Queen is due any day. Walsingham must be here, sir. Let me pass," Gilpin ordered.

"The Queen is due? Our Queen? Where get ye these ideas?" countered the guard.

What was he to do to get this information to the Queen and profit by his work? *I will go to The Cock and the Sow and wait.*

***

Tildy and Sarah worked together making the stews, pasties and pies. Sarah made an exquisite textured pudding and Tildy flavored it with her condiments. Evan was in the field with the cows and the new boy was mucking out the stables.

Sydney was often the subject of conversation, but with fewer tears these days. Tildy knew in her heart that the girl was alive. She also knew that Sydney for all her youth was a capable woman.

Sarah worried about Georgie. She loved him but knew that at his age he needed to establish himself in his own life. His talent with animals could lead to a life with an Earl or even the Queen's stables. One always wished for the best for their children.

"Will we see Morvyn again, do you think Tildy?"

"Aye, I had word. She is on her way and should be here any time now." Tildy pushed the tender dough back and forth. She knew the way of the light and fluffy breads that the customers liked. " I need to let this come up again. Is your puddin' ready fer the oven?"

"Aye, sister, and I'll be puttin' it there directly. It'll be nice to see Morvyn agin. It's been a long while, hasn't it?"

"Aye, but we're not gittin any younger. She be only three months older 'n me, ya know."

"Aye, I know. Think, sister, it must be somethin' important fer her to travel all this way. She were not lookin' too good the last time she were here."

"She be takin' a carriage from the big town. She kin afford it. Never knew why she rode here on them horses to begin with. She really didn't hint as ta why she be comin'. Just that there be some news. I guess she couldna write it in a note."

"Open the oven would ya please. I need ta slip this in now."

"Sister, I have me hands full of dough. Open it yourself. We have a full day today. This dough be almost ready. A couple a more pushes and I leave it to nature. How are the rooms?"

"I cleaned the one what were occupied last night. It be ready ta go. If ye want, I'll give Morvyn's room a quick dust through. Shouldn't be too much. Had someone in it two nights ago. I'll open the windows an' let the breeze blow through."

"That would be nice, Sister. We may should open all the windows for an hour. Freshens up the whole inn. Ah, this is ready. See the stretch? That's how the dough should look just afore restin'. In case I ain't here someday and you need ta make it."

Tildy's afterthought was more prophetic than she knew. Great things were happening, and she was at the center of the whirlwind.

***

Morvyn's arrival was greeted with tears and laughter. Tildy held her away after the first hug and said, "Cousin, you are looking fine, much better than the last time You were here."

"Remember what was happening then? Any news of the girl?"

"Nay, but a man who said he were from the Queen said he would look around. He were here of a night. He were a little scary all dressed in black and skinny the way he were. He loved Evan's ale, though and ate many pasties and bowls. Evan said he were none too generous when it came to stable his mount. The boy done good fer him and he left without warning. There were nothing left from what we was paid, but you know Evan. He give the boy a pence and told him we would make it up to him."

"Cousin let me get to my room and freshen up a bit. Then we must talk. I have some news that only you and Evan should hear, so gather him in and we will have a little *tete de tete*."

Sarah carried Morvyn's bag and showed her to her room. Morvyn sat down heavy on the bed. "Sarah, how long have you been here?"

"A long while since my husband died. Evan and Tildy were kind enough to bring me and mine in. James still be worth nothing, just another mouth ta feed. The older girl is married now, and Georgie went haring off to find Sydney. We ain't heard from either o' them two since. I know they both be old enough, but the circum-stances around Sydney are strange. Rest up a wee bit and I will gather Tildy and Evan fer ya. It be a long trip from the big city."

Morvyn waited for Sarah to leave the room before she opened her bag. There was much she needed to say to her cousins, and she wanted to do it right. Tildy might think she looked good, but Morvyn knew how she felt, and she knew this was her last trip. She had a mild but enduring pain in her chest and a hard time grabbing her breath even after that short flight of steps. *I must make it back to London*, she thought as she laid her head on the down pillow.

***

Sydney looked out the porthole and down the long side of the ship. The drop was not worth it. There had to be another way. She went to the door and looked at the lock. Some fool left the key in the keyhole. There was a possibility. She went to the Captain's desk and found a piece of vellum. Bringing it back to the door, she knelt an slipped it under. She reached into her hair and pulled a long pin from the arrangement. Wrestling the pin through the keyhole was not easy, but when the key started to move, she felt more in control. The more she wriggled the pin the further out the key went. *Oh, please let it fall on the paper,* she thought. One last push and she heard the key fall.

Sydney pulled the paper gently back under the door. She saw the top of the key on the paper and her fingers went for it. Freedom was just a moment away.

***

Gilpin cooled his heels in the center court for more than an hour. This was not acceptable. He called to a guard. "Go and get me Walsingham. I need an immediate audience with him. I have important information. No one will be happy if this news is not made known."

He might just as well saved his voice. *How can I not be known? I am one of the most valuable spies the Queen had. Walsingham said so. I have fulfilled my mission. Now I am brushed aside like so many dead leaves? I have the solution to the Queen's problem.*

Three hours later a page came to escort him to another room. He was not offered refreshment, but at least there was a chair in this place. He heard some commotion in the great hall and tried to open the door to see the cause. The door was locked!

***

Tildy and Evan went to Morvyn's room. Tildy knocked a tentative knock. Morvyn heard it and sat up. "Come in, you two. Listen to me. You need to know what is on the lips of those in London, because it affects you and yours.

"The Queen is leavin' this week to go to 'er home on the sea, East o the Sun. She is lookin' for a solution to the smuggling problem and will hold some military court there. Be ready to receive 'er here at The Cock and the Sow. Gossip says she liked bein' here the last time she passed. That was when Sydney were a child. Do not be shocked when she comes. Just have enough food to feed all and try not to have any guests here." Morvyn took a deep breath. "You don't know the origins of Sydney, do you?" she gasped. Breathing was much harder now. "I don't neither, but I need to ask if you still have anything around from when she came here."

"Of course. I kept all that you brought that wonderful day. Let me get it." Tildy rushed from the room, her senses all agog with the news of the Queen's visit. She only wished that Sydney could be here to meet the Queen once more and let the Queen show how she had grown into a young lady.

Tildy went to her cupboard in the kitchen and got down the packet wrapped in cloth from that momentous day when Morvyn brought her Sydney. Tildy kept everything. Sydney was the answer to all of her dreams.

Running upstairs, Tildy called, "Here 'tis, all of it." She entered the room and dropped the sacred package on Morvyn's lap. "You open it. It is like a gift, and you were responsible. Please, just do it."

Morvyn undid the ribbon holding the packet together. Carefully she unfolded the cloth to reveal the glove used to feed the child and her swaddling clothes. "Tildy, look at this. Feel this cloth. What do you feel?"

"It is very fine linen, certainly made in England. It is finer than anything you could find here. And, oh look, the piece of cloth that named her." Tildy held up the piece of silk, a little holey with age, with the name 'Sydney' in fine embroidery. "Ah, yes, I remember thinking this a very fine hand with a needle. Look, Sarah, as fine as yours, wouldn't you say?"

Sarah starred at the fabric. "Tildy, Morvyn this be silk. You don't get fine silk around here. Only the royals and some in court, who can afford it, have silk. It comes from far away, far east of here. Surely you all saw that. Morvyn, ye didn't ken that this was silk?"

Morvyn whispered, "Many in London town have silk available. The child was supposed to be of noble birth. I was supposed to get rid of it. I thought only of Tildy and her want of a child. The woman what brought her to me was dark and said she were from the north"

Morvyn coughed. "It get harder for me to breathe these days." She changed the subject again. "Just you be ready for the Queen's visit. It be said that she is come to organize the troops and make an end to this smuggling. If you know anything of it, please let it be known. Things are bound to get worse. I just feel it in the nether parts of me.

"Now I need some rest. Tildy think on what we talked of. Sarah be with her. I am not long. This be my last trip here. I pray I make it home to say goodbye ta Jack." Morvyn lay back against the pillows and closed her eyes. Her breathing shallowed and she rested.

"She don't look too good, Tildy. Did you see the blue on her mouth and in her fingernails? When she wakes, I'll be gitten' her another bolster fer her shoulders. She's needing' her air.

"I'll git Evan to take her back to the city, when she be ready to leave. We kin take care o' this place fer a few days or even close. I ain't ne'er been to London and it be not busy here fer travelers."

A weak voice chimed in on the conversation from the bed, "An wot are you plannin' fer me, women?" She sat up and immediately sank back against her pillows.

"Morvyn, Be careful, will you? You are prone to a light head on risin'" Tildy scolded.

"And you needs ta rest more," volunteered Sarah. "We be none as young as we onct was. I git dizzy, if I rise quickly these days." Sarah shot a warning look at Tildy.

"An how much did you hear, cousin?" This from Tildy.

"Only that Evan go wi' me when I decide ta go, cousin." Tildy fussed at the eiderdown as Morvyn slowly sat up. "An' now quit your fussin'. 'Tis time I were arose. I have gardens to see and herbs to buy afore I go. Now leave me."

" There's bread what needs punchin'. I'm goin' down now," said Sarah.

Now alone Morvyn looked at Tildy and said, " I came mainly to warn ya of the queen's travel. I heard tell that she be stoppin' here for a meal and ta see yer daughter. I don't know why, but I do get news on occasion from some,what come ta Jack's pub.

"I might suggest if Sydney ain't here, it could be a good omen. Mayhaps she be wed and on transport ta the New World. You dinna have to listen, but you know I git images o' the future. It be safer if Sydney be away."

"Morvyn, you know Sydney been caught and taken we know not where. She been gone near a month and nary a word about her. Nobody seems to know ought, not when she were took nor where she may be. Truth be told, I hope she be dead, if she been sadly used. Left on her own, she'd be back here by now. She is nay stupid, and she kens nature. She know how to stay warm and dry and what ta eat wots not poison. She'll be back, I pray."

The Castle

Gilpin looked around. There was a window slot, but no other doors to this room. *A master spy is not treated this way. How could the rumors be so wrong? Walsingham is here. I am brushed aside like so much dust.*

He heard a noise at his window slot. "Gilpin?" It was Walsingham.

"Yes, my Lord. I come with important information, My Lord."

"Who do you think you are?"

"I am a spy in Her Majesty's employ. I am sent to discover the smugglers on this coast and find the pirate's treasure."

"Gilpin, Gilpin! Why have I never heard that name if you are indeed in my employ? What made you think..." Walsingham looked more closely at Gilpin through the slot. "Get you near the slot. I cannot see your face clearly." Gilpin moved so that the light lit up his face. "Gilpin? Why do you call yourself Gilpin, Harold? Why did you not make yourself known when you came?"

"Gilpin is how folks around here know me. I am undercover. You know that. You sent me out after your sister died. You said I looked too sad to have around. Remember? Oh, who cares. The point is I have discovered the whereabouts of a pirate ship and the possible connection to the smugglers on this shore. What say you?"

"Harold, I think you are still in mourning for my sister and drowned in your drink. I would know if there be a 'pirate' ship docked around here, don't you think? And another question, how did you know I would be here?"

"I keep abreast of your whereabouts and I also know the Queen is due for a visit, and that she will be here within the week. True or not?" Gilpin asked with a sneer.

"That is none of your business, but where did you hear that?"

"There is an inn about two days walk from here called The Cock and the Sow. I have spent several nights there in the last month and would like to be reimbursed if that is possible. The last night I was there, a messenger came and delivered the information that the Queen would be passing through and would stop for refreshment and rest before continuing. She stopped there before when just in power.

"I must say the food is the best I ever had and there must be something about the water because the inn keep brews his own ale, which is the finest in the land, bar none." Gilpin drew breath and continued, "I have never been in such a clean, fresh place and would stay forever if I had the funds. The stew is sub..."

"You are a walking announcement for the place, Harold. Perhaps I should put you out to pasture in this heaven on earth. Back to the point, the messenger; was he a Queen's man?"

"Nay, he was sent from London by the wife's sister or cousin or such. He was common and swiftly off after some ale and lunch."

Walsingham rubbed his chin with the backs of his fingers. "Common you say. And you, you damned fool, believe it?"

"Stranger things have happened. I found a ship and on this ship, there is a young woman. She is a comely lass with red curls and green eyes and a saucy disposition. There is also a lad who is the nephew of the landlord in this inn. That much I got from the girl, who is in love with the lad."

"The Captain of the ship, a William, is in love with the girl. That much I saw when I was on board."

"Good God, Harold, not William James, tall, good looking well dressed?"

"Sounds like the same person. How do you know him?"

"This I cannot tell you without compromising the Queen's quest. You will stay here until further notice. You are not to leave the castle. I will have a room prepared. We will talk later about your stay at the inn." Walsingham disappeared through the hole in the wall and minutes later the door opened, and Gilpin followed the lackey to a room in one of the towers.

***

"William, would you not let me go and see my cousin in the bottom of this boat. I have missed him so and you have so wrongly locked him up. Please, William, please." Sydney decided jumping out the window was not as preferable as begging to see Georgie. The two of them together could beat any bunch of men. Georgie was strong and she was smart.

William looked into her eyes and fought the impulse to kiss her. He had seen enough of the paper and the key and so instead reached for the hand behind her back and gently removed the key from her fingers and pocketed it once he had locked the door from the inside.

"Nay, my little one. Your cousin is a prisoner. You are a prisoner. I cannot let you two be together. I cannot guarantee your safety in the brig. He will be shot on sight should he escape. What fate do you wish, lass?"

"What would it take to free Georgie? I care not for myself, but he is a simple lad and magic with the horses and other animals. It is a though he could talk to them. You canna' kill him. He be good with the Queen's mounts and such. Why would you want to catch poor Georgie?" Sydney was in tears or so it seemed. She peeked out from between her lashes at William. He had a sad look on his face. Sydney pushed a little more, "You could release him to see the Queen.

You could release both of us. We could go home to our Ma and Pa even if Georgie hasn't got one so he uses me Pa for his'n, and we would never say nothing about your ship or pirates or none o' that. Please, kind Sir, please?" Sydney made a moue and somehow squeezed out a tear for more sympathy.

"Miss Sydney, I am sorry to say but neither of you can be permitted to leave until my mission is done. I am hoping that it will be in a few days. I may have to leave the ship for a day or so, but I promise as soon as we are done, both of you youngsters will be released," and under his breath, "but I don't know for the life of me why I should let you go." William sighed. There was nothing he would rather do than to take this young woman in his arms, kiss her silly, carry her off to the nearest priest and wed her.

***

Gilpin felt good about the interview. Everyone was warned and informed. Walsingham wanted more information about the inn. He was to stay in the Queen's castle. What more could he want? A man servant appeared and asked Gilpin if he wished any food or drink. Gilpin asked for a flacon of ale and a joint of beef or lamb whatever was available. The manservant disappeared as magically as he came. Gilpin was in his reverie and observed little. His chair as comfortable and the room was reasonably warm for a castle. There was a comfortable looking cot in the corner as well as a ewer and bowl for washing and tidying up. Contentment radiated from his entire body. He never tried the door.

***

Walsingham sent orders to William. They were simple: End the assignment, provide for the release of the children after all men were off the ship. William was to put his first mate in charge of the ship and get himself to East O the Sun. His men were to follow. The first mate would set the ship adrift. William would be compensated for his loss should there be one.

William called Sam and issued the order to get his horse from the hold's stable and take care of all the rest.

Sydney and George

Sydney watched William's broad shoulders exit the cabin door. She listened closely but did not hear the turn of a key. *So, I'm not as much of a prisoner as I thought. I need to get Georgie out of here. I can do this, but I have to find him first.* She looked around the cabin and chose a candle holder with a bit of candle in it. She rummaged through William's desk and found an almost spent flint. It would have to do, as would this dress she had on. It was too full and had noisy fabric, but it was that or the other one that was even noisier, and she didn't need her bodice tight for this one, which meant she could breathe and run if necessary. She waited a few more minutes before she cracked the door. She heard movement and shut the door. Sydney sat down on the carpet and waited.

An hour later Syd opened the door and looked around. *Had William left the boat already?* There was no one guarding her door. She slipped out and looked up and down the deck; no one. *Where could they all be. There were always a few men around.* She went out on the deck and started looking for a set of steps to take her 'down below' as the sailors called it. She knew there was a door in the deck planking within view of the captain's deck. Perhaps she could get down that way. She walked casually up toward the prow of the boat, her eyes sharp for any untoward motion. She glanced over the side towards the water. There was absolutely no one on board. She ran to the hatch door and tried to lift it. On her first attempt she felt the weight of it. *It is like lifting a wagon to the side hitches of a horse. Surely there was an easier way.* She walked around the deck looking over the next deck even more closely than before.

The small door was right under the captain's door a deck below. She climbed over the side of the captain's deck and dropped to the deck below. Sydney looked around some more. The ship was empty except for her and hopefully Georgie. She turned the hasp and opened the door. The smell of stale cooking, stale sweat, and moldy wood assaulted her nostrils. *How did these men live this kind of life?*

One more look around told her she had to go, and it had to be now. Down the narrow steps she went, once losing her footing on the worn steps. *I will have a bruise on my bum from that one* she thought. The first landing was hung with ropes and the smell of fresh cooking reached her. She was hungry, but she had to find Georgie. She heard stirrings and pulled back into the shadows, clutching her candle and flint close. There was light here, but what lay ahead besides more steps?

The next steps seemed to spiral down to another deck that smelled mustier than the first. The light dimmed the further down she went. She heard the rustle of her skirts and hoped no one else could. She stopped and listened. *No one is following.* The next deck came fast. The area was dim and hung with hammocks, *for the crew* she thought. *No one is snoring.* The thought passed through her mind. *Strange for the number of men on board.* Sydney edged onward and downward. The next landing was the keel, the bottom of the ship and very dark. She dared light her candle. *This has to be the dungeon area*, she thought, but she saw no Georgie. There were several doors, two with bars. She looked into one and heard nothing. The second revealed a man manacled to the beam of the ship. A large lock looped through a hasp. Sydney looked. "Georgie, Georgie, be that you? I have no key. How do you get fed? Georgie, wake up and answer me, if that be you."

"Sydney? Syd is that you?

"Aye, George. There is no one around that I can find.

"A man comes twice a day and brings me a plate with some bread. He is due about now."

"Does he carry the keys?"

"Aye, on a big ring. I am so tight here that I can move but a couple of feet afore I am jerked back to the wall. You will just have to wait for the food to come. There must be some way for you to get the keys from him and let me out. He watches like a hawk while I eat. He carries a torch as well, so he can see better. Perhaps you can hit him on the head with something."

"You put much faith in my abilities, Georgie. I will do the best I can, but it will not do that the two of us wind up in a cell. I have but this bit of a candle and can see little."

"You don't be a milksop with me, Syd. I know you too well. You can find something out there. This be a ship."

Too well is right, Georgie, she thought. *I don't really want to go from this place, but it be necessary.* She pushed her small candlelight into the darkness, exposing a large keg and some canvas sails. *I don't want to leave William, but we die if I can't get Georgie free.*

"Look, Syd, if he be coming, just hide. When he leaves, you leave. Get off this boat and run like the wind. Go home. You be but a day or three from your Ma and Pa..."

"Georgie, hush. I hear something. And for your information, I don't leave my best cousin to die in a dungeon or on a boat. You say the man be here soon, I think he may be here anon. I will hide. Dinna say naught about me. Do he talk much?"

"He don't talk a'tal. He just bring me a plate and gits to'ther what I et from afore. I wish you would go or we both be sittin' here waiting fer our next meal."

Footsteps sounded overhead. "He be comin'. Git hid. You canna git away now. Go hide."

The key twisted in the lock and the door creaked open. Sydney hidden behind a post clutching her doused candle held her breath. *How had they missed one another?* she thought.

The man entered the dungeon and Sydney slipped in behind him. The shadows were dark, and she melted into them. She felt around behind her and touched something hard. She slipped her hand around it and tried to lift it. Too heavy; she felt some more and found something smaller and lighter. The man bent to put the meal on the floor. "Here be your dinner." Sydney's mouth watered. It actually smelled good. But that voice; he was her kidnapper!

Georgie asked, "How much longer?"

The man grunted and said "Soon."

At the same time Sydney grabbed whatever the object was and swung it up over her head. The momentum carried it down and hit the man on his head. He fell to the floor.

"Good work for a girl." Georgie laughed. "Now you must find the keys an' git us out o' here."

The devil take you, George Lewis. He be the one what bagged me." Sydney felt around the man and found the keys. They were tied to his sash. "George, there be no room and I must roll this lump of flesh."

"Then do it and stop talking. He should be gone by now. Someone might miss him."

"The pox on you! There ain't no one. I wonder why he were still here. I am doing the best I can." Syd rolled the body over and felt for the knot in his sash. The man groaned. Fumbling, she untied it. "Shut yourself or I'll knock you another one harder than the last, ya big lug. You be lucky to be alive, you, you..."

She tore out the knot and slid the keys off. They dropped to the floor when a large hand closed around her wrist. "Drop my arm, ya oaf, or I swear I'll kill ya." The jailor started to sit up, but Sydney pushed him back as hard as she could. He hit the floor with a loud thump and the hand on her wrist dropped away. She grabbed the keys again and stood up.

"Do you ken what key it would be? There must be a hundred keys on here."

"Jesus, girl, what 'ave you done?"

"I hit him on the head with something and then pushed him hard. The floor did the rest. Hush now and help. This is our big chance. I'll get you unlocked. You eat. You'll need your strength." She looked at the keys in the sliver of light. "This one looks possible." She worked her way around the body of the jailor, stepped on his hand and he groaned. "He's still alive, Georgie. We gotta hurry. Will you eat?"

"I kenna reach the plate. He dropped it too far away."

Sydney dropped to her knees and started crawling forward. Her hand hit the plate. Here be your food." She handed him the plate. "Now eat."

Georgie reached for the plate at the same time, a difficult feat in the near darkness of the dungeon. The jailor groaned again as Sydney and Georgie collided and the plate went flying, food dispersed like so many seed pockets from a plant. "So much fer your supper. I've got to try these keys. He'll be coming awake. We best be gone by the time he gets his senses back. Now that I ken your whereabouts, we'll get these keys working and get out of here." She took small cautious steps to avoid falling and dropping the keys. A sense of urgency tingled her spine and even with so much caution made it to Georgie's side in seconds.

"Git me feet. I need to stand and be rid of the fire in my legs."

"Don't move. I will do as you want, just don't wiggle. I need to feel the shackle lock and then try the key. There are many keys on this ring. It could take a little time. All I got is my fingers feeling about." She fussed with the key ring and whispered, "Here is one that might go." She guided the key to the hole for the lock. "Damn, it's too big. I thought t'would fit." She tried another a bit smaller. It fit the lock but would not turn. "Oh, Georgie, this could take a bit of time."

"Just go as fast as you can. Just remember, he won't stay down forever."

"Aye, aye, Captain. Now hush. Let me work" Sydney found a third key. It fit the lock and with a bit of muscle opened the large manacle. "Ah, the charm of three," she giggled as she gently removed the pin from the shackle and then opened it wide enough for Georgie to free his leg. "Move!" she whispered. A groan came from the fallen sailor. The noise frightened Sydney. She heard nothing else. "Move your hands to me, George," she stammered. George leaned over to make her search easier. "Mind you, rub your legs for the feeling and when you stand mind your head. There is not much room above us." Another loud groan filled the small space.

George stood up and fell to his knees. "My legs won't carry me."

"They will when they are less asleep." She felt around and found his arm. "Stand and lean on me. Still, mind your head." She wrapped his arm around her neck and took a step. They fell, tripping over the body of the guard, who let out another loud moan. "Get up, now. We must get out. This is the man who took me from the cabbage patch. Move, Georgie, move now or we will die."

"Die," groaned the man as he tried to get up. "I'm gonna die."

Sydney stood up and took a step—right on his stomach. The air rushed out of the fallen man in a whoosh. "Come on Georgie. Crawl over him if you must. Just let's go." She grabbed his shirt and pulled. "You weigh a ton, George. You gotta help if we are to stay alive and be gone."

"I'm jist catchin' me wind and me legs don't work too well."

"It don't matter. Get up. Be a man. Someone will miss me soon enough. We've been down here for hours."

George stood up and stepped forward. Once more he fell square on the man's stomach.

"Git off a me gut. I canna breathe. And listen, both a ya, git you out a here. I canna take much more. You be killing me. Ain't no one ta find you. They be gone an' Captain William, too. Now git afore you do me in."

George scrambled to his feet. Still shaky he used his foot to find the body and stepped with care over it. He turned back. "There be no one on guard, you say."

"Nay much. Just be careful and stay in the shadows. There be rope in the bow o' the boat. Jist go over and down and head fer the hills. It be on yer way home. Now git. I alles thought it stupid anyway to git ya, lass. Yer more trouble than yer worth."

Sydney hissed at him and then peeked through the slit of the open door. She listened. She heard nothing but the creak of the boat as it wallowed in the water. "Come Georgie, let's go home." She stepped through the door, Georgie right behind her.

The trip to the bow of the ship was without incident. The man was right; no guard to elude. Georgie secured the rope to the low rail. Sydney climbed down first hindered by her voluminous skirts. Georgie started down as soon as she cleared the rail. Once on the ground, George grabbed Sydney's hand and they sprinted to the small copse of trees. They were headed home.

East 'o the Sun

William was at the gate of East o' the Sun. He wondered why the summons at such a crucial time. Something was afoot. Walsingham would make it clear upon meeting. The guards at the gate stopped his ruminations. "Halt!" they cried as one voice.

The guard on the left shouted, "Who goes there?"

"Captain William James of Her Majesty's Army." William cried back. "I have been summoned by Lord Walsingham. Tell him I have arrived."

"Yes sir. You are expected. Enter these gates in peace but make it quick. I will fetch Lord Walsingham immediately. Proceed."

The courtyard was large, and men in uniform occupied training exercises. The villagers were few, and they scurried about with frightened looks on their faces. *Something truly is afoot* thought William.

William got to the castle entrance. The guard there asked, "What be yer business with...."

William interrupted. "I am under orders to report *post haste* to Lord Walsingham, Captain William James. Please grain my mount. My men are not far behind on foot. Please treat them to some decent food and lodgings. Their prior ones were not their custom. They may be men of the sea, but they are used to private ships not musty old fishing boats. Lord Walsingham if you please."

William was allowed entry and was led to Walsingham's rooms. They passed through a grand reception hall hung with rich tapestries. Torches lit the area casting shadows in niches. This hall had the chill of a cave. There seemed to be no doors nor any hall away to lead to the deeper chasms of the castle. No noise of occupancy reached his ears. *The towers must be the areas of activity for this house,* William thought. *There is more to this place than meets the eye. Where are the chapels, the main halls? This is the Queen's castle, and she does come. She is head of the church even in this country and needs have a place to celebrate. Even so, this castle was comfort in name only. This was a fighting place, a place to form and execute attacks. There was no peace here; no comfort. The Queen was coming for the ships, to boost morale and defeat the smugglers from the Irish shores. She was making ready to meet the Spanish!*

William was deep in thought when Walsingham greeted William with a warm hand up as William knelt before him. "William, no need. Stand! What have you to report and why your large contingent? Is anyone guarding the ship?"

"Nay, Sir, my orders were to leave the ship and make sure that it would be released into the sea as soon as all were on land. I left my right arm to ensure that the orders were fulfilled."

"Are you in need of food and drink?" Walsingham asked.

"Nay, but my men will be. They have walked long and hard with no break from the sea. Please see to them when they arrive." William laughed a humorless laugh. "They look like a ragtag bunch, but they are highly trained agents for both land and sea.

"My Lord, I believe we are in great danger and for no good reason. We grabbed a young woman from a pub a day or so from here. She knows nothing. After a few days a young lad shows up. Sam Jones grabbed him and called me. This lad was being the *gallant* to save her. I questioned him and ordered that he be put in shackles, but he knew nothing as well. They are both young.

"Then, shortly after the young lady, a Mr. Gilpin shows up and demands that she be tortured to make her talk. Who is this Gilpin? I know nothing of him and that disturbs me that he knew where we were anchored and why.

Furthermore, there have been no ships by in a month but the posts. My men followed the beach and saw ships anchoring further down and leaving by the same route they came. I fear we are discovered."

"I told none of this to Gilpin. I left the ship unguarded so those two children could use their brains and get out. I left Sam there to "guard" them. I hope he fares better than he did with the girl. She's a lively one." The wistful look in William's eyes told Walsingham the rest of the story.

"William, good work and good thinking. I will dispatch a ship to come round the southern route of the sea. Your crew deserve some leave. You have a trip toward London. The Queen is coming this way in a week or so. You need to meet her and be her eyes and ears. You need to make haste. There is a pub she stops at, The Cock and the Sow. She likes to sup there. Check it out on your way. Intercept her and escort her that far. I will have men to take her the rest of the way with you as scout ahead. After that you have a few days to make things right before your next assignment."

"Sir, have you seen that Gilpin fellow? I believe him to be very dangerous and out only for his own interests. He makes my skin crawl."

Walsingham chuckled, "A good observation. Mine as well. I have him put away safe for now. Your mount and supplies await you. The Queen thanks you. I thank you. I wish there were some more time, but we are against it."

"I am gone, Walsingham. God be with you, the Queen and those children." William saluted and left. The best reward for him was to be on horseback riding on dry land doing real service. This ride on the road to

London would leave room to dream of the red-haired wench that captured his heart.

***

"Tildy, I know she be yer only chick, but chicks do grow to be hens."

"You be good fer me, Morvyn. I hope you're right about the girl. I do miss her so.

"You have customers without. What 'er we servin' t'day?" Evan wore his leather apron newly splashed with drink.

Tildy glanced at the window darkened with dusk. "Oh, I just wandered in my own thoughts. I'll be right out ta get what you needs. We have the usual and a cream cake as well. Where be Sarah?"

"I dinna know, but git the food. These folks be hungry. They be dressed nice, too."

"I'll be right out," Tildy replied with a tinge of annoyance in her voice. "Hold a minute, Morvyn." Tildy went out to the dining room. Four healthy hardy men sat sipping Evan's ale and talking softly. Conversation halted when she approached. "I hear ye be hungry, good sirs. We have meat pasties, a stew, a couple of roast birds, fruit pies and a fresh made cream cake fer ya. We also have tea and a new drink many in this country have called café. You drink it wi' fresh cream and a bit o' sweet. It be pricey, but ye drink it wi' yer sweet if ye want one."

"Just bring some food and we ken it later," one of the men said.

Tildy went back to the kitchen. She gathered the bowls and plates and set up a big plate of fresh bread with a bowl of fresh butter and took them to the table. Again, the men fell silent at her approach. "I will git the rest on my next trip out," And she left.

"Morvyn, slip out to the room and get within hearing distance of the men," she whispered. "They stop talking when I approach. They may know something of Sydney. I'll bring you a tidly of wine and set it on the table behind them when I go this time." Tildy put up some pasties and a large bowl of stew. "I must put in a ladle for this," she spoke out loud, "And some of those roots I baked. They be good." Laden with the tray she made her way to the table and deposited the food. "Enjoy yer meal, gents. I'll leave you be. If you want more drink just let my husband know." She went to the bar and got a small glass of wine, took a sip and casually set it out on the table behind the men, a bench back separating them. Morvyn came and slipped into the bench. The men concentrated on their food and were unaware of the new body behind them. Morvyn could hear every word, and these men were not discussing the whereabouts of Sydney.

"This food is this good. Imagine a cream cake in a wilderness like this."

"I am getting sleepy. Should we stay the night or push on?"

"I vote for staying and another tankard. When have you tasted ale this sweet? Then in the morning after we breakfast, we push on."

"You're always hungry, Ethan, but staying is a good idea." Tildy came to clear the table. The food was gone. "Miss, we'll have some of that cream cake you have and half a pie. Ferget the tea. This ale is sweet enough to go with anything. Oh, and do you have any rooms for let, good woman?"

"Aye, we do. Do you want ta bunk up or have separate rooms?"

"Each his own."

"I kin do it fer you. I'll tell Evan ta bring ale. Your rooms are ready when you are." Tildy left with her hands full, nodding at Evan about the ale. She went to the kitchen and made the desserts ready. She brewed Morvyn an herbal mix to help her sleep and went back out to the pub with all on her tray. At the table she set out plates with forks and the half pie and a generous slice of the cream cake enough for four, if they wanted. She slipped the tea to Morvyn's table unnoticed. It had disappeared by the time Evan brought the pitcher of ale to the table.

The men divided the sweets and a look of joy spread over the first one to taste the cream cake. "This is the best cream cake I ever ate. Even the Queen canna ha'e better. Who be the baker here?" The Scot started to wax poetic. "This food, this sweet, I ha'e ne'er tasted better in court."

"Shut yer mouth, you daft bastard."

"The cook be my wife, the lady what served you. She be the best in these parts"

"Ach, nae, say it isn't so. I am in dire need of a wife and that lass would be perfect. What heaven comes from her kitchen."

The rest at the table mumbled agreement between bites. An hour later, sated with food and drink, one of the men asked for his room when Evan returned once more with his pitcher.

"I'll have me wife show you to your rooms. One last for the stairs?"

"As you say, jest a wee one," responded the Scot, "you haven't any of the strong, hae ye?"

"Nay, we don't serve that here. I'll get my wife. Sleep well my good men."

Evan poured half glasses all around and went to the kitchen. "Your men are ready to whisk you away to be their wife. They are in love with your cooking, my love. They are also in great need of some sleep."

"Aye, my love, I will get them to their beds and us to ours as well. I told the boy to care for their horses."

Tildy went into the pub and herded the men upstairs. Meanwhile, Morvyn, who had sunk back into the dark corner with their going could hardly wait for them to disappear before she slunk into the kitchen to wait for Tildy to come back for the tidying up. She had a tale to tell.

Going Home

Once hidden in the copse of trees the children stopped to get their bearings. "We must work our way to the cliffs and get up over to the road to go home." George whispered.

Sydney looked up. "Georgie, that cliff be too high to climb with me in a dress like this. Close your eyes and unbutton me. Are you sure this is the right direction?" George closed his eyes and fumbled with the buttons. Done, Sydney folded it and stuffed it up her nethers. "I left my sack in the room. Twas not fit for wear anyway. I cut it from stem to stern. I have my nether wear. 'Twill not look too bad should we be seen." Her vest bulged with her new found chest as she turned and faced George with a "How do I look?"

"Like an overblown whore. Let's get going. I think I came in from the bow of the ship. This is the stern. Now get a move on. We needs be gone from this place." George was grumpy. His head spun with unwelcome thoughts. *Is she still pure? If not, was she with child?* These unwanted but persistent thoughts about Sydney kept his mood foul.

"You be brown colored already. I will show up on that cliff in these whites. Either we need to go afore anyone sees us or we need to go further down on the sand before climbing. Either way we needs hurry afore anyone knows we're gone." She grabbed George's hand and dragged him further into the copse of trees. It ended suddenly as it began and before them stretched bare sand and rocks. As she stepped out into the sunshine George pulled her back in the shelter of the trees. Impatiently she pulled her hand from his and said, "George, we have to go."

"Just a minute, let me look." Georgie scanned the beach and the cliff. He saw a great overhang that leveled out further down the naked sand. The sand strewn with rocks had none large enough to hide more than one person. "We will make for that cliff and the overhang. The overhang with shade will help hide us. Do you see where it evens out down the way?" Sydney nodded. "That is where we will try to scale. It should be lower, less steep. Have you ever climbed anything other than a tree?"

She looked at Georgie. "No."

"Start running. I will be right behind you. Stop when you reach the cliff. We can see our way more closely there. Sydney said nothing more. She start to run as if slung by a bow. George ran close behind her. The area was bare; no people, no prying eyes. The two made it to the overhang.

Catching her breath Sydney looked up. "How did you get here? Is there a road up top of that cliff or is it a long walk to the road? Is there any cover to hide us along the way to home?"

George panted part of his answer. "I came through the dark wood beyond and got to the road what follow the cliff. I were at least three days out afore I saw the ship's mast I think. The dark made me lose time sense. Anyway I climbed down a bit into a cave to keep me from the wet of the rain and just missed a unit marching toward Holyhead or the Queen's castle, I don't know which. When the rain stopped, I tried to get out and up but lost me footing and fell down the side. That's why I be so brown, but Syd, that ship.... She be not a pirate ship. Don't ask how I know, I just know."

"Oh, Georgie, you be right. Sir William, that's the captain of the ship, is a spy to capture some pirates or smugglers. I were taken because of Da's pub and the smuggling. They thought Da be a smuggler king or something. I told Sir William that he be daft. Me Da would never do nothing like that.

"There be a man, Gilpin, what came into the Captain's room. He asked me questions, but I didna' know nothing, so he demanded that Sir William start to make me talk. I dinna like that Gilpin. He looked at me like I were an easy girl. Sir William didna like him neither. He told him to go to the Queen's castle, if he weren't happy with my answers. I was his prisoner, not Gilpin's and he needs to leave his hands offin' me.

"And, oh Georgie, Sir William he be so sweet and kind and funny. Georgie, he were such a gentleman. He didna try nothing with me. You know I wish he...."

"Girl, we needs get going if we are to get home," George interrupted. "Syd, are ye in love with him?"

"Oh Georgie, you know I love you, but I think I am. He stirs my innards. Ye never did that. How can I love two?"

Back at the Inn—the Same Day

The four men settled into their comfortable clean smelling rooms. Tildy and Sarah made their way down the hall. Loud snores sounded from the first two rooms. Sarah whispered, "They be more tired than they thought."

"Hush, we needs collect Morvyn and hear what she heard. Hurry! Evan be waiting fer me ta' help, it be not too late. We may have one or two more."

The two women ran down the stairs and stopped short. People had filled the pub in the few minutes the two were upstairs. Tildy recognized one or two of them as regulars. The rest were strangers. Tildy sent Sarah to help Morvyn back to the kitchen. Tildy made her way to Evan. "Whence came these?"

"They be from Bryn a Cywd. They say some of the men going toward the sea saw a pirate ship sail out the bay. They say there be no pirates fer over a month, since the patrols left. Things be stirrin', Tildy,

love. Help me get some ale to these men. Do you have
any meals left? I needs get another barrel on the
ready. Business be good tonight. Go, an I'll be right
back."

Tildy drew a pitcher and passed through the
pub refilling mugs and collecting coin. She glanced
over to the seat where Morvyn hid. The bench was
empty. Tildy relaxed a bit.

As she moved through the crowd, she kept her
ears open. Most of what she heard was about the ship
and how it brazenly swept down the bay under full
sail, flying the skull and cross bones on its tallest
mast. Tildy didn't know that this was highly unusual,
an open invitation to the privateers running patrol to
open fire and ask questions later of any survivors
before hanging them.

Evan reappeared with the new cask. Tildy gave
him the coin she collected and made her way back to
the kitchen. Morvyn and Sarah sat, each with a cup of
herbal tea, one for sleep and one medicinal. They both
looked up and smiled when Tildy bustled in. "Have a
cup'a, Tildy?" Sarah offered her a full cup of tea.

"Come sit and I will tell all," said Morvyn
excitement emanating from her face.

"The house be full. Do you know why that be?
The pirates! Mayhaps the pirate what took my Sydney.
And they just sailed away down the bay in front of
God and everybody. That's what the men from the
village say. Do you know what that means? My Sydney
be gone and possibly ruined." Tildy, sobbing,
continued, "They be taking her Holy Heaven knows

where and she be lost ta' me forever." Salty tears mixed with the sweet tea.

"Tildy, quiet me lass, all may not be lost." Morvyn wrapped a comforting arm around Tildy's shoulders. "Them four gents you and sister Sarah showed to rooms? Them be Queen's men. And they be going to the castle. They say the Queen be comin' and she be staying fer a while. They said a full court contingent and a full regiment be stayin' there too. She intends to rule Britannia from here. They also said Walsingham, her head spy, be there already and he takes prisoners every day. He is running operations from East o' the Sun. Them four be spies.

After they drank of Evan's ale and declared it to be the best they ever tasted. One of them called your cream cake 'the stuff dreams is made of'. The cream cake man said he heard that from some play he saw in London. It were by some guy by the name of Shake-speare. Then they talked about other things I couldn't quite make out.

"Another said it be the best food they ever ate even in London. So, what think you of that, my girl? Oh, an' I fergot to tell ya that I made them some sleepin' tea, so's if you want ta' go through their things, you have no fear. They be socked away for the night."

" Oh, Morvyn, nay. This is not how we do things here. Is that why you served them, Sarah? Be ashamed cousin, sister. 'Twas not right to drug those poor boys. What a head they will have in the morning what with the ale and the tea! Shame on both of you and...." Tildy started to laugh but then teared up again. "It still don't bring back my Sydney."

The women sat quiet for a few minutes, each lost in her own thoughts. Evan appeared, "I be needin' some help out....what be goin' on in here?" He stopped. "Three quiet women? Be I dead and gone to heaven?"

Tildy shook her head and dried her tears, "Evan, I be right there. You need ta know we have four Queen's men abed above. Be sure the boy takes good care of their mounts."

"Jest git out there. I needs another barrel an' some bloke asked fer wine!"

"Mayhaps we needs look at what Morvyn heard ta be true, after all that be why she come back so soon," Tildy gave Evan a quick kiss on the cheek and swept out into the great room. The night went long, and it was the wee hours before they went to bed, exhausted.

***

William prayed that his Sydney escaped unharmed. His concern did not quite reach to the young man, but he knew Sydney might need his protection along the road. *Be safe and well my little love....* he thought. If it is to be.... He put his thoughts on the girl in the safe place in his heart and turned them once more to the assignment at hand. He called for his mount, and as he waited, he thought of the honor of escorting the Queen to her castle. *Something must be afoot for her to come out here for a long term.* A page brought his horse. He mounted up and rode through the gate on his journey to London.

Half a day on the road with no excitement or even any other travelers was a first for William. He spent the day dreaming of a wonderful ending to his story; inherit the title, get the girl, settle in with lots of children. He pictured Sydney, her hair released from the bonds of propriety running about the estate, their children surrounding her in play. She was a wonderful mother and companion. Her presence in court was that of tamed wild beauty. What a wonderful life they could have. His horse stopped and he looked up to see the sign of The Cock and the Sow and a boy ready for him to dismount. This was the place Walsingham mentioned with the great food and ale. The sun was behind him now almost set. He had no idea where the day went. It was time for a bite and a pint. He dismounted and asked the boy "Does this place have beds for the night?"

"Aye, Sir, jest go on in. They be happy ta help ya." With that the boy took the horse and talked to it on the way to the stable. "You will have a nice bag of oats and a good rubdown after your day on that dusty road. A nice rest for the night and you'll love the water, clear and clean from the well. Come along old boy and let's get you settled."

William heard most of this conversation and decided his mount was in a good place for the night; if only the humans were treated the same inside the pub. William opened the door to the pub and walked in. He was glad that he dressed in dark breeches and doublet and eschewed the white ruff so common among the gentry in favor of an inconspicuous presence.

The room was dim as should be a pub, but there was enough light to see the four men to his left deep in their cups and conversation. A shadow hid in the booth behind them. There were a couple of other men standing near the keep, sipping their ales. He went to a table and sat and watched a few more men enter. A sweet looking woman came to his table and asked, "Do you want a dinner tonight? The ale is made here. Can I get you a tankard?"

"Yes, ma'am, a tankard would be nice and a bowl of stew and some bread if you have it. Do you have a room?"

"I'll git your food when my husband comes back with the keg." She placed a flacon on the table and poured from her pitcher. "And yes, we have one room left. It be fer servants but is still comfortable and clean. Do you want it fer tonight?"

William took a sip of the ale and then another his mouth surprised at the wonderful flavor. Putting the tankard down on the table, he said, "I cannot stay. Thank you. And ma'am, if the food be as good as the ale, I am in heaven." His thoughts turned to the ghastly provenance on that ship, which brought him to the red-haired gamin he'd left on board. Once again, he rued not taking her directly to a priest and wedding her. Lost in thought he started when Tildy brought him a bowl of steaming stew, fresh baked bread and butter. "My God I am in heaven." He muttered into his first bite.

***

"Stop, George," she panted. George stopped.

"What now, my queen?" He was tired and hungry and a solution to their problems did not immediately show. His attitude was less than gracious.

Sydney and George had reached the overhang and walked more slowly down the beach to easier access for the climb. They said nothing. Sydney, leading the small march looked over her shoulder every few minutes to see if they were followed, but the coast and the beach seemed clear.

Sydney thought the sun crept closer and closer the further down the sands they went. Night was drawing nigh and a place to rest was in the offing. The overhang disappeared as did their shade and hiding place. They both stopped. Sydney looked up at the sheer cliff of compacted soils. A few straggling plants stuck out but did not look sturdy enough to support their weight. Sydney shifted her purloined dress around so she could breathe easier.

"This is too easy. You don't think they let us go on purpose, do you? We have to walk, but there is no one to follow. Mayhaps we be not as important as we think," said Sidney. *William did this* she thought. *He let her go. What was she thinking; that he would whisk her away and wed and they would live in bliss like Tildy and Evan?* "Oh, I be a fool. Georgie. When can we start to climb?"

"And when there is a little slant to this cliff, and we can find purchase. We be not climbers. Then when we are rested, we will just keep walking. Oh, and get rid of that dress, if it is too much bother. You won't need it onct we be home."

"If we ever get there. We used half the day and we still be on the beach. You said it be not that far. Two days at the most you said, and we still be walking on the beach."

"Damn it, Syd, it be two days onct we be on the road. And we be only a couple of hours from the brig. I do not ken where we be right now. I came in the other direction and if that wee brain of yours remembers, I fell down the cliff. Now if you can't help, just be quiet and keep walking."

"Don't swear at me you brute. My feet hurt. These shoes be not fer walkin' but fer dancin' on a fine flat solid floor. I dinna think any fine ladies go this far with these shoes," Sydney whined.

"By the heavens that be, take the damn shoes off. Go barefoot! It be not that long that you dress so." Sydney scrunched up her face. "Be quiet, and don't cry. Take yer shoes off. I want ta see yer feet." Syd removed her shoes and revealed several nasty blisters and a couple more forming. "Wot did ye do with yer own shoes, girl?"

"I were barefoot in the cabbage field when they took me. I were carried most of the trip in a sack." Sydney rubbed her feet.

"Well, this will ne'er do. You need ta cover yer feet. 'Tis nae good fer ya wi' these blisters. The sand 'll get in and hurt worse."

"I can walk this way fer awhile. This feels so much better without the shoes."

"Nay, ya daft girl, wrap yer feet wi some fabric. Let me get a bit from yer petticoat. Where's yer knife?"

"I...I have no knife. It were took when they caught me after I stabbed a man." Sydney started to yank at the bottoms of her petticoat, tears collecting in the corners of her eyes. It was a pretty one, but William had taken her halbdagger as well as her heart.

The two made a small resting place. George took the first watch as the sun disappeared into the sea. He watched all night.

The next morning at dawn, Georgie and Sydney continued their trek down the sandy beach. George pulled Sydney to the ground and covered her as the sound of horses galloping above reached their ears. Smooshed in against the side of the cliff and flat on the ground they would not be seen unless some sharp-eyed soldier looked down. The horses past, Sydney wiggled under Georgie's weight. "Git off a me ya oaf. They would not see us against the cliff. No one be looking fer us. Now, git off."

"Why? 'Tis the first time I have ya pinned since afore ye left home." A huge grin spread across his face. He was enjoying this. "So, wot say Syd, me love, would ya be thinkin' of marryin' me when we git back home?" He shifted his weight and sat up and back on his heels with her legs beneath him. "Ya know the folks 'ull be expectin' it. They ha' been since we be children and since we be so long together, even if we not be with child, they will think the worst. So, what do ya...."

Sydney heaved her legs and sent George toppling. She scrambled for her balance and sat on his stomach. "Georgie, we canna marry. You know that we be cousins and we wouldna' be allowed. There will ne'er be a child, not ever. Naught will happen. I will bounce a rock on your head first."

"You love me. I love you." George made a slight face that Sydney didn't ken. "Look, I gotta tell ya what yer pa told me afore I left to find you. Sydney...."

Sydney shifted her weight off George. "Sit up, ya oaf. What did me pa tell you afore you left? 'Go find her, George, and bring her back'?"

"Nay, Sydney, it were more important."

"George, what was more important than finding me?"

"Nay, Syd, it were different. Syd, we be not cousins. We be not related at all."

"My pa told you that?"

"Yes, Syd, your pa. You are not really related by blood to yer ma and pa neither."

"Nay, Georgie, I look just like me ma right down to the red hair and all. She be my ma, all right. And my eyes, they be blue just like my pa."

"Nay, Syd, yer pa told me that yer Aunt Morvyn brought ya to them when ye was just a brand-new babe. That you have red hair is just, just what is it called? I am yer Pa's nephew, but ye are not yer pa's daughter nor yer ma's. Oh bother, I can't say it any plainer than that."

Sydney got off George's legs and sat against the dirt of the cliff for support. George looked at her and got a bit scared of her pale face. She looked like a spirit passed over her and took her soul. For the first time in her life Sydney was speechless.

George kneeled in front of her, begging, "Syd, listen to me. We was meant fer each other. We spent our whole lives playing together, eating together and working side by side. I taught you everything I could about the beasties and the fields, and yer ma taught you how to bake and cook. Yer gonna have The Cock and the Sow. I helped Uncle make the ale and he give me his recipe. I hae made it meself wi' no help several times and nobody kenned the difference. We could have a good life together."

"George, listen to me. Before I was taken, I thought that was how our life would be. I was satisfied to share the inn with you. There was ye and there was me and we would carry on the same as me ma and pa but without the bedroom. We would be partners in business only. There would be no children between us. Folks could talk as they would, but we would be all right...."

George interrupted, "Syd, there's something you should know...."

"George, I ain't done yet...."

"Yes, you are. You needs listen to me. Sydney we...."

"George, can we be seen from the top, there? It don't seem so far down, and maybe we can climb where there be twigs to catch and...." Sydney was done listening.

George reached for a low-hanging growth and tested his weight on it. It held. The climb would be easier than that where he fell. They both could do it in a reasonable time. "Syd, we can make a climb here. Your feet should be fine. You have done more than this jest fer fun. Let's do it here afore any more troops pass. We don't know what is above, so I will go first.

Sydney started to climb, Georgie right behind her. "Oh, Georgie, you be my best friend, but I don't want ta marry ya neither.

And Syd, I'm glad you don't want ta marry me. I have...." George began.

"Let's do that climb an' git home. Last one up is sow spore." Sydney closed the conversation. "This climb be easy, Georgie," panted Sydney. "I am goin' up quick. OOPs! The branch come out o' the ground. Watch out. I'm comin' down a bit." She flailed and caught onto another branch she'd used earlier. "You better not be beneath me, Georgie. I might conk ya agin, if'n I fall on yer head."

"Aye, and ye might break yer own neck, too. Jest be careful. This ain't a race."

"'Tis too, an I'm winnin'."

The two scrambled to the top George in the lead. "Sow's spore, Syd. You be sow's spore. Now hush while I look ta see what be about. Be ready ta go down a step or two if I tell ya. We ought not be seen, just in case."

"What see you?"

"Let me look." He peeked over the top of the berm. There was nothing coming or going. There was also no protection in sight. "It be clear, but we needs hurry. There be no trees nor bushes fer hiding, so hie yerself up and over and lets be gone." George lifted himself over the edge and once he had purchase, he reached for Sydney's hand and pulled her up.

She dusted herself off as she looked around. "There be nothing here but a path. Those trees is a bit far off. Do you know where we are?"

"Nay, but I do know we needs get movin' an' I think this way. Let's go home, Syd."

The two walked down the smooth dirt road, Sydney barefoot but for her petticoat wrappings, George with long strides. Gaining a copse of trees or bushes was the immediate object, some place to hide in case of horsemen or even a troop. Walking men would indicate nothing. They saw no one on the way.

They walked for about a half an hour and finally reached a small grouping of bushes when an earth tremor came up through Sydney's bare feet. "George the earth be shaking."

"Syd hide here. Dig into the bush fer coverage. I think they be horses even if we canna' see 'em. Be very still."

The horsemen came into sight. They were a small cadre of soldiers and rode at a furious pace, their concentration bent on the road beneath them with no expectation of interception by a pursuing cadre. Sydney peeked out and thought she saw William. She was about to call out to him when George slammed his hand over her mouth. "Hush, are ye daft? Mayhaps these are the ones what held us." Sydney squirmed in his tight grasp, but the horsemen were out of range already. "We have to pay attention. We can't get caught. I think we be only a couple o' days from the village. How are yer feet? Ready ta try them shoes agin?"

"This be okay fer me. If it gets worse, I'll put them shoes on, but they not be made fer walking on the rough. Let's just get movin'." The two went on each lost in their own thoughts.

***

The inn was busy. The increased patronage made life a bit more bearable for Tildy. Evan and the stable boy were happy with their extra cash. Evan looked forward to the new season for ale making. His hops were close to ripe and the grains were various shades of golden in the fields. Another month or so would bring the fall and he would be busy with the harvest. He missed George. The new boy was good and kind, but he hadn't the rapport with the animals Georgie had, and he didn't work quite as hard as Georgie did. And there was no Sydney for him to play with. Evan leaned on his rake before washing up for his breakfast. Life just wasn't as rich even with the extra cash.

Tildy looked out the kitchen door. She could see her little darling playing in the garden, but that was years ago and her little darling was a young woman now. *Life brought interesting and sometimes sad experiences,* she thought as she kneaded her famous bread dough.

Morvyn lay back on her pillows. *I am not going to make another trip to this place,* she thought. *Nothing makes my heart beat faster. I feel it slow in my body and my breath comes harder every day. No, I will not be back here once I leave. I must get up. Breathing is easier when I am up.* She sat up and edged her legs over the side of the mattress. A few more breaths and she stood and proceeded with her morning rituals.

Sarah had a small commission for her needlework. She looked up from the fine work and rested her eyes, glancing out the small window in her loft house. She missed her Georgie. *By this time, we would have a wedding and perhaps a babe on the way. My sight is getting too weak for this kind of work. I am better suited for bringing the food to the patrons. This be my last commission. I needs go to Branwen's house and see the progress there. I could hold the new one and sing again. Oh, Georgie, where are you?*

The Way West

The day was hot and there were no clouds in the sky promising a cooling shower in the afternoon. There was no chance of doffing jacket and vest. One must be properly dressed in the presence of the Queen.

William rode at the front of the 'parade'. The Queen was on the move and the entourage went forward at a fast pace. William had no time for thoughts of Sydney. He was the lookout for outlaw thieves on this road. It was common knowledge that, if one traveled by land, bandits were there to take your worldly goods if not your life. On the seas it was the pirates. *Thieves are thieves*, thought William, *but to be stupid enough to assault this group of soldiers and Queen's Guards was foolhardy.* Still he kept his eyes and ears open and alert. At this pace they were at least a day from that wonderful inn of a week ago.

***

George and Sydney walked down the dusty path. George mumbled to himself about location and Sydney just marched on ignoring him. It was hot out and the dust they raised by just walking cooked into their sweat.

Sydney knew there was a hard crust forming on her outsides just like the one she was forming in her mind about George and her parents and...well maybe not William just yet. That would take some time to jostle around. At least her feet didn't hurt, and the blisters were dried up mud scabs. And her 'new' petticoat was ruined forever. *Damn you Georgie!*

"George are we going in the right direction? We should have come to something by now, don't you think?"

George stopped so short that Sydney bumped into him. "Quit yer whinin', Syd, and be careful. Do you think it easy fer me? I think we be lost, and I don't know how. The sun be in the right direction and now it be hot enough that I am wet with me own juices. Any hotter an' I be cooked. An' look at you wi' naught but yer underwear. You be the cool one, but you'll be burned by the end o' the trip. Don't tell me your hurtin' or you want water. I ain't got none, an' I don't see any trees ahead where a pool or a crick might be. And yer right, Syd, we be lost, and I should na' be yelling at ya' fer my mistake. I think we went too far along the beach and we be on a road south o' where we should be.

"We been walking for days and there is no water nor food. If there be nothing in the next mile, I say we go in the right direction by the sun before it get dark."

"Good idea, my girl, good idea. I shoulda thought of it meself. Why wait? The sun be at our back and that be west, so we needs just go right fer awhile. Let's move an' see what we get in ta afore dark."

They left the road and finally were headed in the direction of the Cock and the Sow, George hoped. He did not know that they were several miles, less than a day's walk from the inn.

***

Gilpin figured it out. He was in gaol. Walsingham had him imprisoned and for what? He was only doing his job. His important information would save this land and stop the smugglers forever. What was the problem? He knew somewhere someone could hear him. He started yelling.

A passing chamber maid heard the noise and thought that spirits were in the walls. She ran crying to the housekeeper. Gilpin did not cry out in vain.

The Stop

The Queen was hungry for a hot meal and a rest from the constant motion of the carriage and the petty annoyances listed in the papers on her lap. She knocked on the wall and a head appeared in her window. "Yes, Ma'am"

"How far are we from an inn or a pub?"

"A few miles, Ma'am"

"We will stop for a break. Send someone ahead to clear the way" She dismissed the coachman with a nod and got back to her work.

"Captain, the Queen wishes to stop for a meal and a rest. What is in front of us?"

William said, "The Cock and the Sow. Best food and drink I have ever had, and it stuck here in the countryside."

"Her Majesty requested that the way be cleared, and the inn notified of her coming."

"She will not be unhappy with her choice. I will order that the way be cleared and let the inn know of our arrival." The cavalcade kept moving and William dispatched a corporal to the inn with specific orders for the number and stabling of the horses for the stay. They needed rest, too.

The Arrival

In the late afternoon, dusty and tired the two escapees arrived at the kitchen door of the pub. Sydney burst in. No one was in the kitchen. *Where were they? Her mum was not cooking. What happened in the short time she was gone?* George bumped into disrupting her ruminations.

"Where is everyone?" he asked

"I'm going into the pub," she said, "This is strange, and it is giving me butterflies."

She went through the passage into the pub and stopped short. Everyone was there, Mum, Da and... and the Queen? The room was packed with people eating, drinking and talking in the middle of the day. *And what is the Queen doing here?* Sydney's thoughts ran rampant.

George bumped into her in his haste and peeked over her shoulder. His jaw dropped and with mouth gaping he arrived beside Sydney. Evan was the first to notice them and their condition. He walked over to them and shielded them with his body. "What, where ha' ye been? George. You found 'er but what took so long? Sydney are you all right? He ha' touched you? You're both filthy dirty and the Queen bein' here and all. Go wash and straighten yer clothes and come back in dressed proper, wi' shoes, Sydney. Go now an' I will tell your ma."

"Yes, Da," replied Sydney and turned to go, dragging George with her. In the kitchen, she said to George, "Go and wash up at the trough. I needs get some clothes from the back. I canna be looking at the Queen dressed like this."

George looked at her and said, "Sydney, you look just like the Queen, freckles and all."

"You are daft, Georgie. She ha' no freckles and she be dressed so nice even for a carriage ride. Go wash up. Do you have a clean blouse and pants for your presentation? Go quickly. I'll be ready when you come back. We both have to get the sweat and dust off us."

"I have all of that in the stables. I'll take a few and bathe myself clean and change for your majesty."

Sydney threw her court shoes on the table and went to the water trough by the sink. She soaked her face and head in the leftover water. She grabbed a clean towel and wet it enough to wash her arms and feet. She dragged the green dress from her middle and shook it out. It was a rumpled mess, but it was better than being seen in her undergarments. She smoothed it the best she could and put it on. She felt like a queen in this green silk. She reached the court shoes from the table and put them on her feet. She wished she had stockings to protect her new shoes and look more ladylike, but this would have to do for the moment. Never had she longed for the white muslins of her childhood.

George was back just as she fastened the last buckle on the shoes. He smelled good and looked clean. His shirt was snowy white and his pants his regular browns, but clean. "Are you ready?" She asked.

"Much as I'll ever be." He said.

They proceeded to enter the pub in a decorous fashion more than the push and shove of a few minutes ago. Evan looked up from his pouring and dropped the stein on the floor. It shattered at his feet and he didn't know it. The sound of the pottery breaking stopped talk around the small shelf and when that stopped more looked at them. Within seconds all eyes were on the girl in the green dress and the farm hand beside her. They were holding hands, a slightly terrified look in their eyes.

Tildy glanced up from her service and dropped the plate on the table. Her Sydney was back. She rushed over and wrapped her arms around the girl. Sarah did the same with George. Morvyn who was ensconced in her usual seat, sent a silent 'thank you' to the universe and the Queen of England looked up at the girl and boy. Her eyes widened in recognition. Silence washed over the room for enough of a moment that the comment '...looks like the Queen..." was very audible from a lone male voice somewhere in the dimness.

William walked in the room from the stables. When he opened the door, he stood in the light, so his face was not visible, but he saw Sydney. He stood stock still and his heart clutched with recognition.

Sydney glanced over her Ma's shoulder. The shape in the door looked, well, familiar, but then any tall person with pants looked familiar in the half light of the pub. She moved away from Tildy's arms and headed to the kitchen. A page touched her arm. "The Queen wants you," he said.

"The Queen? Where is she? I am not dressed." Sydney replied.

"Follow me." The page led Sydney to the back corner of the pub, a small but more private table. The Queen, being the Queen, sat ramrod straight, the leader of her people. To Sydney's thought she was almost doll-like, not real.

Murmurs spread through the pub like a small wave lapping the shore of a lake. The click of a fork on a plate or a stein hitting the table and some variant whispering was all there was to be heard for the next few minutes.

"Bring some light. I must see this person, who looks like me. It could be useful someday." An attendant brought a candle and the two of them were bathed in the soft glow. "I saw you when you were two years old. You have grown up into a beautiful woman. Are you happy here, my child? What is your name? I don't remember. How old are you?"

Sydney curtsied the best she could in the heeled shoes and long rumpled dress. "Sydney, Your Majesty. I am fifteen years old. I am very happy to be home. You see I was kidnapped. I have been gone a long time and it took many days to get back here. My cousin George rescued me and now he says he isn't my cousin, but that can't…"

"Silence, my child. I didn't ask for your life's history. Ah, you do look like me. You are beautiful. I suppose we all have a common ancestor here in England."

Sydney replied, "This is Wales, not England, so that is not possible, is it Ma'am."

"No , I suppose not. Still it is uncanny, is it not?" The Queen smiled. Her secret would be safe. There was no one else alive on earth that knew, that could possibly put the puzzle together. Her father journeyed from England on a hunting trips. He used the castle East 'o the Sun, she was sure. "Thank you for talking with me, lass. You have grown up fine and healthy, and you have a beau in that young man. You may go now and have a wonderful life. Daniel, give the young woman this." And with that Sydney's audience with the Queen of England was over. Daniel pressed a small bag of coin into Sydney's hand and the Queen turned to finish her tea. Sydney curtsied to the Queen's side and left the table.

***

Morvyn overheard everything. She thought of that long-ago night when the serving wench brought the lovely girl child to her for murder and burial. She thought of the clothes Tildy had hidden in her room from the day the child was delivered to The Cock and the Sow and joy lit up the old pub as never it had been before.Morvyn knew she had to do something to preserve what she now knew. Sydney was the rightful heir to the throne of England upon Elizabeth's death.

***

William looked in wonder and sadness at the girl in the green dress. She did look woefully like the Queen of England, perhaps the afterthrow of good King Henry, the Queen's father. The likeness was astounding. Still, the girl had a mind, and William still desired her with all his heart and body.

***

Tildy and Evan were overjoyed at the return of both the young persons. After the Queen turned away, Tildy grabbed Sydney and ushered her into the kitchen. Evan welcomed George back and asked how he was. George let him know if his services were needed, he could help. Evan sent him to the stables by way of the kitchen where he could pick up some food and drink. There were so many questions and more food needed to be brought. The questions would have to wait. Tildy had some for Morvyn as well. Tildy plunked a plate of food in front of Sydney. "Eat, child, and tell me all."

"There is no time with the crowd out there and Ma, I am very tired. Me an' Georgie ha' walked most of four days to get here once we was free of the pirate ship. Did you know he ain't got no sense of direction and had us go more than a day wrongly? We had no food and nor a spare drink in a stream somewhere. And Ma, you have a lot of questions to answer." She put a spoonful of stew in her mouth and didn't talk until the bowl was empty.

In a spare moment Tildy and Evan gave a small hug and a smile. The joy was back in his home. Evan knew from the light in Tildy's face. "Our girl is back. Are you happy?"

"Oh, Evan, you know that this is almost as great a joy as when she were first brought here as a babe. Of course, I am happy, but you know we must now plan fer a wedding. Her and Georgie out there fer four days together. We don't know what happened. If she be with child, we must protect both."

"Tildy, now is not the time nor the place. Let's get through tonight and tamorra an' we will figure it all out in the peace after time. Now we have lots of thirsty, hungry, tired people out there and just the three of us to handle all."

***

Gilpin was free. He was being kept well fed and comfortable, but as a prisoner he was a complete failure. "Ha! Walsingham thought he could keep me. What a fool! And he the head of intelligence?" Gilpin talked out loud. "Damn fool guard. I hope he enjoys the tray when he awakes. 'Don't pull no tricks,' he says. I am sorry about the teapot, but what is a piece of crockery to my freedom. I needs be off and find that girl." He gathered his cloak about him and made his way to the gate door. "A horse, a horse, the kingdom for a horse. I will never make London in time." He snuck back toward the stable area. It was beneath ground, but easy to access. There was no guard on the door, so he walked in and found a mount that looked to have speed. He saddled the roan, mounted and was on his way. He rode to the gate door and reached down to open it. No one interfered. This is the Queen's castle and there is no security. He thought, strange, I know she is to come here soon. Little did he know he had stolen the Queen's favorite mount, just brought the day before.

He rode out the door, leaving it open for all to enter, albeit, one at a time. A wall sentry reported his departure to the day officer, who in turn reported directly to Walsingham. "Let him go," said Walsingham. "There is naught he can do now to harm this situation."

Gilpin rode hard and fast toward London. He knew he could not stop at The Cock and the Sow for a meal. He must find the Queen before she left. He rode all the rest of that day, stopping only to rest and water his steed. He passed The Cock and the Sow with fond memories of great food and ale, but pressed on, missing the Queen he sought by his haste.

A mile down the road he pulled the horse up to a stop. That pub looked very busy for a weekday. Insurrection, he thought, they are planning an insurrection or another smuggling date.

***

The Queen was sated with food and drink. She wanted to move on. The entourage was mounted and awaited her order. She beckoned William to her table. "I am ready to leave," she said.

"We are always at your command. I will escort you to your carriage when you are ready," said William.

"Summon it and let us go. I wish to make the castle before dark, and we have several hours to go if I remember."

"Yes, Your Majesty. We may still be able to make your ride, if we hasten and drive the horses a bit." William offered his arm. A nod from him brought the carriage around. The Queen arose and took his arm.

"Go," she said, "The sun will not wait for me."

They were gone from the inn not twenty minutes when Gilpin arrived. He burst through the door. "Where is she? What have you done with the Queen's daughter?" Gilpin screamed. The pub was now empty. Evan gathered steins, Tildy and Sarah gathered plates and eating ware. They looked up at the shadow in the doorway screeching at them.

Evan responded first. "Ho, what are you, man or vapor?"

Gilpin strode into the pub, "Turn her over. I am Her Majesty's secret intelligence. I will brook no interference. Turn her over immediately," he ordered.

"What do you speak, apparition?" Evan's quiet voice belied his agitation.

"The Queen's daughter, where is she?" Gilpin's agitation showed no bounds.

"You are speaking through your bung." Evan met the man half way across the room and grabbed his tunic at the chest. "There ain't no 'Queen's daughter' here and you will be quiet lest you scare the ladies with your yellin' and screamin'. I will not have disorder in my house. Sit and I will bring you a glass of cold ale. You have seen too much sun, I wager." He half dragged Gilpin to a bench and sat him down hard.

"The Queen will have your head, oaf, manhandling me in that fashion." Gilpin straightened his tunic. "Just give me the girl and I will be on my way."

Evan in his quiet way drew a stein of ale then, as the anger built, slammed it on the table in front of Gilpin. "You're nothin' ta me and if you don't stop your yellin' an orderin', I will shut you in the stable and send fer the authorities. There be soldiers all over this area, and they will gladly take you someplace to make your stupid accusations. Queen's daughter indeed. The Queen be a virgin and your sovereign, and all know that. There be just me an' me wife an' me sister what live here. My daughter and nephew be here, too. There be no Queen's daughter here. From whence did ye come? Go ye hence to the west and find the Queen herself. She left here not an hour ago with a column and servants. If there be a queen's daughter she would know, would she not? Drink up an quiet yourself."

Gilpin took a sip of the ale afraid of what Evan might do. The Queen herself here an hour ago, and he did not pass her on the way. How did he not see her? Gilpin, confused, took another sip and then another. Evan glared down at him. "Good sir, is there anything to eat? I have gone awhile with no nourishment and if I remember right, this inn has the best food in the kingdom. I will gladly pay." Evan still glared. "Whence goeth the Queen? I did not pass her on my way here."

"Mayhaps you were not looking. And what business was it of yours? Mayhaps ye are sent to do her damage? Go back the way you came, if you want 'er so bad." Evan glowered and stood with his hand out. This was a first. He never asked for payment until the meal was over and the last sip was sipped. "It is my thought that you be gone with your last bite, so drink up, eat and leave."

"I do not have to take this treatment from a peasant. I will be on my way and I shall not pay for this abuse."

"You will be on your way onct I am satisfied ye ha' paid fer your meal else I'll send me lad after the lawmen, and have you shaken fer my lot." Evan said.

Gilpin shoved the last ort down his gullet and took a long draught of the ale. He threw payment on the table and strode out a haughty, nasty look on his face. "This is not the last you'll hear of this." He threw out over his shoulder.

***

"My little love," Tildy reached up to the neck of the girl who was a smidge taller than she and gave a big hug. "How were your trip?"

"Oh, Ma, you ken I was taken up in a smelly sack and kept on board a pirate ship that were no pirate ship, but a spy ship on the pirates? I got this fine dress and these pointy shoes from it, but only because my own dress was torn and dirty and those lazy men tossed it overboard rather than wash it.

This color suits me, don't you think?" Sydney turned and laughed. "There was a man what was the captain, and he held me in his quarters so I wouldn't scream, and he ordered the cook to make me special plates. If I weren't away from you and the fresh air and the garden, I would've had a good time. How long is it now-weeks? And no one laid a hand on me but for the kidnapper what shut me in the sack and whomped me bottom fer screamin' in 'is ear, and then wrapped my mouth in a dirty scarf. No one heard though. We was in the forest far from any place I knew, and I was lost. I might have been a meal for a ferocious beast, if he let me go. And this were the only dress what fit me on the whole ship. The color goes with me.

And tell me about the Queen. Were she here long afore we arrived? And why did she want to see me? I ain't nothin' to her."

"Adventures is good, child, but you must see that there ain't no 'ferocious beast' what would want such a vain girl for dinner. Find your dresses and let's see if they will still do fer such a princess." Tildy kept cleaning and Sarah was laughing in her sleeve as she stowed the dinnerware away for the next night's business.

Morvyn said, "What kind of a monster are ya, ta think the Queen of all England would be interested in ya, an ugly redheaded wench with a green dress from a pirate ship? Git over yerself and get ta work like yer Ma asked. She been busy enou' wi' all this by 'erself." She took a sip of tea and added, "I think I will go and take a rest. This be a wearin' day."

"Go wi' your auntie and make sure she is comfortable then git down here an' start helpin'," Tildy said. "And Sarah, go find that boy o' yours and make sure he be fit. Bring him here and I want to look at him, too." Tildy waited until Sydney was out of earshot. "Evan and me, we both missed the lot o' them bein' gone fer sech a long time. We needs get them married."

"Thank you, Tildy. I do want ta give him a good welcome home. Them comin' at sech a busy time and all, he went ta the stables and helped the boy with the horses. I did miss him; you know with the girls gone. I love all o' you but there is something about your own offspring what... married did you say? Tildy what be the matter? Why are you cryin'?" Sarah put her arms around Tildy.

Tildy sobbed, "You know Sidney be me own daughter. I raised her from a babe, but she weren't from Evan and my seed. Morvyn brought her to us when she were but a wee one only days old. Now she be ready fer marriage but ruined in George's eyes. Evan told George afore he left to find her. Now all may be for naught."

Sarah comforted, "You know Georgie will do the right thing by her. Why don't we just get them together and talk to both of them with Evan and Morvyn. Morvyn sees things. She knows."

Tildy wiped her eyes. "That is a good idea. There be nothing wrong with that. We will wait until her nap is o'er and put the question to her."

At the same time, Sarah, grateful for the return of her son said, "Georgie, I have missed your presence and I know the inn missed your way with the grand beasts. I noticed a goat or two that was pinnin' fer you, too," She laughed.

"Oh, Ma, tis good ta be back wi' you. It were not long I were gone, but do you know Syd is a spoiled piece of a girl? She done nothin' but complain the whole way. She were why I got put in the brig o' that

ship. I think we was left loose on account o' she bein'
so hard ta' manage. She be a grand pain in me arse."

Georgie, me lad, one question: did you, is she, I
mean..."

"Ma, I ain't had naught to do wi' 'er. It were
ne'er allowed here an' why would I do that afore she
be married? There be others to care for those urges. I
don't know about while she were alone on that ship,
but I know after I rescued her there be nothin' goin'
on. Are ye goin' ta make me marry 'er? You ken I love
the baker's daughter in the village. We be more easy
wi' one another. But I will do what Evan an' Tildy
want."

East O the Sun: The Queen's Chambers

A very perturbed Queen reached the outflung
castle. She and her ladies proceeded to take refuge in
the upper chambers for the rest of the day. Their
supper was light, and the women worked well into the
night unpacking and arranging the Queen's clothing
by day and evening wear and for court appearances.
She requested that all who were in the traveling
entourage be present at an informal court the next
day. She requested William to come to her chambers
with Walsingham that night.

Gilpin arrived at the castle just after the
Queen's entourage passed the gate. One of the guards
recognized him and rang the alarm for Walsingham's
men. Gilpin was put into custody, once more raving,
how he had seen the Queen's daughter. His
accommodations were not as luxurious as before.
Walsingham ordered him to cease and desist under
penalty of death.

***

William entered the Queen's chambers quietly and with a great deal of consternation. *What could she want with me? I am a dead man. Just my luck. Live with it for as long as you can,* he thought. *It is a good life, but nothing as rich as with the gamin. I am glad she got home.* The door opened. Behind this door was his life. He started saying his goodbyes.

A guard stood aside as he entered the anteroom to the Queen's chambers. Ladies-in-waiting sat doing various activities needlework, stitching, one was even tending the fire. The richness of their costume was impressive. William gazed and thought of Sydney dressed in the finest silks and satins. The Queen favored white for her ladies, but all William could see was his redheaded vision in the richest of greens.

The guard announced his name and one of the women, it was Lady Walsingham, came to him and said, "William, welcome. Her Majesty will be with you in a few moments. Let me introduce you."

Introductions over, William stood at ease in the vast room looking at the various doors to unknown chambers. He had only been with Walsingham in the large greeting hall beyond the courtyard. Lady Walsingham resumed her seat next to the embroidery frame and got back to her diversion.

The door to the Queen's chamber gave a squeak. "Oil those hinges!" came the command from within. Word was transferred quietly from person to person. When the next call came. "Where is that Lord James?" The voice was querulous and tired. "I ordered him here at six. It is what Lady Anne, about five minutes to?" Muted sounds came from the chamber. "Then, bring him in here when he arrives. I will not stand on accuracy for this visit."

A woman in the palest blue opened the inner chamber door. "Is Lord William James present?"

"I am here my Lady Anne. It is very good to...."

"Enter the chamber at once Lord James. The Her Majesty wishes your presence immediately."

William strode to the door and bowed deeply in the entranceway. "Come William, get your scrawny arse in here, my boy. My, but you have grown to a bonny lad. Come in, come in and stop all the bowing. I have a problem only you can solve. Lady Anne, close that door with all of you ladies on the other side. This is to be a very private audience. Send for a secretary to be ready upon the conclusion of this meeting. I wish to dictate some letters."

The ladies exited the room, a bouquet of pale lavenders, pinks, blues, and greens. The last one out shut the door and the Queen spoke in a quiet voice, "William, I am so glad to see that you are well. You've done some dangerous jobs for me and done them well. Walsingham keeps me informed.

I have a big one for you now and it involves sea travel. I assume that you are good with being on a ship from your last assignment?"

"Yes, Madame, the sea and I are good friends. I love my time on the water."

"Good! This next assignment involves marriage as well. Are you good with that or are you secretly and inextricably betrothed or married to some country maven?"

"Madame, there is one who is my heart's desire, but I will obey any order you give me, since you are not available." William knew the Queen loved a flirt. "How soon do I need to be ready?"

"You are such a bad boy! It is not your want. William, you are a good and faithful servant as was your father before you. I don't have much to say about that wastrel brother of yours, but your sister is one of my ladies, as you are well aware. She is in the country giving you a nephew or a niece in a month or so." The Queen paused and then, "But what I am asking is beyond that. I am asking you to marry sight unseen and be gone from this land for a very long time. I want you to go to the New World and gather information. I need trustworthy eyes there. I need you to stay, observe and then come home again with your information. If you bring good news, you will be dispatched again. I would ask that you leave your bride in the New World, if at all possible, when you make your journeys back to me. If that is not possible or the place is too wild for us to establish, then by all means return with the tides, but do what you can do while there. Above all, stay alive and your wife with you. What say you?"

"Madame, you are my Queen and the only one to whom I owe allegiance. If you can give a month or so to put all of my affairs in order, I am ready to do your bidding. I will marry immediately if that is necessary."

"Good! The marriage will be in a week's time. You will have more than a month, for I have to get a ship seaworthy enough to carry you across the ocean.

I have heard tell there are natives that are cruel and murdcrous. I will provide enough to trade and build you a shelter. Your lady will have clothes enough to wear in all weathers and you as well. News has reached me that some parts of the new land are inhabitable. I also grant you land adjacent to your current estate for income when you return. What say you?"

"Where is the wedding to be, Madame?"

"Here in this castle. It will not be large, but there will be witnesses and cake. It will be here in next Saturday, if that meets with your schedule."

"Madame, your schedule is my schedule. I will be here and thank you. You are all I ever imagined. I will make this arrangement work and bring you any information I can gather."

"You are dismissed. Have my women come to me. I have needs to make the arrangements. You may billet here or go to your own home. It is close by is it not?"

"Yes, Madame, it is, and I shall go there and prepare. Adieu, My Lady."

The door to the chamber opened and William bowed his way out. The ladies streamed in around him. It was a river of color and scents. He had no thoughts for any of them. *Married in a week,* he thought. *I cannot see that midge of a girl. She will have a good life with that young man. Perhaps the Queen will have the pub owner's wife make the wedding cake. At least something good can come from all this.*

"Send in that scribe!" was the last word William heard from the Queen of England that day.

The Cock and the Sow

When put in motion the Queen's will gets done quickly and well. A courier arrived at The Cock and the Sow within a night. He met briefly with Tildy and Evan and when done an order for a wedding cake, pasties, and several barrels of ale was placed as well as an order for a bride-to-be with all of the clothing befitting a new bride to be provided.

Georgie held the horse for the courier and gave it a carrot from the garden. *What message could be that important that a Queen's man came galloping up to the inn?* He led the horse to the water trough and eased the cinch on the saddle to give it rest. Within minutes the man came out and George gave him his horse back after securing the saddle. The courier thanked George and gave him a coin for his services.

Evan came to the stable and asked Georgie to join them in the inn. "We have some news," said Evan, "And you must hear it on account it concerns your life, too. Wash up a little an' come. An remember, I love you like me own son. Ye needs come right now."

Georgie entered the kitchen, face shining wet with water, an expectant look on his face. Tildy and Evan stood together, and Sarah was on Evan's right. Morvyn sat at the table.

"George, we have just received news. A message from the Queen of England that wants to have Sydney at the castle by Saturday. She wants to marry Sydney to someone. We don't know who, but we are going to follow the royal order. I don't want you too disappointed about not having Sydney as your bride." Evan finished and cleared his throat. A grin covered Georgie's wet face and a blush went all the way to the bottom of his blouse. The women were taken aback at his reaction. Evan had a good idea of the reason for the smile.

"Are you not upset by the news, boy?" Tildy asked. "Did you touch 'er an' now you are happy not to have to wed 'er? Oh, Evan, what if she nay be a virgin? Will they cancel the wedding?"

"Woman, you blither on about things you know nothing of. George, here, swore he ne'er touched her. He told me...."

"I kin speak fer meself, Uncle. I ne'er touched Sydney. I proposed on the road an' she said 'Nay'. She ne'er believed me about not bein' cousins. I have a girl in the village who you would like Ma. She be the baker's daughter. You all know her. Gladys? We been keepin' company fer a year now, but I thought I had to have Sydney after what Evan told me. I was relieved when Syd said 'No'. She be a hellion, she be, and grouchy to boot. I were not made fer that sort of person. Nay, Gladys be the one fer me. I think Syd had her eye on someone different, too. She were different after the boat."

"Your daughter be pure. She say she weren't touched an' ya ought ta believe 'er." wheezed Morvyn. "You brought 'er up right. You should be proud o' her."

Georgie said, "Aye, she be smart, too. She got us outta a bunch o' problems on our walk. She even noticed we was going the wrong way an' she only been to town onct a week and then only ta market. She were took away in a sack an saved 'erself on the boat. But I tell ya, she really ain't the one fer me fer a lifetime. She be too smart fer me."

The women let it rest. George left the room and Sarah said, "I be not happy about the boy's choice of mate. She has a reputation for being a wiffle-waffle. She don't think fer herself an Georgie 'ull have ta make all the decisions. He may be good wi' the beasts o' the fields, but he ha' bad taste fer the ladies." Sarah sniffed, looked at the others and was quiet. She knew Morvyn would call her a bad mother-in-law. She didn't want that. She never interfered with the marriages of her girls, but her only son was a different story. He would carry the name and she didn't want it sullied. She was not happy with Sydney to be married to an unknown by order of the Queen but had to abide with that decision.

Evan and Tildy were overjoyed. Sydney was not, when told of the upcoming ceremony. *Marrying someone without meeting is cruel isn't it? But the Queen must be obeyed. That was why she is the Queen. Why me?* thought Sydney. *What have I done? Where? And back to why? Georgie must know about this. It does solve my 'Georgie' problem though, but what about William.* Sydney's thoughts took her in circles, and she was not prepared to accept all of this without a battle. *Why can I not know who my groom is? Oh, that's right I have no choice in the matter.* Even the thought of new dresses did not make her happy.

Tildy and Sarah made sure Sydney was washed and brushed within an inch of her life. The soaps were scented with her mother's herbs and she did feel better, even with Sarah scrubbing her calloused dirty feet until they were soft and pink. No more barefoot adventures with Georgie, she thought. The day before she traveled a trunk was brought and several women fitted her into the confines of her new clothing.

Tildy, Sarah and Evan got new garments fit for a wedding at court. Tildy and Sarah were busy baking. Morvyn kept them company and was official taster for all. "Of course, you are coming, Morvyn. I couldn't leave you home at a time like this. Our girl is marrying and at the Queen's request."

"I will not be welcome. They have sent no clothes for me, so I will be in the courtyard not in the castle for the wedding. I do not wish to travel that far right now. I am not strong enough. Why do you think I am still here?"

The two women were quick to assure Morvyn that she should be there. After all, with her history....

"That is what worries me. I don't wish to be seen. Just let me be. Tell me about it when you return. That is my desire."

Morvyn planned to be gone by the time the family returned to the pub. Later she ordered a carriage from the village by way of a stable hand going into the village for some sport. He took her coin and promised that the carriage would be there when she desired.

The Queen's men arrived with a carriage for transport on Friday, with the wedding planned on

Saturday. There was enough time to travel, rest and dress for the big day. The food was already on its way, to be stored in the larders of the castle. Tildy supposed what wasn't eaten Saturday would be kept and eaten later.

Sydney, wearing a traveling dress and cloak, climbed into the carriage. Tildy, Sarah and Evan followed. They did their best to make room in the vehicle, but with all of the fabric in the clothes, they were hip to hip. The journey took less than a day and they were nicely ensconced in their own chambers after arriving at the castle.

***

Sydney looked around in awe. Never in her life did she imagine herself in a castle like this one. Exploring was next and Sydney managed to sneak out of the chambers and walk in the courtyard. She asked a guard, "Where be the horses?"

The man answered, "They are in the stables under the courtyard." He showed her the entrance, a long downward sloping path. "You kin see the stable doors from up here if you lean over fer enou'." Sydney leaned over and there they were.

"Can I go down?"

"Nay, there be only stable boys and horses and the Queen don't like others down there. She be here or I could show ye meself. Someone stole her favorite mount a day or two ago and it come back all frothy and sech. You should git ta where you should be afore the sun go down. It be dangerous outside the castle."

"Where be the kitchens?" Sydney asked.

"They be up that turret at the top. It be airy and cool up there e'en wi' the ovens blaring in the summer and cozy in the winter. I wouldna go up there, though, since there be a marriage tamara and the cooks be busy gittin' already ta serve. The marriage ta be at noon and food be brought in fer it from some pub. There were a ton of it an' I hope we git some.

"The Queen's chambers be in that turret. She have the whole thing. She made the wedding on the morrow, so they be busy up there as well. You should git indoors now. It be too dark for us ta be here. I needs be goin', but I'll see you to the door."

Sydney thanked the man and reentered the castle doors, it being dark in the courtyard. She wandered around the ground floor and came to several chapels and a large nave. One of the chapels was decorated with flowers and the altar was set up. She supposed her wedding was to be there. She went in and knelt at the altar to get a feel of it. Her family never were big churchers and Aunt Morvyn were of the old religion still even though it be illegal. Sydney liked Morvyn's religion. It was natural and held outside. Sydney would miss the gardens at home and Morvyn's instructions in herbs and their uses.

Syd wasn't tired and she wandered for a bit more time. She headed back to her family and their chambers and discovered she was lost. She found a guard who looked at her surprised. He sent her in the right direction without a word, but when he encountered another of his sort, he mentioned that there was a young queen in the building. When she arrived, she slipped into her room and undressed herself. Tomorrow would come soon enough she thought, soon enough.

***

Morvyn looked around at the empty pub. With a great deal of effort, she made her way to the entrance. Evan had left a CLOSED sign on the door. There would be no one coming. There would be one going. Morvyn gathered her things and left a note about her leaving.

'Don't worry about me. I am fine. I will send a messenger when I reach The Witch's Brew. I know things went fine. Good will to you all.

Love Morvyn.'

She left the note on the kitchen table. Then she hoisted her small baggage and left the inn in the carriage she ordered from the village.

Questions

Sydney appeared in the chapel at the castle, the one she'd seen the night before. There were few people there she knew. Her father and aunt stood toward the rear of the space deep in conversation. *There is no bridegroom or groomsmen,* thought Sydney. She looked at her dress from the top. The corset that bound her, unaccustomed as she was to being bound, was not uncomfortable. Her gown swept around her a beautiful silk of palest yellow with rich gold beads and silk flowerettes placed on the overdress. The chemise was the finest cotton with lace her aunt made especially for her wedding. The intricate patterns decorated the neckline, which showed just above the edge of the overdress. Sydney wondered aloud, "The undercoats are heavy considering the number of them. What happened to my simple muslins? And who is my groom? Why have I not been told at least to whom I will be married? If it were Georgie, he would have told me already somehow. I feel like I am imprisoned for a crime." Sydney's thoughts made her unhappy on what should be the happiest day of her life.

Her father and aunt saw her at the same time and her father rushed to her and said, "Syd, you shouldn't be here. Go back to your room until someone calls for you. There is still a bit of time before your wedding. Go child and my darling, you look beautiful." Sarah took her arm and started to lead her back to the private room.

Sydney stopped and gave her father a quick hug and whispered, "Pa, who do I marry? Do you know? Will he be good to me?"

"Darling girl, I know that the Queen herself picked him out. I suppose he will be good to you. I can't imagine anyone mistreating you and, my girl, love can come after. Working together makes a bond that turns to friendship and then to love."
"But Pa, you and Ma loved each other before marriage and, and.... Oh, Pa I am a little frightened. And where is Ma?"

Evan held her at arm's length. "She is still getting dressed. She has a maid to help her, and when I left, she was moaning and groaning about her corset, but she looked mighty pleased with herself since they had to get two sizes smaller than what they thought." Evan laughed, "And she is having her hair done up the likes I have never seen. Your Ma is the most beautiful woman in the world to me and my best friend. I hope that for you." Evan took Sydney by the shoulders and turned her around. With a little pat on her rear he said, "Now get on with you. Go to your room and wait a little longer. I love you and will miss you."

Sydney did as she was told, but not before she said, "You don't love me like you used to. You think I am tainted. I didn't do anything. How can I make you understand? Now, I am to marry some old man. This man will never be happy with me. I will cross him every chance I get. You will rue the day you did this and so will he! How dare the Queen?"

Sydney's thoughts got blacker and blacker. There was no justice for her. She had done nothing and because some person kidnapped her and brought her to a pirate ship, she was ruined. Well, her new husband would have a big surprise. She could stay a virgin forever, just like her Queen, if she only knew.

***

Tildy fussed about not seeing Sydney. "Tis a mother's right to see her daughter the day of her wedding. There are certain things a daughter must be cautioned about so she does not make mistakes that could cost her a happy home."

"Tildy, do not carry on so. This is not the croft and Sydney was chosen by the Queen of England herself to be the bride of this man. The Queen must have her reasons and there is no point in causing a disturbance and landing in the Tower, even if you do get that trip to London out of it. Surely someone will give the girl advice. Don't forget she saw all matter of pigs and cows and even the dog do the deed at the inn. And you know we never had fancy women there, but there was talk and all those soldiers were never that quiet. I am sure she has some idea of what happens in the bedroom.

"I know I did before I married Euan, and we had a happy marriage to the day I discovered him dead." Sarah rearranged a curl by her ear. She was a widow, dressed in a lovely brown silk gown. She was tired of the drab color, but the dress itself was well made and a pleasure to wear. She thought of the things she could fashion from the fabric once the wedding was over, and all were back snug in the pub.

"And Tildy, remember, this will bring more business to the pub and you could get a business of your own with the baking you do." Sarah was smug about this. She was planning on her own little business making fashions for those in court with fine Welsh lace and embroidery. She could still see well enough to sew a fine seam." Why some might even get seen in London, and the girls and I could make a nice penny from it," she said. "Even if married, it is well to plan and save."

An escort knocked on the door. "Your presence is demanded in the chapel immediately. The wedding will begin when the chimes strike. The glass leaves little sand in the upper chamber. Hurry now."

Tildy and Sarah gathered up their voluminous skirts and hurried as fast as the tight corsets would let them. The escort waited until they caught up and then set out at a merry pace again. The stairs were treacherous for the two women unaccustomed to fine full skirts and heeled court shoes. When finally they reached the main floor of the castle, Evan greeted them. "How fine you ladies look today. Tildy, our daughter looks beautiful, but the look on her face does not bode well for her new husband. There is no one who will reveal his name, only that he has a title and an estate and is highly thought of by the Queen."

"Why all the secrecy I wonder?" said Tildy. "They could let us know who, don't you think?"

"It is not that important. I understand he is a rather young man and has served the Queen well." Evan took both women by the elbow, one on each side and hurried them along to the chapel.

"This is beautiful!" said Tildy. "Our daughter will have a beautiful wedding. Do I get to talk to her beforehand?"

"Why are we kept in such secrecy?" asked Sarah. "You would think"....

"Hurry, do you want to miss your daughter's wedding?" whispered Evan to Tildy. "I hear the first chime and I must walk her on the sixth." Evan led them to the front of the chapel. "Sit here. Stand when we enter."

The two women sat, their faces sour with displeasure. Weddings were women's work. Evan took the pleasure right from their hearts. Where was the music? No fiddles played, no horns gave cadence, there were only those infernal chimes counting the hours by quarters as the sand drained from the glass.

The sand was gone, and the sixth chime sounded. The hush over the small congregation was audible and the priest and the processions made their

separate ways to the front of the chapel, the priest
from the side door and the bride from the rear. The
groom was nowhere to be seen. The bride was heavily
veiled. No one would know her countenance until the
unveiling.

"I canna see anything but shadows," Sydney
whispered. "I wonder why all the mystery. At least my
groom won't know my face until the vows are over. I
hope he likes a redhead with a temper. What fool I am
to do this today. I should have run before the carriage
came. Damn! Damn! Damn!"

***

William was late. "She wants me in white and
black is more suited to my mood," he said to himself.
He was dressed in the white doublet and bloomers,
white stockings and white leather slippers. The sleeves
were slightly puffed, as were the bloomers. The
doublet was embroidered in gold thread, love knots
abounded. His hat or capotain was white with a long
white feather. A caplet covered one shoulder which
denoted a military assignment of some sort, although
the look was more French than English. "Damnation,
there is the third chime," he muttered. "Now I am
going to be late. Ah, my little Sydney, where are you? I
should have moved when I had the chance. She could
not ask me to marry unknown if I were already
married. Damn! Damn! Damn!"

***

William made his way to the chapel very
slowly, an unwilling sheep to slaughter. *Sydney,
forgive me. You have a good life. I will live with my*

choices and allegiances. These black thoughts made for a very sour countenance as the bridegroom made his way to the chapel for his endgame. His life for all intents was over, at least the life he knew.

***

The bride proceeded up the aisle, her father with a very firm grip on her elbow pulling her along. The groom made his way to the priest's room for a side entrance. There he bumped into a figure veiled and dressed in black. Her back was to him as she peeped through the hole in the door. "Excuse me. I need to get to the altar before my bride," he said.

"By all means, young man." She stepped back and he opened the door to proceed into the chapel.

Who was that? He thought. He glanced down the aisle and saw his bride on the arm of her father? *Oh my, what luck be mine and thank the gods for this!* he rejoiced. *It's her father, the pub owner, where I supped and drank. What luck, what grand and glorious luck,* was his final thought before the couple reached the altar. His heart danced in his chest.

Who is that? Sydney thought taking a peek through the veils that covered her face. She made out a white ghostly figure emerging from the priest's chamber. *I should just say 'no' when I am asked. I don't want to do this. Two men in my life and I can't have either of them. Oh William! Oh Georgie!*

Sydney stepped on the edge of her gown and nearly tripped. Evan held her arm firmly. He leaned over and whispered, "Don't you try anything, daughter, you just go through with this. I'll naught have the Queen's men on my back for the rest of my life. You will have a good life, and should all come to naught, you will have the pub and the grounds when yer ma and me don't need it anymore. I know you think this should be a happy time for ya' and I agree, but sometimes things don't happen the way ya think they should. I don't know what put this flea up the Queen's skirts, but just go with it. You ain't the first." They made the altar and the priest descended to be level with both.

The new words in English fell from his lips, "Who giveth this woman to be married?"

"Her father." Evan said, a sadness in his voice.

"Are there any objections?" the priest intoned.

The room was silent. *Come on Ma, somebody, say something. Stop this!* thought Sydney as her father held her arm a little too firmly. *Why is Pa doing this to me? They think I am soiled! I did nothing.*

A new figure took her hand and drew her close to him. "Sydney?"

The voice was so familiar, so longed for, Sydney snapped her head around and peered through the veiling. "William?" Her body flushed with the joy of it all. How this happened, she didn't care. "I do!" Her voice rang out over the priest's words.

William spoke his 'I do' and the priest pronounced them man and wife. With great care William retracted the veils to look upon her face. "You are mine. Thank the gods. I dreamed of this," William whispered in her ear and then they turned to the congregation, small as it was. Both grinned and they held hands tightly so neither could escape.

"They are now man and wife," intoned the priest. He left the room for the priest's chamber.

The woman in black made her way through the halls, a smile on her face. The princess was safely married and on her way to a new land, until she was needed to fulfill her duties as the once and future Queen.